A Dangerous Engagement

OTHER TITLES
BY MELANIE DICKERSON

Regency Spies of London Series

A Spy's Devotion
A Viscount's Proposal

Medieval Fairy Tale Series

The Huntress of Thornbeck Forest
The Beautiful Pretender
The Noble Servant

Fairy Tale Romance Series

The Healer's Apprentice
The Merchant's Daughter
The Fairest Beauty
The Captive Maiden
The Princess Spy
The Golden Braid
The Silent Songbird

A Dangerous Engagement

The Regency Spies of London

MELANIE DICKERSON

Waterfall
PRESS

Published by Waterfall Press, Grand Haven, MI

www.brilliancepublishing.com

Amazon, the Amazon logo, and Waterfall Press are trademarks of Amazon.com, Inc., or its affiliates.

ISBN-13: 9781503938656
ISBN-10: 1503938654

Cover design by Mike Heath | Magnus Creative

Printed in the United States of America

A Dangerous Engagement

CHAPTER ONE

Spring 1815, London, England

Felicity took the young gentleman's arm as they moved away from the dance floor. He was quite handsome, with brown hair and a gentle manner.

"You dance very well, Miss Mayson." He smiled shyly at her.

"Thank you, Mr. Kellerman."

"Would you honor me with the next dance?"

"I would be—"

An older woman walked up behind Mr. Kellerman and tapped him on the shoulder. She glared at Felicity as she took Mr. Kellerman's arm.

"You are not to dance with that young woman again." The woman spoke in a harsh whisper, loud enough for Felicity to hear.

"Mother, please. I already asked her." His cheeks were turning red.

"She has no money. No money." She punctuated her words with a tug on his arm. "Go and dance with Miss Gandy over there."

His face flaming red, he turned toward Felicity and bowed. "Excuse me, Miss Mayson."

"You are excused." She held herself with as much dignity as she could and matched his ugly mother stare for stare. They both turned and walked away.

Felicity stood alone by the wall. *I will not care what those supercilious, grasping people say or think,* she recited over and over in her head. If only her friends Julia and Leorah were there, she wouldn't feel so embarrassed, but neither of them had yet returned to town for the Season.

The rest of the night, the only people who asked her to dance were her father and the host's fifteen-year-old son.

In the carriage on the way home, Felicity announced, "That was the last ball I ever plan to attend, unless it is given by the Withinghalls or the Langdons."

"Oh, you do not mean that," Mother said.

"I certainly do." But she wasn't sure anyone heard her, for two of her brothers and her sister began to argue.

"You're taking too much room! Move over."

"You move over! You're sitting in my lap."

"Your hair is in my face!"

Her father was wealthy enough to live in Mayfair and be invited to assemblies and balls but not wealthy enough to give each of his five daughters a significant dowry, and he had to do at least a little something for each of his eight sons. She had never been lonely growing up with so many siblings, but being one of thirteen was not helpful in securing a husband.

From now on, she would do what she liked, and she would give not one thought to marriage or eligible men.

She had been studying Chinese in the hope of traveling to the Orient, ever since hearing the impassioned words of a missionary at a lecture hall a few weeks before. But truthfully, she wasn't even sure she wanted to be a missionary. She might just write a treatise on what was wrong with the conditions and restrictions society placed on ladies, its dictates on who should and shouldn't marry whom, and on how money was a crude and unfair factor in marriage.

Perhaps she could be a sort of young Hannah More.

All she really knew was that she wanted to dedicate herself to something besides standing around waiting for a husband who wouldn't snub her for her tiny dowry.

***

"Have you heard? Napoleon is in Paris, and the king has fled France."

Felicity looked up from her book. Alas for the French. It seemed their government was always in turmoil.

Tom's eyes were bright, and his voice pulsed with excitement. "The war will be recommencing, and my regiment leaves tomorrow."

And alas for England, joining in another war. Felicity's friend Casandra had lost a brother to the war a few years ago. And Felicity would have to be blind not to notice all the soldiers who had come home missing an eye, an arm, or even both legs.

"Tom, you will be careful, won't you?"

"What kind of fun will it be to be careful?" Her brother grinned.

He was full of the prospect of adventure and danger and the courageous acts he would be lauded for. Felicity shook her head and went back to studying.

"Not still trying to learn Chinese, are you?" Tom snatched the book from her hands. "Father will never allow you to go to China. Besides, aren't you afraid you'll faint at the first sight of such a foreign place?"

Felicity took back her book and glared at him. It was embarrassing enough that she had twice fainted, but to have her brothers constantly bring it up . . .

"I suppose it is all well and good for you to go get your head shot off in France, but I am not allowed to be a missionary in China."

"Why don't you marry a good soldier and forget about China? You don't want to end a spinster, do you?"

Felicity held up a finger. "First of all, why would I want to marry a soldier who will only get himself killed or maimed? And secondly . . ." She huffed out a breath and turned away.

Mother entered the room waving a letter.

"Lady Blackstone has invited you to Doverton Hall for a few weeks."

"Lady Blackstone?"

"Your aunt. You remember. She was married to my brother briefly before he died. Then she married a baron. She is inviting you and your sister. Unfortunately, Elizabeth will be in Surrey for a fortnight with the Harrisons, but Aunt Agnes can accompany you."

"Must I go?" The thought of a house party with strangers was not appealing. "I'm so tired of everyone expecting me to find a husband." And tired of being rejected.

Mother gave a slight smile. "I suppose I shouldn't tell you that Lady Blackstone writes that there will be several eligible young gentlemen there, including one in particular she wishes you to meet."

Felicity heaved a sigh.

"Oh, my dear," Mother cried, "do not look up at the ceiling in that rude way. Who has taught you that terrible habit?"

Lady Withinghall, her dear friend, often rolled her eyes, but Mother probably already knew that.

"Forgive me, Mother." Perhaps she could try a different tactic. "But why would Lady Blackstone be having a party at her country estate at this time of year? It is the middle of the Season, and everyone will be in London."

"I don't know, but it will not be for the entire Season."

"Are you certain Lady Blackstone and her parties are quite respectable?"

"Why would they not be? She is the widow of a baron, and surely at her age—she must be five and forty—she is beyond the sort of behavior that ruins reputations."

"I suppose."

"You must get your things packed, then, for you leave tomorrow."

"Tomorrow?" She didn't even want to go, and now she had to leave before even getting used to the idea?

"Enough time to see me off," Tom said cheerfully.

Mother turned her attention to Felicity's brother, fussing about how he should take care to keep his feet dry and talking of where he might be sent and what he should take with him.

There seemed to be no help for it. She was off to Margate on the coast to engage in the kind of frivolities—card games and dancing and flirting—that were supposed to bring pleasure.

She should refuse. She should tell Mother she wanted her life to count for something, not just be an exercise in futility, standing about trying to attract the attention of someone—anyone with a shred of wealth—who would marry her.

But Mother could be quite determined, and Felicity would save her reasons for her treatise on British society's hypocritical marriage restrictions.

***

Lady Blackstone's smile lit up her entire face as she traversed the enormous entryway of Doverton Hall toward Felicity. She embraced her quite warmly.

"And here is your delightful aunt, Miss Appleby. How good of you to accompany dear Felicity." She squeezed Auntie's hands and looked into her eyes.

"Yes, here we are," Aunt Agnes said. "I've never been to Margate in the whole of my life. The air is quite moist, but everyone is always saying how healthful the sea air is for—"

"Yes, yes, it's quite healthful." Lady Blackstone turned away from her. "And now, Felicity, let us get you both settled into your room."

Felicity and Aunt Agnes started up the stairs behind Lady Blackstone. On the landing, a young man seemed to be waiting for them.

"Oh, how fortunate you are here, Mr. Ratley, so that you might meet my lovely niece and her dear aunt. Miss Felicity Mayson, Miss Appleby, please allow me to present Mr. Oliver Ratley."

Oliver Ratley. That was the name Mother had mentioned from Lady Blackstone's letter, the young man she thought would be a good marriage prospect for Felicity. Well, with brown hair, brown eyes, and even features, at least he was handsome.

Mr. Ratley took her hand and squeezed it. Felicity smiled, but she drew her hand back as soon as possible. He should not take the hand of a young lady with whom he was not well acquainted.

He smiled agreeably, as he was fortunate enough to have straight white teeth. His hair was thick, and his neckcloth was tied neatly. His style of dress was pleasing—neither too foppish nor too austere.

"I am very pleased to make your acquaintance, Miss Mayson." Mr. Ratley bowed, then turned to Aunt Agnes and took her hand as well, which caused her face to twitch. "Miss Appleby, I am very pleased to make your acquaintance. I hope you shall both be down later for a game of whist and some conversation. The afternoon will be most dull if you do not."

"Perhaps we shall," Felicity said. Then she and her aunt followed Lady Blackstone the rest of the way to their room.

Once inside with the door closed, Felicity glanced at her hair in the mirror. Good. It did not appear too messy after their long carriage ride.

"The young man, Mr. Ratley, was amiable and gentlemanlike, though I did not expect him to take my hand," Aunt Agnes said. "I did not have my spectacles on, but he seemed handsome as well."

"Yes. I had thought I might spend most of this house party in my room," Felicity said, "but I may as well satisfy Lady Blackstone by getting to know Mr. Ratley."

"Yes, of course," Auntie said. "You should go down and see if he is as agreeable on further acquaintance."

"And you must go down with me."

"Oh, I had rather thought I would read. I have a new book—"

"Auntie, please. I shall not force you to go to all the festivities, but it is the first day, and I don't know anyone except Lady Blackstone. And though she does treat me so familiarly, I hardly know her. Please? You must."

Aunt Agnes glanced around nervously. "Very well, very well. But I shall bring my book and my spectacles with me, and if I can find a quiet corner, I shall sit and read."

"Just as you wish, Auntie."

***

Downstairs several people were gathered in a large sitting room, and at least two card games were underway at two separate tables. But . . . everyone in the room was male. Not a single lady was present.

"Aunt Agnes," Felicity whispered, bending her head so her aunt could hear, "I think we should go look for Lady Blackstone."

They turned to leave when Mr. Ratley and Lady Blackstone suddenly appeared in the doorway.

"You are not going back to your room?" Lady Blackstone asked.

"We were afraid . . . that is, this seems to be the gentlemen's card-playing room."

"Oh, never you mind those men. They have been instructed to be on their very best behavior when you are around. Nevertheless, we shall go for a walk, the four of us, in the garden. Will that suit you both? Oh, you shall love my garden, shall they not, Mr. Ratley?"

"Yes, indeed, it is a splendid garden."

Felicity wanted to ask where all the female guests had gotten to, but Lady Blackstone was hustling them away.

"I should get my bonnet and a jacket before venturing out of doors," Aunt Agnes said.

"No need to get your bonnet, Miss Appleby," Lady Blackstone said. "It is a lovely day with not a speck of wind, and the sun is safely hidden behind the clouds. You shall be quite warm and cozy between Mr. Ratley and me, and Felicity can take the gentleman's other arm. You see?"

They were out the back door before Felicity knew where they were going.

Though Lady Blackstone bore the facial lines of a lady of forty years, her hair was not yet gray but rather a light brown. She tucked Aunt Agnes's hand inside her elbow. Mr. Ratley gave Auntie his arm, then offered his other arm to Felicity. There was nothing in his manner to give her alarm—his gaze was gentle, though intense—so she accepted his arm and kept her eyes on the garden walk ahead.

"Miss Appleby, I have heard from my sister-in-law, Mrs. Mayson, that you are a great novel reader. Pray, tell me, what are your favorite novels?"

With Lady Blackstone engaging Auntie's attention on her most beloved subject, Felicity was very aware of Mr. Ratley and the quiet way he was inclining his head toward her. And finally, he spoke.

"Lady Blackstone has kept the garden very much as it was when the monks of Doverton Abbey owned it. Here you can see their herb garden amongst the flowers and shrubs."

"Are you interested in horticulture, sir? Or botany, perhaps?"

"No. That is, I know a little of the subjects, but very little. I was a soldier before my father died and left me a substantial fortune."

Well, she was not sure what Lady Blackstone had told him, but she would let him know right away that if he wished for a wife with a large fortune—

"So I may marry as I wish. It is a luxury, a consequence of inheriting such a great fortune."

"I do not believe most heirs would share your opinion of the business, Mr. Ratley." She nearly laughed. "In fact, most would feel as though they now had the opportunity to improve on their fortune by marrying an equal or greater one."

"I understand you, Miss Mayson—you do not mind my calling you Miss Mayson?"

"Of course not. It is my name."

"I only mean that . . . Lady Blackstone refers to you by your given name, and I hope I do not make a mistake and call you Miss Felicity."

"If you do, it is all right. I am not the oldest daughter in my family."

"Felicity is such a pretty name, so charming and feminine. It suits you perfectly."

His cheeks turned red, and he seemed to have difficulty looking her in the eye.

Felicity did laugh. "You must accustom yourself as best you can to it, I suppose."

He shook his head. "Forgive me. I was prepared to admire you, as Lady Blackstone had told me you were a remarkable woman, but I do not often meet with such beauty as yours."

Felicity wasn't sure which urge was greater—the urge to laugh or to roll her eyes. "I think it best if we talk of other things, as my mother taught me never to receive flattery."

"Forgive me. I was quite forward."

"Not at all." The moment was becoming awkward.

"But I believe we were speaking of the rather indelicate subject of fortunes. Miss Mayson, you must think me terribly ungentlemanlike."

"What?" Lady Blackstone cried. "You have very gentlemanlike manners, Mr. Ratley." Lady Blackstone leaned forward and stopped walking. They were all forced to stop as well.

Felicity was determined to set forth the truth. "Mr. Ratley was just informing me that he has inherited a great fortune, but Mr. Ratley, I do not think you ungentlemanlike at all. Rather, I admire your forthrightness, and I shall attempt to duplicate it by divulging that I have no fortune at all."

They all stared at her.

Should she set his mind at ease by excusing him now from further flirtation?

"But I thought your father was very successful in his business in London?" Lady Blackstone's brows drew together.

"He is successful, but I am one of thirteen children, my lady, and can expect little when I marry. My father has settled only a hundred pounds per annum on myself and my younger sister."

There. The truth was out, and Mr. Ratley could shun her as he pleased.

Mr. Ratley gazed down at her and squeezed her hand, which rested on his arm. "As I said before, it is well that I do not need to care about the dowry of the woman I marry, since I have my own fortune."

Felicity again felt the urge to laugh. Surely this man was in jest, as no one said such things. He could not be so disinterested. She'd never known anyone to take such a view. And yet, he seemed perfectly serious.

"Dear Mr. Ratley," Lady Blackstone said, "you have shocked our poor Felicity—I can see it on her face. And well she might be shocked, for the *gentlemen* she's accustomed to meeting care only for a lady's fortune. Is it not so? But I shall not press you about the matter, my dear. No, no, we shall not dwell on unpleasant subjects. We shall be merry and leave sad things behind for a month or so."

They all agreed that was a good plan, but Felicity continued to feel unsettled, though not unpleasantly so, as they explored Doverton Hall's gardens with the handsome Mr. Ratley.

***

While Felicity was dressing her hair for dinner, a knock came at the door.

"Come in."

Lady Blackstone entered the room and closed the door behind her. "You are looking so lovely. No wonder Mr. Ratley was so smitten with you."

"Smitten?"

"He could not take his eyes off you. I cannot blame him."

"He did seem inclined to think well of me, though I cannot think why. He has never met me nor any of my family, and I informed him of my lack of fortune."

Perhaps she was being *too* honest. But she rather prided herself on her honesty, and her friend Leorah had encouraged it. That lady's courage was too great to worry about the consequences of speaking her mind.

"Have men often reacted unfavorably after they learned of your lack of fortune?"

"Very often. Once a man said, in my hearing, that he would not dance with me because I was the daughter of a merchant and had no dowry. And sometimes a gentleman will dance and flirt with me at a ball or party, and then the next time I see him, he will ignore me and pretend not to know me. People often say that women are mercenary and only want the wealthiest man they can acquire, but I believe it is the men who are the mercenaries. Rather than wishing to marry for love, or to cherish and care for the woman of their choice, they wish to be financially cared for by the woman. That is not chivalrous, nor is it biblical."

"And do you think British society discourages such ungentleman-like behavior?"

"Indeed, society does not discourage it. It practically demands it."

"You are so right, my dear. The rich care only for the rich. I am glad you think as I do." Lady Blackstone's eyes were wide and glittering. "I did not misjudge you. I knew you were a spirited young woman with a mind of her own who does not allow society to dictate her beliefs. Given half a chance, you would fight such an unfair system as we have in this country—the elite classes dictating to everyone else, never allowing the poor their equal part in government and in life."

Felicity stared. What did Lady Blackstone mean? Fight the unfair system? Perhaps she had been too strident in her opinions.

"But this is a party. You are young. You want to enjoy yourself." Lady Blackstone's smile was back in its usual place. "I have arranged for you to sit with Mr. Ratley at dinner. He will entertain you quite satisfactorily, and your dear Aunt Appleby will be seated nearby." She caressed Felicity's cheek in a most familiar way.

Why did the woman treat her as if she was a long-lost favorite relative? They'd seldom been in each other's company, and Lady Blackstone and Felicity's uncle had no children. The baron she married shortly thereafter died a year ago, leaving her once again a childless widow.

Lady Blackstone chatted a bit longer before going to greet the guests who would be arriving before dinner, leaving Felicity to wonder at her hostess's strange words. Could Lady Blackstone be a reformer? Or a suffragist, perhaps? Felicity might almost think her capable of being a member of one of those oath-taking societies that were illegal, and that, from time to time, had been brought to light and summarily squashed by Parliament and the Home Office. Some members had even been hanged for plotting treason.

But, no, Lady Blackstone could not be part of anything so frightening.

CHAPTER TWO

Philip McDowell glanced around at his parents and all three of his brothers gathered around the breakfast table—a rare occurrence. His mother was smiling, and his father was frowning.

"So, you're finally going to fight in the war against Napoleon?" his oldest brother, Damian, asked Philip, taking a sip of tea and following it with a bite of bread.

"Not exactly."

"Leave him alone, Damian," Nathan, his clergyman brother, said. "He's probably spying on some evil frame-breakers union or a bunch of lawless men bent on burning mills in Manchester. He can't tell us where he's going or he'd have to kill us."

"That's right," Thomas, his second-oldest brother, added. "But don't mock him. If he gets a commendation from the Prince Regent, we'll all be shown up."

"Well, I am very proud of Philip," his mother said. "He's been serving our country in the Home Office, and whatever they ask him to do, I'm sure he will do the job very well indeed."

"Thank you, Mother."

"When are you getting promoted?" his father demanded. "I haven't heard anything about a promotion for more than a year. What do you do in the Home Office anyway?"

"Whatever I was doing, Father, I'll be doing something else for the next several weeks. I only told you so you will not worry if you cannot reach me. And I will probably not be able to write to any of you."

Philip wished he had not told them anything. Let them find out when it was all over. But his mother did not deserve to have her letters unanswered without an explanation.

He should expect some teasing from his brothers. As the youngest, he was used to it.

When the meal was over, Philip made his way downstairs, thinking he might play some billiards for an hour before he had to leave. On the way down, he met Clara, his mother's maidservant.

"Good afternoon, Clara."

She smiled but then seemed unable to meet his eye. "Good afternoon, Mr. Philip."

His mother, distraught, had told him earlier that morning that she suspected Clara was with child. "I am very sad to get rid of her," she confided. "But what choice do I have? I cannot have her here. It isn't done. What would everyone say?"

He almost said, "Why do you care what everyone will say?" But he knew how cruel people could be if one disobeyed society's "rules." Instead, he said, "Do you know who the father is? Perhaps he will do right by her and the child."

She shook her head. "I have not asked her yet."

"Perhaps she has family who can care for the child, and she can come back to work after the baby is born."

Mother smiled at him. "Even though you are my youngest, you always were the most mature." She stood up straighter, as if casting off the burden that had been weighing on her. "I am sure all will be well.

It is certainly nothing for you to worry about, Philip, and so we shall speak of it no more."

Now, as Philip made his way down the stairs, he noticed his brother Damian was behind him. Philip glanced back just in time to see a significant look pass between the maidservant, Clara, and his brother—Damian's look was stern while Clara's eyes filled with tears. After she passed by him, she practically ran the rest of the way up.

Philip's heart sank as he continued down the stairs.

"Why don't you play a game of billiards with me?" Damian took the steps two at a time, catching up with him. He clapped his hand on Philip's shoulder.

The game was friendly, up until Philip won.

"There's a first time for everything." Damian curled his lip. "Why don't you tell me where you're going? Did you get some girl pregnant and have to stash her away somewhere?" He laughed, a loud, ugly guffaw.

Philip felt the heat travel from the back of his neck to his forehead. "No, Damian. I have not slept with my mother's maidservant, as you have clearly done."

Damian stopped short, his jaw hardening. "How did you know about that?"

"How could you take advantage of a servant girl in such a way? You are a Member of Parliament. You should adhere to a higher standard than the average man."

"Who made you my judge?"

"Do you plan to marry the girl?"

"Are you daft?" He snorted. "She's only a servant."

"Is that why you aren't interested in any of the ladies Mother has tried to match you with? Well, I think you should tell Mother. She might treat the girl better if she knows she's carrying the first McDowell grandchild."

Damian's face flamed red. "Listen to me, little brother. You are not to tell Mother anything." Damian took a step toward Philip, his hands clenching into fists.

Philip stood his ground. After all, he was no longer the *little* brother. Philip had kept growing long after his brothers, and he was now two inches taller than the tallest of them. "I hope you will do right by the child, at least."

"Keep your mouth shut and your nose out of my affairs." But Damian's voice had lost its bravado. With one last look, he stalked off.

Philip let out the breath he'd been holding. But this was not over. When he returned from his mission, he would make sure Damian took steps to ensure the child was taken care of, at least.

He supposed his brothers would never treat him respectfully, nor did they seem inclined to grow up and behave as men. When they were children, they had often used Philip as the butt of their jokes, had left him behind, and had treated him as if he was incompetent. As a consequence, he had worked harder than any of them to learn and succeed. He could make friends with anyone, could decode secret messages, and could even infiltrate secret societies. He'd wanted his brothers to finally respect him, to be different now that they were adults.

Perhaps things would be different if this assignment at Lady Blackstone's house party proved as dangerous as he anticipated.

***

As soon as Felicity and Aunt Agnes changed out of their formal dinner clothes, her aunt sat down with a book by the lamp.

"Did you enjoy yourself tonight?" Auntie asked, holding her book in one hand and her spectacles in the other.

"It was less dull than most dinner parties."

"That nice Mr. Ratley was flirting with you again." Auntie's brown eyes crinkled as she smiled.

"Do you really think he was flirting?"

"Come now, Felicity. I may not see as well as some, but I'd have to be blind not to see that he is showing an interest in you. Even Lady Blackstone said he was smitten with you."

"But why should he be? He hardly knows me. You may have noticed—there are not very many women here. It was rather scandalous, but there were only six females at dinner, including you and myself, and there were fifteen men!"

"Yes, it was very many." The same intimidated look crossed Auntie's face as when she had first seen the other dinner guests.

"And I had never met a single one of them before. I may not know more gentlemen than the average twenty-two-year-old in London society, but you would think I would have recognized at least one person."

"I would have thought so."

"You must come to dinner again tomorrow, Auntie, even though I know you do not like to. I need to feel a bit less outnumbered."

"Oh, you are safe, surely. You have Lady Blackstone," Auntie said. "But what of your Mr. Ratley? Was he as pleasant and agreeable as he was on our walk earlier?"

"He was." Felicity couldn't help smiling. He had been attentive and complimentary. She had only known him for one day, but she could not help feeling flattered by the attentions of a handsome young man, especially one who claimed to have such a large fortune that he did not need to marry well.

But that seemed a mercenary thought, as well as a hypocritical one, after all her self-assertions that she was no longer interested in getting married. The truth was, she would like Mr. Ratley even if he were poor. Still, happiness in marriage depended at least somewhat on being able to support oneself and one's spouse. It would be unwise for her to marry a poor man with no prospects.

"Perhaps you should write to your father and mother to ask them to make inquiries about Mr. Ratley."

Felicity hesitated, then said, "Yes, perhaps it would be good to see what we can discover about him and his family." She disliked the thought of investigating his claims, but she also had no wish to form an unwise attachment to someone who was misrepresenting himself.

"I shall write the letter in the morning, then."

***

Philip McDowell arrived at Doverton Hall while the sun was high, its rays sparkling off the gray stones of the massive Tudor-era house. The manor house's three stories towered over even the trees in the old hunting grounds several yards to the west side of the house.

Wrangling an invitation to this party had taken months. He only hoped it would prove worth it.

As he was taking off his hat and handing it to the servant, Lady Blackstone appeared.

"You must be Mr. Philip Merrick! How delightful to welcome you to Doverton Hall."

"Thank you, Lady Blackstone." He already felt comfortable with his borrowed name. He took her extended hands and smiled. "It is so kind of you to invite me. I have been looking forward to meeting you and your guests."

"Mr. Ratley and Mr. Cartwright have told me so much about you. How is your poor mother? Has her condition improved at all?"

"Sadly, no, but I thank you for inquiring."

"Come. We shall make you merry, I dare say. Do you like to shoot?"

Lady Blackstone drew him forward, and soon he was meeting several of the guests who were playing billiards. He only knew a few of them but recognized many of the names that he had managed to learn from Oliver Ratley, and he noted the names he had not heard before, branding them on his brain so he could write them down later in his room.

After spending an hour with the other guests, Philip started up the stairs to his room where he encountered two ladies on the landing.

He was arrested by the green eyes of the younger lady whom he was certain he had seen at a ball, perhaps two years before. She had been standing and conversing with Nicholas Langdon's wife, Julia Grey, before the two were married. But what was a respectable young lady, a friend of Julia Langdon's, doing here? Had he been mistaken that this was to be a time of planning for the coming revolution?

No. He had heard the seditious words with his own ears, spoken by the very people attending this party. But surely Mrs. Langdon's friend was not involved in an organized rebellion against the government and monarchy of England.

Whether she was or not, it was his job to discover the truth. The lives of many depended upon his being able to uncover whatever was happening here. And if he misinterpreted something or failed to convey correct information back to the Home Office, innocent people could be transported far away from their homes and families, or might even be wrongly executed. It had happened before.

But even worse was to allow an insurrection to endanger the safety of England's government, monarchy, and people.

***

"All of the guests have now arrived, and you are certainly the most beautiful and ladylike of all." Lady Blackstone had entered Felicity's room rather suddenly.

Felicity looked up from where she sat at the little desk in front of her bedroom window and closed her book.

"And Mr. Ratley talks of nothing but you." Her hostess clasped her hands and made a tiny noise like a muffled squeal.

"He does?"

"What is that you are reading?" Lady Blackstone stepped forward and picked up the book Felicity had been studying. She opened it and took a step back, her face going pale. "What is this?"

"It is a book on the Chinese language. I am trying to learn it, but I do not get on very well."

"Why in heaven's name would you want to do that? Learn Chinese?" Lady Blackstone laughed—a harsh, brief sound.

Felicity's cheeks burned. "I thought perhaps I might be a missionary there someday."

"My dear, you cannot be serious." She barked another laugh. "Only plain girls become missionaries. Besides, you would not be allowed in the country. They would cut off your head and eat you." She handed Felicity her book back and continued smiling, as if amused.

Felicity cradled the book to her chest, her cheeks burning even hotter. "Perhaps."

"Oh, forgive me, my dear." Lady Blackstone turned back toward her. "I am insensitive sometimes. But I came here to tell you what a very good impression you have made upon our Mr. Ratley." Her smile left her face, and she put her hands on her hips. "But you look as if the news does not please you. Perhaps you have handsome young men with large fortunes fall in love with you every day."

Felicity did not speak for a moment, unsure of what to say. "I did not mean to offend."

"Pishposh. What do you say of Mr. Ratley's love for you?" Lady Blackstone leaned forward, her eyes wide again and her mouth agape.

"I . . . I say he does not know me yet. Not very well, at least."

"Are you always so guarded? Cannot a man admire a girl he has just met?"

"Yes, of course. That is, of course a man can—"

"I can easily imagine men falling in love with you, for you have the prettiest, most delicate features—so irresistible to men—and the most beautiful green eyes. But tell me truly, how many men do you know who are completely disinterested in the fortune of the woman they will marry? Do you not think it does Mr. Ratley credit that he cares not a whit that you will bring no money or property into your marriage? But perhaps you do not care for his company."

"On the contrary, I enjoy his company."

"Yes. I knew you would." Lady Blackstone's full smile returned, showing remarkably well-looking teeth for a woman of her age. "I knew just how it would be," she went on. "I saw the two of you in my mind's eye, as Shakespeare says, and could see how happy you would be together. But I am pushing too hard. You must forgive me for being overly romantic. I simply cannot help it. Romanticism must always be forgiven." She clasped her hands together again.

Just then Aunt Agnes entered from the dressing room wearing her spectacles and carrying a book.

"There you are, Miss Appleby. We missed seeing you last night at dinner, and it is such a shame you were not there. Mr. Ratley insists you come down for tea, as he wishes to become better acquainted with Felicity's dear aunt."

"Oh. Well, I am not certain I can . . ."

"But you must. What enjoyment can you have hidden away in this room? I insist you come down for tea and talk with our guests."

"Oh." Auntie was glancing about the room in that darting way of hers. "I am certain Mr. Ratley cannot . . . That is, he does not wish to speak with me. It is Felicity he wants, wants to—"

"Please do come down and join us for tea, Miss Appleby, if you are able." Lady Blackstone's tone was considerably gentler. "I promise there are no monsters or fiends amongst my guests, though they are mostly men."

Auntie chuckled, then nodded, plucking at her sleeve. "Yes, of course."

Lady Blackstone said a few more words before squeezing Felicity's hand and telling her she would see her at tea.

When she was gone, Felicity turned to her aunt. "You do not have to go down to tea if you do not wish to."

"No, it will all be well. I shall bring my book and sit in an out-of-the-way corner. Lady Blackstone was so insistent, but no one ever minds me when there are lovely ladies about—such as you, Felicity." Auntie smiled. "I am pleased you have found a young man who seems worthy of your attention."

Felicity suddenly remembered something. "Auntie, did you notice the young man we saw on the landing earlier?" He was so tall and handsome, she'd realized too late that she had been staring at him.

"I did not have my spectacles. Wasn't he young and handsome, with red hair?"

"Yes, and I believe I have seen him before." He had looked surprised to see her. Why should he have looked so surprised?

"He did not speak to you as if he knew you."

"We have never been introduced, but I believe he was at a party or a ball some time ago that I attended. I think he may be acquainted with Nicholas Langdon."

"I suppose you shall meet him very soon."

"Yes, I suppose so."

CHAPTER THREE

Felicity made her way down the stairs with Aunt Agnes, who was nervously plucking at her sleeve while carrying a book and her reticule, where she kept her spectacles.

As they entered the sitting room, at least ten pairs of eyes turned to look at them. Mr. Ratley crossed the room to greet them.

"Won't you sit by me?" Mr. Ratley seated them on a sofa, which was also near Lady Blackstone. "Miss Appleby, it is so good of you to join us. I hope you are comfortable. I understand you reside with Miss Mayson and her family in London."

He proceeded to draw Auntie out and encouraged her to talk about herself and about Felicity's family. He seemed skilled at listening and asking the right questions.

But from the corner of her eye, Felicity watched the red-haired gentleman, who stood talking not far away.

Soon Lady Blackstone began to pour the tea. Everyone talked quietly with their neighbor. Mr. Ratley divided his attention between Felicity and Aunt Agnes, who actually seemed less nervous while Mr. Ratley was talking to her. It was to his credit that he treated her so deferentially. Felicity sipped her tea and finished her sliver of cake while admiring Mr. Ratley's patient manner.

"Felicity." Lady Blackstone approached her and stood with the tall red-haired man. "I would like to introduce Mr. Philip Merrick. Mr. Merrick, this is my dearest niece, Miss Felicity Mayson."

Her eyes met those of Mr. Merrick's, and again she had the feeling she had seen him before. She could even picture him wearing a dark-green waistcoat and jacket, standing in a ballroom, talking with Nicholas Langdon. Now he wore a dark-blue waistcoat with a fashionably tied snow-white neckcloth. And rather than cropped short the way many redheads seemed to prefer, his hair was thick and a bit long. She could appreciate that he was not ashamed of the color, since her own hair was a pale reddish blond. His was a few shades darker and more reddish brown.

His eyes, she noticed, were bright blue.

"I am pleased to make your acquaintance, Miss Mayson." He bowed.

"She lives in London," Lady Blackstone was saying, "and cannot possibly mind our abundance of gentlemen. After all, she has so many older brothers."

"Do you have many brothers and sisters?" Mr. Merrick asked.

"I am the twelfth of thirteen children." Felicity usually blushed when she said the words. Such a large family often caused people to raise their brows or even exclaim, "Heavens!" One wealthy gentleman's wife, after hearing the number, had muttered under her breath, "How vulgar."

Mr. Merrick did not hesitate. "You must feel fortunate to have had so many playmates as a child and so many friends as an adult."

Felicity couldn't help smiling up at him. "Yes. My sister Elizabeth is nearly always with me, but she was not able to accompany me on this visit."

"You visit Lady Blackstone often, then?"

"As a matter of fact, this is my first visit to Doverton Hall. Lady Blackstone and I have only met a few times in London."

"But my niece is quite devoted to me just the same. Is that not so?" Lady Blackstone smiled, but an unexpected look shone in her eyes, questioning.

Mr. Ratley turned from Aunt Agnes and moved to Felicity's side.

"Merrick, I am so glad you are meeting everyone. We shall have to go out shooting later."

"Yes. Lady Blackstone tells me the pheasant and grouse are as thick as bulrushes in a marsh."

Perhaps Felicity was imagining that Mr. Ratley was edging his body in between herself and Mr. Merrick. Could Mr. Ratley deduce that there was something about Mr. Merrick—perhaps because he was so handsome or because of the way he looked at her—that made her feel mildly unsettled?

Mr. Merrick soon moved away with Lady Blackstone, who was continuing to introduce him to the other guests. Mr. Ratley stayed with Felicity and Aunt Agnes and kept them company. He often smiled at her and asked what books Auntie enjoyed reading and what they had done all winter when the weather was bad, and he complimented Felicity over nearly everything she said. Surely this was how it felt to be courted, how other, more sought-after girls of fortune were treated by gentlemen in search of a wife. Felicity would hardly be human if she didn't have a bit of tender feeling for Mr. Ratley. In truth, whenever she saw him or heard his voice, her spirits lifted. Was this how it felt to fall in love?

Mr. Ratley hovered nearby until all the other men began filing out of the room to go shooting, then he took his leave.

"He is a very attentive young man," Auntie said.

"Do you like him?"

"I cannot help but like him. His manners are very pleasing, and he seems kind. The most important question is, do *you* like him?"

"I do. As you said, he is very pleasing."

Auntie plucked at her sleeve. "What shall we do if he makes you an offer of marriage?"

Felicity's heart skipped a beat. "I am not quite sure. But it seems unlikely a man would ask for my hand so soon after meeting me."

"It is quick, but just think, he has heard about you from your aunt, perhaps for some time. He probably feels he knows you very well. And he made a point of talking with me and asking many questions." She raised her brows and stared down at her hands.

"Did you think him impertinent?"

"No, but he certainly wants to know as much about you and your family as possible."

"I hope Mother will write to us soon."

"Today would be the soonest we would receive a response."

"I am anxious to get it."

***

Philip moved from his hiding place behind the open door just outside the room after Felicity Mayson and Agnes Appleby quitted it. He needed to get his gun and join the other men, but he was glad he had stayed to hear the ladies' private conversation. It seemed as if Miss Mayson and her aunt Appleby did not know Ratley very well. And yet, would he show such a preference for a young lady whose loyalty he was unsure of? Could she be unaware of this entire group's plans to overthrow the government? He couldn't explain, even to himself, why he did not believe she could be a ruthless revolutionary, except perhaps for the fact that she had such an innocence about her—her expressions, her voice and manner. But of course, he needed real evidence. The Home Office would not approve of him acquitting her of wrongdoing on the sole basis of her innocent expressions.

He should find out eventually, in any case.

Philip took the steps two at a time to fetch his gun and catch up with the other men.

Once the men were all standing in an overgrown field, leaning on their rifles, he realized this was a planned gathering. Lady Blackstone stood on a stump with her fists clenched.

"Gentlemen," she said, her big floppy hat pulled low over one ear, reminding him of a thief he'd once helped apprehend on the streets of London. That thief had been forcing children to walk the shallow areas of the Thames in bare feet to hunt for coins and other valuables.

Strange that he would think of that now.

"Gentlemen, amongst those devoted to our cause are mill workers in Manchester, weavers in Nottingham, and cotton factory workers in Yorkshire. The downtrodden and oppressed will rise up and fight to overthrow our unjust government, but they need leaders to guide them. That is why I invited you all here. You are the leaders, the very ones the people need to show them how to fight."

"We are ready," Simon Beckwith, the illegitimate son of a wealthy cotton merchant, spoke up. "Why should we wait? Let us make a plan and put it into action now."

Lady Blackstone said, "That is another reason we are here: to plan and discuss all our options and collectively decide on the best course."

"Have we decided against peaceful reform, then?" That was Perceval Blankenship, the third son of an earl who had disowned him for his gaming debts.

Someone cursed.

"Peaceful? The time for peace is over," a Mr. Adrian Sproles said. "The only kind of reform that arrests their notice is violent reform."

"Agreed!" another man shouted. "Tyrants never listen to peaceful protests. They only pay attention when their lives and livelihoods are in danger."

Others bellowed their agreement.

"I believe we have all realized that peaceful efforts avail us nothing." Lady Blackstone stared at Perceval Blankenship, not blinking, for several long moments.

"Of course," he said finally. "So we have."

"I am glad we are agreed that the Prime Minister, Parliament, and the monarchy have become so corrupt and unfeeling as to warrant drastic measures. We shall be the leadership now. You are the true and loyal sons of England, protecting the people who have been trodden underfoot for generations, men crushed under the heel of an aristocracy that cares nothing for those who work for wages that are not even enough to keep alive themselves, much less their wives and children. We are tired of men, women, and children going hungry, fathers and mothers falling ill due to lack and want, dying and leaving their children to starve in the streets. The true sons of England will not stand by and allow it any longer."

Another shout of solidarity went up. Philip did his best to shout with them, but his heart was sinking. Would this be the end of the British monarchy? Would these men—and Lady Blackstone—incite riots to assassinate the Prime Minister, Members of Parliament, and even the Prince Regent and the royal family? They could instigate a bloodbath in the tradition of the French Revolution, following the path of Robespierre and his Reign of Terror, in which thousands were guillotined because of their loyalty to the king, simply because they were born into titled families, or because someone accused them of opposing the revolution. Philip's own family could be in danger.

"We must stir support stealthily at first, so as not to arouse suspicion," Lady Blackstone went on. "We will assassinate several of the highest people in government—Lord Liverpool, cabinet members, and as many from the House of Lords as possible—then the rest will be thrown into confusion. We can capture the royal family and execute them as well while our armed men from outlying areas will march on London and seize the government buildings and institutions."

"How will we arm so many men?" one man asked.

"We have stockpiles of arms in various counties, in barns and factories and warehouses, but we need more. That is one of the most important tasks. We must acquire arms by whatever means possible. Buy them, steal them, donate them from your own collections, but we need as many as we can get between now and our glorious revolution, which we shall implement in May, a month from now."

But did they have enough people for such an insurrection? Philip wanted to ask, but he thought it best not to draw attention to himself.

The men spoke of their plans and ideas about how to procure more guns. Certainly these men—the leaders, as Lady Blackstone had called them—were the wealthiest of their secret group, and some of them were rich enough to be able to afford to buy quite a few guns. They began to talk of how to purchase a large amount without raising suspicion.

Philip needed to find out the exact locations of those stockpiled weapons Lady Blackstone had spoken of. If he could get word back to the Home Office, they could confiscate them, thereby crippling their entire rebellion. But that might not be so easy.

CHAPTER FOUR

Felicity watched the next morning as the servant brought round the letters that had come by post. Sadly, there was no reply from her mother.

She sat in one of the drawing rooms with the few other young women in the group. All of them were married, she discovered, besides herself and Aunt Agnes. Beside her sat Mrs. Josephine Cartwright, who was just her age. Her husband was playing cards with some of the other men.

Mrs. Cartwright was embroidering a silk pillowcase while she spoke. The bright thread flashed in and out of the cloth with seemingly little effort.

"I can never seem to stop sewing." She smiled and shook her head, barely glancing up from her work. "I hope you don't mind. Whenever my hands are idle, I simply cannot concentrate on conversation or any-thing else."

"I don't mind at all." Felicity had set aside her book on Chinese, and she now took up the needlework she had brought downstairs with her.

"I am looking forward to dancing. Lady Blackstone said we would have a dance soon and I can test out my new skills. I've been learning from a dancing master since I got married, but this will be my first real ball."

It was very unusual for a young woman to learn to dance after she was married instead of before, but Felicity thought it best not to comment on it. Likely she was from a poor family and had married someone of means who wished his wife to know all the social graces, including dancing.

"Lady Blackstone said you are from a large family. I had seven brothers and sisters, but three of them died before they were a year old. I hope to have a great many children. My husband says the more the better." She looked up and smiled before pinning her gaze back on her embroidery.

"There are many good things about having a large family." Felicity worked a knot loose from the sampler she was stitching for one of her nieces. "I am thankful for my sisters especially, but my brothers are my good friends too—mostly."

"Oh, girl children are the best, to be sure, though the boys are the most useful to their fathers." She glanced up with another smile.

"There you are." Lady Blackstone stopped abruptly as she rushed through the doorway. She was looking down at Felicity. "Mrs. Cartwright, you don't mind if I steal Miss Felicity away, do you?"

"No, I—"

"Felicity, come. I want to show you something in the garden."

Felicity began stuffing her needlework back into her bag. She hoped Mrs. Cartwright didn't feel slighted, but it was rather flattering to be singled out.

"Don't worry about your things. I'll have the servant take them to your room. Come." Lady Blackstone laid a cloak over Felicity's shoulders. "I don't want you to get a chill."

Lady Blackstone hurried her out of the house to the garden. "Whew, it's good to be out in the fresh air, away from the clucking hens." She laughed, then sent a side glance Felicity's way.

Felicity looked about her. "It is a beautiful day, but I was enjoying the conversation with Mrs. Cartwright."

"Oh?" Lady Blackstone's lips were slightly parted as she stared at her. "Was she telling you of intrigues and conspiracies?"

"Not at all." Felicity laughed.

Lady Blackstone laughed too, as if relieved.

"We were only speaking of dancing at the ball and the benefits of having a large family."

"Oh yes, Mrs. Cartwright is quite the little wife. Her husband rescued her from near starvation."

Felicity stared. "What do you mean?"

"Well, her father worked as a weaver, and when he got sick, he was unable to feed his wife and children. Mr. Cartwright found her on the street one day trying to sell some of her embroidery. He took pity on her and fed her. His mother took her in as a servant and . . . he fell in love with her. But you are not shocked that I would tell you such a story? Your mother might not approve of you knowing such things."

"No, I am not shocked. I think it is a very sweet story. And my mother allows me to visit the Children's Aid Mission, so I am acquainted with stories of the poor street children of London."

"Yes, of course." She was all smiles. "When I learned of your work there, I knew you and I were kindred spirits. But do you really think it is a sweet love story? That is, you agree, do you not, that a girl's marriage-ability should have nothing to do with her circumstance of fortune or birth? For Mr. Cartwright has some money and property, and his family was not very pleased at his marrying such a poor girl."

"I believe that, as long as each partner is well pleased with the other, where there is love, economy, and enough to live on, there is nothing more one could wish for."

Lady Blackstone squeezed her lips together in a sort of triumphant smile. "I knew I was impulsive to ask you here, now, but my instincts proved true. You do not approve of arrogance, and you are just the compassionate sort who will wish to thwart the cruelties of our society."

Something in the wildness of Lady Blackstone's eyes made Felicity cautious. "I do believe in caring for the poor and needy. It is a Christian's duty, as I think most people accept."

"Yes, they *say* it is their duty, and yet they cheat their workers out of a living wage. Their actions show they care nothing for the poor. They think of them as dogs and worse."

Lady Blackstone's expression as she spoke was completely different than it had been but a moment before. Her eyes were hard and flinty, her voice cool, her jaw rigid.

Her expression changed again as she smiled. "Forgive me, sweet Felicity. You are too kind and innocent, your parents far too excellent to have ever allowed you to be exposed to the evils of this world. But believe me when I tell you that you would not be able to stand for the atrocities that are inflicted on the poor by the wealthy in this country."

Felicity's heart ached at the pain behind both Lady Blackstone's words and her eyes.

Lady Blackstone brightened again. "But I wanted to show you these roses. I believe you said you loved pink roses, and mine are blooming."

Felicity did not recall saying she liked pink roses, but she looked at the beautiful blossoms, bending to sniff one and touch its cool, velvety petals. "They are lovely."

"You know, Mr. Ratley is a natural-born leader. He will be a strong advocate for whatever he believes in."

Felicity smiled and nodded, hoping to encourage Lady Blackstone to tell her more about Mr. Ratley.

"He has a very good heart, a true Briton's heart. I believe he thinks of me as a second mother. His own mother died some years ago. Here he is now."

Mr. Ratley rounded a bend in the walk, appearing from behind a tall hedge.

"Miss Mayson. Lady Blackstone." He joined them and began chatting about the garden and the weather, the last time it had rained or snowed. After a few minutes, he asked, "Miss Mayson, did you know that the seaside at Margate is only a short carriage ride away?"

"I did not."

"Have you ever been to the sea?"

"I visited Grimswood Castle in Lincolnshire, which is on the sea. It was a beautiful sight."

"And that is the only time you've been to the seaside?"

"It is. And I only saw it from the castle tower, but it was quite an impressive view."

"Then I propose a trip to the seaside, just for the day."

"Oh yes!" Lady Blackstone cried, laughing as if he had just told a great joke. "Miss Mayson would enjoy that above anything."

"Miss Mayson?" Mr. Ratley turned to her with a humble look. "Would you and Miss Appleby accompany Lady Blackstone and me to the seaside tomorrow?"

"I cannot definitely speak for my aunt, but I believe we would both enjoy the seaside."

"Excellent. Then we shall plan to leave in the morning." Lady Blackstone looked pleased.

When she was back at the house, in the bedroom she shared with her aunt, Felicity spoke to her about going to the seaside. Auntie agreed.

Later, when they were both sitting in the drawing room again having afternoon tea, the servant came bearing letters. "For Miss Felicity Mayson," he said.

Felicity took the letter. It was from her mother. She excused herself to go to her room and read it.

Dearest Felicity,

I am pleased you are enjoying yourself at Doverton Hall with Lady Blackstone and her guests. As for your inquiries about Oliver Ratley, your father says that he has a fortune left to him by his father, who was a successful merchant. He knows nothing of the son, and of the father he knows only that he was a clever businessman. Your father and I will make further inquiries, but if your aunt Lady Blackstone approves of him, then I think he would be a great match for you.

Mother went on to give the news from home, of various colds, disagreements, and household intrigues that were interesting or amusing.

"Is that a letter from your mother?" Aunt Agnes asked.

"Yes, it finally came." She relayed the information about Mr. Ratley first. "And everyone is in good health, and Tom has arrived with his regiment in the Netherlands."

"Mr. Ratley is an honorable man, then? It does sound as if your mother would approve of your forming an attachment to him."

"Yes." Still, Felicity would have preferred if her mother had more information or had known his mother or father personally. All she really knew was that he was truthful about his situation in life. She was left to make up her own mind about his character—and about how trustworthy Lady Blackstone's opinions were.

Felicity gave Auntie the letter to read for herself. She stared down at the seal, holding her eyeglasses close to it.

"It almost looks as if the seal was pried off and melted again. The seal is warped. Would your mother have done that?"

"I suppose she might, if she had forgotten to say something after sealing it. But would she not have just sealed it again with new wax?"

Felicity examined the seal herself. It did indeed appear as if some-one had melted the wax again, as the edges were smudged and the seal was slightly blurred.

"The weather is not warm enough to have melted and smudged it," Felicity mused aloud.

Aunt Agnes's brow creased. "It was just so in a book I read. The nefarious uncle intercepted the heroine's letter and opened and altered it."

Felicity examined the letter again. "It is certainly Mother's hand-writing and her style of writing. Nothing seems amiss about the content of the letter. Besides, who would want to intercept and read my letters?"

She smiled, trying to shrug off the uneasy feeling her aunt's words had given her. It was silly. Auntie had read too many novels.

"I'm sure you are correct, my dear. No one would interfere with your correspondence with your mother." But the crease between her eyes lingered.

***

While most of the other guests were readying themselves for dinner, Philip came downstairs to see if anyone was about. He did not want to miss any clandestine meetings or important conversations.

He found Miss Felicity Mayson sitting by a window with an open book as she wrote on a sheet of paper.

His eyesight had always been excellent, so while she still had not discovered him standing there, he tried to see if he could read what she was writing from across the room.

The writings were similar to tiny drawings, or even just random markings. He stepped a bit closer. They looked even less like words. Was she writing in some sort of code? Or perhaps learning a code?

His stomach sank at the thought that she was one of this group of revolutionaries. What other reason could there be for her learning to write in code? She had such an expression of goodness in her face

36

whenever she spoke. Mr. Langdon and his wife would be most disappointed to find that their friend was a traitor to England.

He stepped forward, letting his footsteps be heard. Miss Mayson glanced up and closed the paper inside the book, turning the book over so that its cover could not be seen.

"Good evening," Philip greeted her.

"Good evening." She placed her hands over the book in her lap.

"I hope I am not disturbing you. I can leave you alone if you like."

"Oh no, that is not necessary." She smiled. "I was only giving my aunt some time alone in our room. I thought I would do a bit of studying downstairs."

"Studying?"

"Yes. I enjoy novels, but I also spend time studying. Mr. Merrick, isn't it?"

"Yes, Miss Mayson. You have a good memory." Another trait of a spy. Now that he thought about it, women would make good spies; they were such mysterious creatures.

"Thank you. I have met quite a few people since coming to Doverton Hall, but I cannot say I remember all the names."

Was she telling the truth?

"Do you mind if I ask what you were studying?" He carefully watched her face for her reaction.

"You will think me foolish." She fingered the book in her lap.

"Foolish? Why?"

"I am trying to learn Chinese."

He let out a pent-up breath. "Chinese?"

"You can laugh at me if you wish, but I thought I might perhaps be a missionary there someday."

"That sounds very noble." He could not be sure she was telling the truth, but in his heart, he was relieved to have an explanation for the "code" he'd seen her studying. He took a deep breath and let it out.

"Most people tell me it's foolish, since unmarried women aren't allowed in the country. But I want to do something in life, something important. I thought perhaps if I were a missionary, I could write something that would be meaningful to others, similar to Hannah More." She shook her head and looked down at her lap. "You must think me foolish for telling you all that."

"I don't think you foolish at all. It is refreshing to hear someone speak so openly about honest ambitions."

Indeed, most girls he knew only cared about "bettering" their situation in life by marrying the wealthiest man. They schemed and simpered and spoke flowery, flattering words until one was left to guess what their true thoughts were. And they were rarely interested in *him*, as he was a fourth son and would inherit nearly nothing.

At least now he could go back to admiring her pretty eyes, delicate brows, and perfectly shaped mouth.

He probably should not be noticing the latter.

Felicity Mayson was different, especially if she wanted to be a missionary. Of course, she might only be pretending to feel and believe things she did not.

But he had yet to discover: What was she doing *here*?

CHAPTER FIVE

Felicity blushed at how much personal information she had revealed to this stranger. She had never opened up that much to anyone except a few friends and her mother. What had made her say so much to Philip Merrick? Perhaps it was his friendly, empathetic expression, how he looked her in the eye and nodded. She was accustomed to her brothers laughing at anything serious she might say, but Mr. Merrick did not even look as if he wanted to laugh.

But where were her manners? She shouldn't be only talking of herself.

"And what are your ambitions, Mr. Merrick?"

"My ambitions?" His look turned more sober as two creases formed between his brows. "I am the fourth son of my father. He is a gentleman of some means, but a fourth son must have plans and an occupation. That suits me well, for I enjoy a life of activity." He seemed to make an effort to smile, but the somber crease remained. "I shall make the church my profession, if other aspirations do not develop."

"Other aspirations?"

"Yes. The sort of aspirations the rest of the men are here for."

She looked inquiringly at him.

"We are all hoping for positions of leadership."

"I don't understand. This is a party, is it not?"

"Then you don't know?"

"Know what?" Felicity's chest tightened.

He stared at her as if unsure what to say next, but there was a hint of compassion in his eyes, unless she read him wrong. Her heart was beginning to pound.

"There you are!" Mr. Ratley entered the room. "Miss Appleby told me I might find you here." He turned his attention to Mr. Merrick. "Did you tire of the game in the billiards room, Mr. Merrick?"

"I was searching for a quiet place to read when I happened upon Miss Mayson."

"Then I shall gladly whisk her away so that you may have your solitude. Miss Mayson, would you like to take a turn around the garden with me?"

Felicity acquiesced, and she once again found herself in the garden with Oliver Ratley and Lady Blackstone, wandering about, talking of the flowers and their trip to the seaside the next day, eagerly anticipating the short jaunt.

But what had Mr. Merrick been speaking of? All the men here were seeking positions of leadership, he'd said. Whatever kind of positions could they find here at Lady Blackstone's country estate?

***

Felicity and Aunt Agnes sat across from Lady Blackstone and Mr. Ratley in that gentleman's carriage the next day as they set off for Margate. Lady Blackstone's voice was animated as she spoke about first one topic and then another with a ready smile on her face, while Mr. Ratley kept glancing out the window to relay their progress, commenting on how slowly the carriage was moving, and dabbing at his face with his handkerchief.

Meanwhile, Auntie plucked at her sleeves and mumbled under her breath.

"What did you say, Auntie?"

"Oh, I was saying the weather is warm for this time of year, but I am glad I brought my warm cloak."

The carriage came to a halt, and Mr. Ratley sprang out, helping each lady down, Felicity being the last one out.

"How do you like it?" Mr. Ratley bent to look into her face.

The ocean was before her as she stood on a sand dune just above the shore.

"It is lovely." His face was so eager, so expectant, that she went on. "I love the roar of the sea. And the expanse of it is simply wonderful. The way the water continues to meet the sand is unlike anything I've seen before."

"I'm so pleased you like it."

"Come," Lady Blackstone called to them from several feet away where she stood holding Aunt Agnes's arm. "We must go down to the shore."

Mr. Ratley dabbed at his face again. He had lost some of his color.

"Are you well, Mr. Ratley? You look pale."

"Oh no, I am quite well." He smiled, but the corners of his mouth trembled.

What could the matter be?

They started off, and he appeared strong enough. He helped her down some stone steps that led to the beach. She was careful, though, not to lean on him.

At the bottom, her foot sank into the sand. The gritty grains entered her thin leather shoes and settled between her toes. A white seabird ran along the edge of the water in front of them as the frothy water rushed up to meet it.

Felicity shaded her eyes with her hand to gaze out at the ocean. The rippling sea was like a thousand sparkling jewels glinting in the sun.

The roar of its ceaseless motion filled her ears the way it seemed to fill the whole world, all encompassing.

She glanced to her right. Lady Blackstone and Aunt Agnes were surprisingly far down the beach and walking still farther. She turned to her left. "Should we not follow th—"

Mr. Ratley was down on his knees beside her. Sweat beaded on his forehead and upper lip.

"Mr. Ratley!"

Was he ill? Should she go and fetch a physician? He reached and grasped her hand.

"Miss Felicity Mayson, will you make me the happiest man in the world by agreeing to become my wife?"

Felicity's heart pounded. He gazed up at her, fear and expectation all over his face.

No man had ever asked her to marry him, except the one time when a surgeon's young son had asked her in the vestibule of the surgeon's home when she'd come to fetch him to set her brother's broken leg.

Now, she stammered as she had done then. Except this time, she said, "I will."

But did she mean it? Did she truly want to marry Mr. Ratley?

Mr. Ratley seemed to love her, if his nervousness and attentiveness were any indication, and he had a large fortune besides. They would not quarrel about money or be in want. Wasn't this her opportunity to have the kind of love that her friends Leorah and Julia enjoyed? What else could she wish for?

He jumped to his feet, still clutching her hand. "Oh, thank you, Miss Mayson. I am so . . . thank you for accepting me. I shall endeavor . . ."

He let her go and raised both arms high in the air to wave at Lady Blackstone and Aunt Agnes.

Was this the right time to discuss when he would speak to her father and when the wedding should take place? She rather imagined when she became engaged that her fiancé would kiss her or at least embrace her. But that was foolish. They were in a public place.

Lady Blackstone and Aunt Agnes were walking back toward them now. Mr. Ratley put his arms around her and lifted her off her feet. He bent and kissed her with wet, limp lips.

Was this how a kiss felt? All slobbery and awkward?

Then he set her on her feet again.

Her cheeks burned at the thought that Lady Blackstone and Auntie had seen him kiss her, her very first kiss, which she had not realized would feel so . . . unromantic. But one could not expect perfection when he had—she hoped—never kissed anyone before.

When the two ladies reached them, Mr. Ratley announced, "We are engaged."

"Truly, I wish you both the best of everything life has to offer." Lady Blackstone's smile stretched from one ear to the other. "I could not be happier if you were my own children. That is, if one of you were." They all laughed.

Aunt Agnes was plucking at her sleeves. "Yes, very happy."

They continued walking down the beach, her hand on Mr. Ratley's arm. Felicity could hardly pay attention to the beauty of the ocean. Had she done the right thing? How could she say no to him when he had that vulnerable look on his face? Besides, he must love her to ask her to marry him. But truly, what did she know of him, of his beliefs and his wishes and his thoughts on important things such as faith in God, how many children they should have, and . . . There must be a great many important subjects they had never discussed.

They wandered along the seaside, watching the birds and the waves as they got their shoes soiled and sandy. Mr. Ratley kept his hand on hers. Would he be a kind and affectionate husband? He gave every indication that he would be. Surely her life would be pleasant and comfortable married to this man.

On the way back to Doverton Hall, no opportunity to speak privately presented itself, of course, since Lady Blackstone and Aunt Agnes were with them in the carriage. If only she could speak with him, he would surely dispel this uneasy feeling in the pit of her stomach.

***

Philip noticed a restlessness in the men while their leader was away sightseeing at the seaside. They drank far too much brandy. But by dinner Lady Blackstone had returned with the others, and the guests' drinking slowed to normal.

The dinner seemed especially fine and fancy tonight as their hostess managed to get everyone's attention, a broad smile on her face.

"I have an announcement to make. Or perhaps I should allow our dear Mr. Ratley to make the announcement."

She looked down at the young man, and he stood. He made a show of clearing his throat.

"Dear friends, I would like you all to share in my joy, as Miss Felicity Mayson has agreed to become my wife. We are engaged to be married."

There were a few cries, then cheers, as the room erupted in exclamations.

Felicity Mayson was smiling, but in her eyes he read an emotion that had nothing to do with joy. But perhaps he was imagining that she was putting on a brave face, pretending to be happy.

After dinner was over and the men joined the ladies, Mr. Cartwright came over to him.

"Perhaps now we can speak more freely about our revolution."

"Now?"

"I forgot that you were not here the first day." He glanced behind him. "Lady Blackstone and Mr. Ratley asked us to behave as if we were at a normal house party and not mention anything about our activities and plans in front of the ladies, particularly Miss Felicity Mayson and her aunt."

"But why?"

"I suppose it was because the ladies did not know our true purpose for being here. Or perhaps Lady Blackstone was not sure we could trust them. Either way, if Ratley has asked her to marry him, it must mean that they consider them safe."

Philip became aware of two men, Sproles and Rowell, arguing. Both had had too much to drink, and their voices rose as they drew closer to each other.

"I should be in charge of the weapons," Sproles yelled in Rowell's face.

Philip's whole body tensed as he calculated how to place his body between the two men and the ladies, who, unfortunately, were not sitting in one location.

"You?" Rowell shouted. "You don't even know the meaning of loyalty to our cause. You would turn your back on us all if the Crown offered to pay your gaming debts."

Sproles roared and throttled Rowell, and they fell on the floor in a heap of flailing arms and legs.

CHAPTER SIX

Felicity screamed and then covered her mouth as two men suddenly attacked each other and fell to the floor. She glanced around her, then remembered Auntie was upstairs. She'd claimed a headache after their outing and declined to come down for dinner.

Lady Blackstone's face turned crimson as she started toward the two men. Mr. Ratley stood, but Mr. Merrick sprang forward, and he and another man pulled the two fighters apart.

Lady Blackstone said in a loud voice, "How dare you behave in such a way!"

"How could you disrupt the evening of my engagement?" Mr. Ratley said.

"You two don't get to decide who is in charge of anything," another man said, pointing at Sproles and then Rowell.

What were they talking of? It made no sense, but her uneasy feeling had been correct. Something was going on here, something subversive. But what?

She looked to her fiancé for answers, but he was stepping closer to the two men whom Mr. Philip Merrick was holding by the scruffs of their necks, keeping them separated by the span of his own arms.

"This is unacceptable!" Lady Blackstone was livid. "I shall not have this kind of behavior at my dinner table."

Felicity's stomach tied itself in a knot as several men looked angry or made a resentful remark. Then someone touched her arm. Mrs. Cartwright stood at her side.

"Perhaps we should go to our rooms and let the men sort this out amongst themselves."

"Yes, perhaps you are right." She couldn't help staring at Mr. Ratley. Wouldn't he notice that she was leaving? Could he not see how much she wished to talk to him? But as she and Mrs. Cartwright left, no one seemed to notice, and soon they were walking up the stairs and bidding each other a good night.

"Mrs. Cartwright," Felicity called out from just outside her bedroom door.

"Yes?"

"What were the two men fighting about?"

"The two men?" Mrs. Cartwright bit her lip and did not look her in the eye. "Oh, who knows what men fight about? They are like children sometimes. I am sure they will have it all smoothed over by tomorrow."

"Yes." Felicity's heart sank into her stomach. She and Aunt Agnes must be the only two people at this party who did not understand what was going on.

***

Felicity went down to breakfast at the time she thought Lady Blackstone most likely to be there, but she must have missed her. Instead, Felicity ate with Mrs. Cartwright and three men, who talked quietly amongst themselves.

"You look very bright-eyed and cheerful this morning," Mrs. Cartwright said after she had seated herself directly across the table from Felicity.

Felicity almost said, "Even though I barely slept, my eyes are red, and I look rather pale?" But she refrained and finally answered, "Thank you."

"I am eager for the ball tonight, though I'm a bit nervous about dancing." Mrs. Cartwright smiled, but there was an almost brittle quality to her voice and a wariness in the way her eyes darted repeatedly to the men at the other end of the long table. "I am sure Mr. Cartwright will help me not to make too many mistakes, but I shall be too afraid, I think, to dance with anyone else. I do believe it rained last night." She rushed into a new topic without even taking a breath. "The ground may be too wet to take a walk in the garden today, which will be such a shame."

Obviously, she was trying to avoid speaking about what had happened the night before. Felicity did not wish to make her uncomfortable—she sensed the young woman might cry if she questioned her about the incident—so she ate her food, smiled reassuringly at her new friend, and asked the others in the room, "Do you know where I might find Lady Blackstone?"

They all answered in the negative, so she excused herself and left the room.

Felicity looked through all the rooms where the guests usually gathered, but she saw no one. Finally, she found a servant and asked her, "Do you know where I might find Lady Blackstone?"

"No, miss. Have you tried her bedroom?"

"I have not. Thank you."

Felicity did not like to knock on her hostess's bedroom door, but she went up the steps anyway.

"Felicity. Darling." Mr. Ratley stood at the top of the stairs, then started down. "I was just looking for you."

Felicity took a deep breath.

"Darling, is something wrong?"

When Mr. Ratley reached her, he took her hand between his. His touch was so gentle and his expression so attentive.

She took another deep breath and let it out. "I think something is wrong, but I don't know what it is. And yet, I feel everyone else here does know."

His gentle expression changed slightly, and he no longer looked her in the eye. He nodded. "I should have realized you were too astute not to discover the truth. Come with me." He put her hand through his arm and led her into a nearby sitting room and closed the door.

"I am sorry the argument last night was disturbing to you. The truth is, we are a group of politically minded Britons, spread throughout the country, who are determined to right the wrongs of society."

When he did not continue, she asked, "Right the wrongs of society? What does that signify?" The skin on her arms and the back of her neck tingled.

"I know that you are too kind and intelligent to misunderstand the wrongs I speak of. People are downtrodden and unable to feed their families. You are too shrewd not to have heard of the atrocities that are perpetrated by the rich and privileged. And nothing will change until we change it."

Memories of hangings and transportations for treasonous activities and unlawful oath-takings in recent years flooded her mind. She tried to force her expression not to change, to listen calmly, but she felt the blood draining from her face.

"I've been told I'm not good at explaining things. I need Lady Blackstone to help me explain."

He started to rise from his seat, but she grabbed his arm. "Tell me the truth. Are you trying to overthrow the government?"

He sat down beside her and took a deep breath. "Lady Blackstone warned me not to tell you all at once. She said you should learn everything gradually. I should have asked her to do it. But you must try to understand." He pursed his lips together and rubbed his chin.

She whispered, "How will you mount this . . . this insurrection?"

"Darling, people are starving. The wealthy in this country do not care, and we must make them care." He still would not look her in the eye, and his brow creased more deeply with every word. "You would not have people—innocent, good people and their children—starve in the streets, in the villages, because the mill owners and the masters refuse to pay them a decent wage. You are too kind and gentle to want to see that continue in our country."

Of course she would not allow that if she could prevent it, but she stared back at him without speaking. Her mind was churning, searching for a way out. *O God, help me be wise. Give me a glib tongue to say the right thing.* What would he and Lady Blackstone do to her if she did not agree with them?

She had engaged herself to a man who was bent on revolution.

Still, might she not be able to persuade him?

"You cannot know what you are involved in," she began, leaning close and practically forcing him to look her in the eye. "What you are plotting is sedition, and it is punishable by death. You will be hanged, or at the very least, transported to a faraway country for many years. Your actions could cause the death of innocent people—you amongst them."

"Darling, you know I love you." Finally, he was looking her in the eye as he caught hold of her upper arms. "Please do not be angry with me. All will be well. We have many, many followers. We are very strong, and once we are in power, we will make things better for all people."

"And what if I do not agree with your methods for making things better?" She thought of her brother engaged in military service out of loyalty for his country, fighting Napoleon in a foreign land. She thought of the Prince Regent, King George III, and all the royal family. She thought of her friend Lady Withinghall and her husband, the viscount. Would they be murdered as the French revolutionaries had murdered thousands of innocent aristocrats and their families, even their young children?

Her fiancé suddenly looked like a stranger, and a dangerous one at that.

"Listen, darling. Our intentions are good. We would not hurt any innocent people."

"Surely that is what the French revolutionaries said as well."

"Please don't look at me like that." His voice turned wheedling. "I thought you would understand. Lady Blackstone said you were as tired of the hypocrisy as the rest of us, that you disliked society's cruelties toward the less fortunate. Don't you want to see people helped and lives made better? The hungry fed and the naked clothed?"

Felicity might have asked him how he planned to accomplish such things, but she didn't trust her voice not to tremble and break. What had she stumbled into? To what had Lady Blackstone invited her? Had she truly seemed the kind of person who wanted to join with revolutionaries to overthrow the government?

"Darling." He took her hand in his and leaned in close. "Together we will make this country a better place for all. Lady Blackstone says we are very close to our goals. We could make an advance on Parliament in just a month or so."

"Make an advance on Parliament? What does that mean?"

Mr. Ratley actually smiled. "Now don't you concern yourself about any of the details. Lady Blackstone and I and the rest of the men here will take care of the particulars."

He bent and kissed her on the lips, a quick action that she had not anticipated.

"But I must ask your father's permission to marry you. Isn't that what society dictates?" His smug smile made her stomach churn. "A letter will be sufficient, don't you think? No need to go all the way to London. Shall I write to him directly?"

She should say something. She should say, "I beg you will not write to him at all." But fear gripped her, paralyzing her insides. She said nothing.

"Darling, you are not still worried, are you? Listen, we will go and find Lady Blackstone. By the time she is finished explaining it all to you,

you will be as eager as the rest of us to begin at once. Lady Blackstone can use your sharp mind to great advantage in the planning. A woman who has the gumption to study Chinese on her own . . ."

He looked as if he might laugh.

"I beg you not to trouble Lady Blackstone. I believe I should like to go to my room and rest." And write to her father to send a servant and the carriage for her and Aunt Agnes. Immediately.

Mr. Ratley squeezed her hand. "I shall escort you. But you must speak with Lady Blackstone now that I've bungled the business of explaining it all to you."

He was not smiling now, and his eyes darted about as he stood and walked to the door.

They left the room, with Mr. Ratley holding her hand on his arm in silence.

Once they reached Felicity's door, he looked into her eyes. "I love you, Felicity. You are just the sort of girl I always wanted to marry. Just know that I love you."

It was on the tip of her tongue to say, "You don't even know me." But she bit her lip instead. She nodded and broke away from his touch, entering her room and closing the door.

Felicity's breath came faster as she closed her eyes. "Oh, what have I done?"

She walked to her bed and lay across it without a thought for wrinkling her dress.

She had pledged to marry a man who was involved in sedition. How could this have happened? And still, she wanted to believe he loved her and all would yet be well. How desperate for love was she to even hope . . . ? How desperate was she to engage herself to a man she did not know, had only been acquainted with for a few days?

Lady Blackstone, her fiancé, the people at this party, were all traitors to the Crown, to England.

She was cold all over, her mind numb with horror. She stared up at the canopy over her bed.

A knock sounded at the door.

She sat up. "Come in."

Lady Blackstone swung open the door and strode in even before the summons was out of Felicity's mouth.

"Felicity, my dear." She moved to stand in front of her. Lady Blackstone's expression seemed chiseled from stone. Her eyes were dark, almost black. But then she pasted on a brittle smile.

"Mr. Ratley tells me you are confused about our ideals and plans." She moved a stool closer to Felicity and sat down. Only then did Felicity notice that Mr. Ratley had also entered the room and was standing near the door.

"You may not realize it, but there are many atrocities being visited on the people of our great nation. You also may not realize that there is a movement afoot to make right the wrongs that have been done. Now, I knew you were an intelligent, kindhearted girl, just the sort of person who would understand what we were trying to do and would join us, seeing the rightness of our actions and our ideals. I saw in you the kind of courage and dignity that would stand up to tyranny of every kind."

Fierceness seemed to flash from Lady Blackstone's eyes. Felicity got the impression that she was exerting extra effort to soften her tone, as it went from strident to quiet and back to strident again.

"I also saw in you the perfect soul mate for my dear friend, Mr. Ratley, who wished for a wife to be by his side, supporting him in his noble fight. He wished for a sweet girl, a compliant but wise woman who would love him and receive his love in return. And you are that woman, Felicity."

Lady Blackstone took hold of Felicity's hands. Her touch was icy cold. Felicity shivered.

"We have brought you into our fellowship, believing in you, trusting that you would see the good in what we are attempting to do." Lady Blackstone drew her hands in closer, forcing Felicity to lean in, bringing her face within inches of Lady Blackstone's. "You will not disappoint us, will you, my dear?" She said the words in a quiet, steely tone.

"As . . . as you said, I am confused. Please explain things."

Lady Blackstone did not release her hands or even loosen her grip. "Mr. Ratley told me he botched the explanation. But just know that all will be done in an upright manner. We shall not allow the kind of confusion and barbarity of the French Revolution. Robespierre was unable to gain control. We shall not make the same mistake, I assure you. Our objectives are clear, our plans are precise, and we will not allow anything . . . anything . . . to prevent us from attaining our goals."

Felicity swallowed. A response seemed to be required, so she said, "I see."

"And since you are engaged to our dear Mr. Ratley, and since you are now privy to our intentions, you must realize . . . you are one of us now. You may as well embrace us."

Lady Blackstone's smile sent a chill down Felicity's spine.

Mr. Ratley stepped forward, his eyes wide and his lips parted. He knelt in front of her beside Lady Blackstone and reached for her hand.

"Darling, as I know you love me, I also ask that you trust me. Our cause is noble. Truly, it is. If you will only trust me, I shall protect you, and when our group is in power, we shall be rulers, and your own ideas will be considered and respected in the decision-making of our country. How many other women in history have had such privilege?"

"Of course, of course," Lady Blackstone said, her voice suddenly placating. "Felicity cares about the poor, and she is loyal to me, but most of all, she is loyal to her husband-to-be."

Her hard eyes seemed to bore into Felicity's thoughts.

What could she say? What *should* she say? The thought of marrying a revolutionary made her feel sick, but what would they do to her if she refused her loyalty to Mr. Ratley, Lady Blackstone, and their cause? People's lives were at stake, not to mention their precious cause, if she should leave there and alert the authorities. They would all be hanged for treason.

"Why me?" Felicity spoke carefully, trying not to betray her true thoughts so as not to stir their suspicions. "Why did you ask me to come here when I had nothing to do with your cause and you did not know if I would support it?" *And why persuade Mr. Ratley to fall in love with me?*

"When I was visiting in London, you said some things about society's rules and the way the aristocracy treats its women and the poor that led me to believe you would be very receptive to our ideas."

She tried to recall to what Lady Blackstone was referring. Felicity must have been talking about her favorite author Hannah More's latest book or treatise, of the hypocrisy Miss More always pointed out.

"I saw a kindred spirit in you, Felicity." Lady Blackstone's expression became fiercely earnest.

Felicity could almost believe in her sincerity.

"I also knew"—Lady Blackstone glanced away as she spoke—"that Mr. Ratley would fall in love with you, and you with him, if only you had the opportunity to form an attachment. And my party was that perfect opportunity. You are so well matched, and it gives me pleasure to make others happy."

"But are you quite certain," Felicity said, still carefully weighing her words, "that this will all end the way you intend it—the revolution and the overthrow of the government?" She couldn't even say the words without her throat going dry. "I am concerned for your safety."

"Do not forget," Lady Blackstone said with a sly smile, "that our safety is your safety. You are a part of us now."

"Of course." Felicity's voice sounded strangled.

"But you are tired." Mr. Ratley squeezed her hand and rose to his feet. "I think we should leave her to rest, as she had asked to do."

Lady Blackstone reached out to pat Felicity's cheek. Felicity forced herself not to cringe.

"Mr. Ratley will come and check on you later. Rest well."

CHAPTER SEVEN

Felicity watched them leave, then clutched at her throat, leaning forward. "What have I done, what have I done?" she mumbled, rocking forward and back.

She jumped up off the bed and paced to the window. She had to think, had to find someone who could help her escape. But to whom could she turn?

Aunt Agnes walked into the room holding a book.

"Oh, Auntie, I'm so sorry." Felicity wrapped her arms around herself as the cold, weak feeling came over her again.

"Whatever is the matter?" Auntie put her eyeglasses on and came closer, peering at her.

"I have endangered us both by coming here and engaging myself to Mr. Ratley." She spoke softly, just above a whisper.

"I don't understand. Do you regret agreeing to marry Mr. Ratley? I'm sure it can be undone."

"No, no. It is not only the engagement." How could she tell her poor nervous aunt of the danger surrounding them? Of the nefarious plans of the people at this party? That they were now trapped?

"Auntie, haven't you noticed something strange about this party? The men outnumber the women almost three to one. This is no party but rather a political meeting to plot how to overthrow the government."

Auntie's mouth opened. Her hands started twitching. "Surely you cannot . . . That cannot be. Lady Blackstone is your aunt. She would not be involved in such a plan."

"We hardly know Lady Blackstone. She was married to my uncle many years ago, and we've hardly seen her since he died. She has been married and widowed since then and been amongst the Lord only knows who. She may have become enamored of these seditious ideas at any point in the last ten or twelve years."

"Could your mother and father have been so ignorant of her character and activities?" Auntie's hands plucked furiously at her sleeves.

"Lady Blackstone would of course take care to hide her unlawful activities. She must have deceived many people, including my family. I only wish she had left me out of her schemes."

A pain stabbed Felicity's midsection. If only she had refused to come to this party. If only she had not allowed herself to indulge Mr. Ratley's attentions. If only she had not said yes to his proposal.

But it was all done now, and there was nothing she could do to change any of it. She simply could not imagine a way out of this situation, and yet she had to be wise and think of a way out for herself and her aunt. Poor Aunt Agnes.

"Forgive me for telling you all that. It could serve no purpose." Felicity was speaking more to herself than to her aunt, who was now mumbling to herself and still plucking at her clothing.

"Do not worry, Auntie." Felicity tried to get her attention. "I shall find a way out of this. We shall write to Father and ask him to bring the carriage and fetch us. Truly, all shall be well."

She did her best to sound confident.

"I am not a child."

"No, of course not. I just don't want you to worry. Mr. Ratley may be persuaded to assist us. If he loves me as he says, I should be able to make him see reason."

She would at least try, if she could think of no other way of escape. But if he was more loyal to Lady Blackstone than he was to Felicity, their likelihood of escape was quite small.

***

Felicity walked beside Mr. Ratley in the cool of the evening in an area where the servants had just lighted a few torches for them. Everyone else was changing for dinner, but she'd asked to take a private walk with her fiancé.

"Darling," she said, "I don't wish to be obtuse, but I am still confused about what is happening and about your role here." She chose her words carefully, keeping her voice quiet and even. "When I agreed to marry you, I had no idea of any of this."

He focused his gaze on her face, his brows drawing together. "It was a great deal for you to take in, I know, but consider the fact that we were actually sparing you, in many ways, in the future by allowing you to be acquainted with what is happening and what is about to take place."

"How did you become involved?"

He seemed to think for a few moments, and he led her to a bench and seated himself beside her.

"It must have been a shock to you. Forgive me for not explaining my situation first, but I wanted to marry you so badly, I could not stop myself from asking you when I did. You are not sorry you said yes to me, are you?"

What could she say? "I enjoy talking with you and being in your company, and I was pleased to say yes to your proposal, but now I am . . . a bit afraid. As I said, I am confused." *God, please let him reassure me that we do not have to be here, planning an insurrection, that if I am uncomfortable with our involvement in this revolution, we can leave and distance ourselves from this.*

"Darling, you must trust me." He gave her that condescending smile she had not seen until after she'd agreed to marry him.

"Trust you? Believe me, I want to, but I am unused to . . ." Revolution? Unlawful plotting against king and country?

"You must try to understand and sympathize. Lady Blackstone doesn't like to speak of it, but her sister married a man who forced her to work in a cotton factory, and she died in an accident in which she was crushed. The factory owner was so far from caring he left her on the floor and ordered everyone to continue working.

"And Lady Blackstone's first husband beat her and starved her when she was with child. She lost the baby because of it and was destitute when he died. She credits your uncle, her second husband, with saving her life. It was very much like Mrs. Cartwright's situation.

"When I met Lady Blackstone, I had just lost my father, and it was around the time Lord Blackstone died. We formed a bond, much like a mother and son, I believe—she being childless and me without a mother since I was five. So you see, we are fighting for the country's freedoms together now, as she wishes to right some of the wrongs that have been done, preventing the type of terrible fate her sister met as well as her own early situation."

"I am glad you and Lady Blackstone were able to form such a bond, and it is our Christian duty to help the poor. But how did you become interested in revolution?"

"How else are we to help the poor? Lady Blackstone has quite a vigorous mind, and she showed me how impossible it is to alter the way things are done in this country without a complete regime change— without revolution. I'm sure, once you hear all her plans and ideas, you will agree. But, Felicity"—he leaned toward her on the bench and took her hand in his—"I need you to pretend to agree with her, even if you do not yet understand everything. She can get very upset when she thinks someone is being disloyal." He took a deep breath and let it out slowly. "Please, just tell her you approve of what we are doing. I promise you will agree with everything eventually."

"If she doesn't like people disagreeing with her, I wonder that she invited me to this party when I was completely ignorant of what she and the rest of you were plotting."

Mr. Ratley pursed his lips. "I hope you are not going to be difficult about this."

A cold tingling spread to her fingertips.

"I am trying to be patient," he went on, his dark eyes boring into hers. "You must understand the seriousness of our situation. Everything, even our very lives, depends on everyone's discretion. We must remain united, and above all, we must not allow anyone to hear of our plans, or all will be lost. You understand that, do you not?"

Indeed, she did. "Yes."

"That's a good girl." He patted her on the hand. "Now kiss me like a good fiancée."

She leaned away from him. It was an involuntary reaction, as her skin crawled at the thought of kissing him now.

His expression changed from satisfaction to disapproval.

"Someone might see us here. Hannah More says engaged couples must be discreet until the wedding day. Please humor me." She forced her lips into a smile. Truly, she did not know if Hannah More had ever said any such thing, but it seemed to mollify him.

"I suppose young ladies are often sensitive to such things—not wishing anyone to see them display affection with their sweetheart." He smiled condescendingly. "Very well. I shall humor your sensibilities."

He stood and tucked her hand inside his arm.

Being so near to him set all her nerves on edge. Her limbs ached with the tension.

They joined the others who were awaiting the announcement that dinner was served.

She needed to hold herself together through the next few hours of tedium and conversation. She had to stop her mind from dwelling on the facts of her situation. But most of all, she must not let Lady Blackstone and Mr. Ratley see the fear and dread and panic in her heart.

***

Philip watched Lady Blackstone and Mr. Ratley both glancing often at Felicity Mayson—Lady Blackstone with shrewdness and suspicion, and Mr. Ratley with a bit of fear and perhaps even anger. Had something happened? Was Felicity a potential traitor to their cause?

Or was it only wishful thinking on his part?

Felicity Mayson, on the other hand, was quick to laugh at the other guests' jokes, and she avoided eye contact with both Mr. Ratley and Lady Blackstone. There was a strange tension in the way she held herself erect and in her jerky movements.

After dinner, when the men rejoined the ladies in the drawing room, he watched Felicity Mayson get up from her seat and sit next to Mrs. Cartwright on a settee that was made only for two, as if she was trying to prevent any of the men from sitting too close. But Mr. Ratley pulled a chair up next to her.

What newly engaged woman would try to avoid sitting with her fiancé?

Philip noticed Miss Mayson only spoke when Mr. Ratley spoke to her first. Then she slipped away before anyone else, and Mr. Ratley said, "Miss Mayson had a headache and went to bed early."

He did not look concerned about her and immediately joined a conversation between Lady Blackstone and two of the men.

Philip would not be able to solve the mystery of Felicity Mayson and her loyalty tonight, so he drew near to Lady Blackstone's group to eavesdrop on their conversation.

***

Felicity got up as soon as it was light and took out a sheet of paper and pen and ink, sitting down at the little desk in the bedchamber she shared with Aunt Agnes. She'd been writing this letter in her head for the last hour and a half, changing her mind every minute as to how much to say and how to say it.

> *Dear Mother,*
> *I do not wish to alarm you, but I need you to send Father and the carriage at once to take Aunt Agnes and me home. I don't want to say too much in a letter, but there is danger here, and I'm very afraid.*

Felicity's hand shook as she wrote. What if Lady Blackstone came into the room and read her letter? Would she murder her and hide her body? What would happen to poor Auntie?

Felicity closed her eyes and tried to steady her breathing.

She would finish the letter, seal it, and place it downstairs with the outgoing mail. All would be well. But what if they opened her letter and read it? Surely they would not do that. What other choice did she have but to send the letter? She could think of no other way to escape from the nightmare in which she had found herself.

She continued her letter, her hand still shaking.

When she finished, she read over it. The handwriting was not the steadiest, but it was legible. She folded the paper, held her stick of wax over the candle to melt it, and sealed the letter.

Should she take it downstairs now while everyone else was still asleep? That would give her hostess more time to get suspicious, take her letter, and read it. Perhaps she would wait until it was almost time for the servant to post the letters.

Felicity set the letter down on her desk, but it looked so incriminating lying there. She covered it with some paper.

But what if her letter was the only one going out? What if the servant waited until more letters had been brought down before taking the trouble to post them?

Her chest began to ache, and she felt as if she could not breathe. Never had she been so frightened in her life. Her gaze caught upon a copy of the *Book of Common Prayer* lying on a shelf.

Oh. *I should pray.* Why had she not thought of that sooner?

Felicity knelt by her bed and clasped her hands, then whispered, "O God, I beseech thee to hear my prayer and save me from this danger. Let this letter go safely into the post, be sent quickly to my mother and father, and let them come and save me. And please, please, do not let my letter be intercepted. Let it be invisible to those who would do me harm if they were to read it. In the meantime, let them not despise me, but let me be safe from the wrath of these insurrectionists. Truly, I am sorely afraid. Please save me."

She was becoming even more afraid as she prayed. Instead of letting anxiety overwhelm her, she should make a statement of faith.

"O Almighty God, you are not without strength and power to save. Save me with thy mighty right hand. Send your angel with his flaming sword to defend Auntie and me and keep us safe. For yours is the kingdom and the power and the glory. Amen."

Feeling encouraged, she got up, took her letter from the desk, and went downstairs. She would trust God to keep her letter safe and carry it to her parents in London.

CHAPTER EIGHT

Philip heard a door open. He waited a moment, then stuck his head out to see who it was.

Miss Felicity Mayson walked to the staircase and started down. He waited another moment and followed her.

She passed by the breakfast room without slowing down and headed for the large entryway on the ground level of the great house. She seemed to be holding something in her hand, perhaps a letter, as she turned the corner out of sight.

He continued the rest of the way down the steps and turned the same corner—and nearly ran into Miss Mayson herself.

"Oh, pardon me," she said, her eyes wide and her hand over her heart.

"Forgive me, Miss Mayson, for nearly colliding with you. I was not looking where I was going."

"Of course. Now I must go . . . look in on my aunt. Good morning to you, Mr. Merrick."

"Good morning." He waited until she continued on her way, then went to see what she had gone into the entry hall for.

A stack of letters lay on a salver on the small table, waiting to be posted. Philip picked them up. There were only three, and the one in the middle was addressed to Mrs. Robert Mayson of Grosvenor Street, London.

He took Miss Mayson's letter and slipped it into his pocket, turned, and went back upstairs to his room.

He fetched his knife and heated the tip of the blade over a candle flame. Then he carefully pried the wax seal up around the edges until it popped off.

He unfolded the letter and read it quickly.

Dear Mother,

I do not wish to alarm you, but I need you to send Father and the carriage at once to take Aunt Agnes and me home. I don't want to say too much in a letter, but there is danger here, and I'm very afraid.

I have become engaged to Mr. Ratley, but it seems he and Lady Blackstone, much to my horror, have involved themselves in an insurrection, a revolution against the law of the land, against Parliament, and even against the king himself. I am afraid for my life if they find I have written this letter or that I am not loyal to their cause. Please come quickly to save Auntie and me.

Your faithful daughter,

Felicity

What a dangerous letter to have written and left in plain sight!

He tapped his fingers against his leg as he imagined what Lady Blackstone and the others would do to the poor innocent girl if they found this letter. And they certainly would have seen it and taken it and opened it, just as he had done.

They would have killed her immediately—gone to her room, given her poison, then paid the doctor to say she died of natural causes.

He held one corner of the letter over the candle and let the flame catch the paper on fire. He made sure it was completely burned, dropping the last corner, which contained no writing, onto the brass candleholder.

The poor girl. What she must be going through, what terror and regret she must feel. His heart crashed against his chest at how close she had come to getting herself killed.

What could he do to help her? He could not jeopardize his mission by rescuing her and taking her away from here. No, he must simply warn her not to write any more letters like that and to be careful what she said.

Philip opened his window and fanned toward it to remove the smell of burning paper, and he considered how he would accomplish the dangerous task of speaking privately with Miss Mayson.

***

Felicity couldn't stop thinking about the letter she'd left downstairs on the table near the front door. Would Mr. Ratley and Lady Blackstone read it? What would they do to her?

Felicity sat at her desk trying to study her Chinese text. But the more she thought about that letter, the more her stomach churned and her hands turned cold and damp.

Auntie had stayed up late the night before reading and so was still asleep. Felicity closed her book and stood. She put on her heaviest redingote, as the weather had turned much colder, took her bonnet, and left the room.

She stopped herself from wringing her hands. She tied her bonnet ribbons under her chin as she headed outdoors.

Felicity took a turn about the garden, following the hedgerows and the little path that led through the less formal part of the garden. Finally, she sat down on a bench beside a wall that was covered in rose vines, leaned forward, and closed her eyes.

What had she done wrong? Accepting an invitation from a distant relative she didn't know very well? That was more her mother's mistake than her own, although she could have refused her mother's wish. Accepting a marriage proposal from a man she had only just met? But even if she had not engaged herself to him, she and Aunt Agnes would still be in this terrifying situation. Still, it certainly did not help that she had accepted him. If she'd unequivocally refused him, he and Lady Blackstone might have let her leave this place without ever revealing their true plans.

A tear tracked down her cheek, and she covered her face with her hands. "I'm so afraid," she whispered, muffling the sound with her hands. "God, please send me someone to help me. Surely you can send a friend, an angel, to save Aunt Agnes and me from this predicament."

Footsteps crunched on the walkway. She sucked in a deep breath, wiping her face with her hands before plucking her handkerchief from her pocket. She pressed it to her nose and looked up.

Her stomach sank. Lady Blackstone and Mr. Ratley were approaching. Had they seen her letter? Did they open it and read it?

"Sweet Felicity, you're up early this morning." Lady Blackstone was smiling, but it seemed a cold smile. Or was that only Felicity's imagination, her fear getting the best of her?

"Darling, are you well?" Mr. Ratley sat down beside her.

"Oh yes. I was only taking a turn about the garden when I grew a bit tired and sat down to rest." She smiled up at him.

"You are not worrying about what we spoke of earlier, are you? Because there is no reason at all for you to worry. Once we are married, you never need concern yourself with matters you do not wish to. I know I said you could help make decisions, but if that makes you uncomfortable, you need only leave it all to me and the others. I love you too well to push you into distasteful or frightening tasks."

Frightening? Yes, frightening was a good word for the tasks they were planning. Also, unlawful, immoral, and—

"My dear, your countenance does not put our hearts at rest. What is it you are thinking?"

"I am . . . a little worried. I do not wish anything to happen to either of you. I love you both too well, and this revolution might not be entirely safe for you." It wasn't a lie, as she did not wish anything to happen them.

"Darling." Mr. Ratley took both her hands in his. He lifted them to his lips and kissed them.

She shuddered.

"Now don't fret about such things," Lady Blackstone said. "Once everything is set into motion, you will stay here at Doverton Hall, and Mr. Ratley and I will go to London and implement our plans, but we shall hardly do any hand-to-hand fighting." She smiled as if the thought was amusing.

"And how soon will all this take place?" How long would she have before she could escape and tell the authorities?

"While Parliament is in session," Mr. Ratley said, still squeezing her hands. "Probably in about a month."

Lady Blackstone was staring at her rather shrewdly. Did she suspect Felicity's disloyalty?

To make it look more convincing, Felicity leaned her shoulder into Mr. Ratley's. He put his arm around her.

"You will be safe, won't you?" She gazed up into his face. Could she truly have married this man and loved him and had his children? She told her heart to pretend it was true, to pretend he was not a revolutionary but an ordinary man. But her skin crawled with imaginary bugs at being so close to him.

She looked away and saw Mr. Merrick coming toward them. Thank goodness. Now she could move away from Mr. Ratley with the excuse of propriety.

Mr. Ratley became aware of Mr. Merrick's presence and waved him over to them.

"Good morning." Mr. Merrick had a much friendlier look than the other men here. What a shame he was one of these lawless revolutionaries. He was actually very handsome, with his red hair, muscular build, and ready smile. There was something about him that drew her to him.

After a bit of talk about the weather, Felicity was persuaded to take another turn about the garden. She was quickly paired with Mr. Ratley while Lady Blackstone took Mr. Merrick's arm.

Were they only pretending friendliness toward her? Had they read her letter, and were they now planning to kill her secretly out here in the garden?

Mr. Ratley looked down at her and patted her hand. Was he plotting her murder even now?

Her heart thudded sickeningly in her chest, and her knees went so weak she could barely walk. *O God in Heaven, am I about to die? Jesus, please receive my spirit.* That was what some saint in the Bible had said. Would her role model, Hannah More, hear of her murder someday at the hands of insurrectionists who had discovered she was loyal to her king and her country?

"Miss Mayson, are you well?" Mr. Merrick was staring at her. "Forgive me, but you seem a bit pale."

"Oh no, I am very well." She plastered a smile on her face. Did she seem suspicious? Should she play the part of the fainting female? She had fainted a couple of times before and might actually be near to that again. "I am enjoying the fresh air, but perhaps I would like to go back inside. I think I rose too early this morning."

"Of course, my darling." Mr. Ratley was all attention now, holding her arm with both hands, as if to keep her from falling. "We shall get you inside right away. Right away, of course."

She smiled up at him, trying to look grateful and doe-eyed, but her heart was still beating hard, and her knees were still shaky.

"You look as if you have a headache." Mr. Ratley's forehead was wrinkled. "You should get into a dark room and lie down."

"You are so kind." Felicity leaned into his upper arm.

He seemed to catch his breath and stand up straighter, then he put an arm around her shoulders as they walked into the house. They went up to her room, leaving Lady Blackstone and Mr. Merrick talking at the bottom of the stairs.

"Is there anything I can do for you?" Mr. Ratley held her hand as they stood in front of her door. "What shall I have the servants bring you? Tea? Some laudanum to help you rest? Some bread and milk?"

"Oh no, I think I just need to lie down."

"Very well. But if you need anything, please do ring for a servant or send for me."

"Of course, I shall."

Felicity slipped into her room before he might try to kiss her.

***

Philip spoke with Lady Blackstone until she excused herself, saying she had some letters to write.

He went into an empty drawing room. Would Felicity Mayson's fiancé have left her alone by now? He had to speak to Miss Mayson before she tried to send any more letters. He'd been alarmed to see her looking so wan and pale, and he marveled that her fiancé had not even seemed to notice. But every time she turned on her smile, he inwardly praised her. She at least was wise enough to pretend she was still in love with her blockhead of a fiancé.

He stood at the foot of the stairs and listened. When he was assured there was no one talking at the top, he went quietly up the stairs and came to Miss Mayson's door. He stood for a moment, then knocked.

"Come in," came the muted voice.

Philip quickly glanced to the left and the right, then let himself inside and closed the door behind him.

CHAPTER NINE

Felicity drew in a breath as Mr. Merrick came into her room and closed the door.

"Sir? You have come to the wrong room, I think." Would she be able to scream if he attacked her? Auntie was downstairs in the library and might not be back for some time.

He held his hands palms out, almost in a defensive position.

"Forgive me, Miss Mayson. I mean you no harm." He spoke in a deep, quiet voice. "I need to speak to you, and this was the most private way I could think of. Forgive me for coming into your room this way."

"What is it you wish to speak about?"

"You must be careful not to leave any more letters for the post. Lady Blackstone and Mr. Ratley will not hesitate to read your private correspondence, and they will be ruthless if they think someone here is not loyal to their cause."

He wore a serious but not unkind expression. But was he not loyal to their cause? Her breath left her, and she thought for the hundredth time of the letter she'd left downstairs.

"What makes you think I am not loyal to their cause?"

His sober expression lightened. "Miss Mayson, you can be honest with me. I took your letter, and I read it."

Her cheeks burned. "How dare you!" She pressed her hand to the ache in her chest as she struggled to breathe.

"Please don't alarm yourself. I was sent here from the Home Office to discover this group's nefarious plans. You are safe with me."

His gentle tone helped her draw in another breath and another.

"Forgive me, but it is a good thing I did intercept such a letter. It is very dangerous to write down anything that this group might not like. I had to warn you, because such a letter could get you killed."

He said the word softly, but it still sent a shock of fear through her. She sat down on her chair but did her best to breathe and keep her voice steady and her hands still.

"Thank you, Mr. Merrick."

"And, forgive me, but I burned the letter. It was too dangerous to take it to the village to post."

"I understand."

"I hope you will not trust anyone here. I am the only safe person."

"Oh."

"But please understand, with your views, it is very dangerous for you to stay here. If there is any way to safely get you back to London and your parents, I will do it."

"Oh, thank you. I would be so grateful."

"At present, there does not seem to be a way to do that. Unless your fiancé and Lady Blackstone believe they can trust you and believe that you are wholeheartedly supportive of their efforts, it will be nearly impossible to escape."

"So I must make them believe that I agree with them? I must pretend I'm not horrified to be engaged to marry a revolutionary?" She let out a soft, brief laugh.

"Exactly. And if I may make a request, I and your government would very much appreciate if you could tell us any information you might learn."

"Information?"

"Such as where they're storing their arms and any specific plans, dates, and definite targets."

"Yes, of course. But how will I let you know?"

"Don't write it. You must find me and tell me when no one else is around, or if no one is near enough to hear."

"In the garden, perhaps?"

"Yes, or if it's very urgent, you might come and find me in my room late at night."

She must have raised her eyebrows, because he immediately said, "Please know that I will never take advantage of you, Miss Mayson. I realize you do not know me at all, and I have naught but my word to recommend me, but you can trust me."

"You are acquainted with Nicholas Langdon, are you not? I saw you talking with him once at a party. Did you work together on the case against Julia Langdon's uncle?"

"We did."

She had little choice but to trust him. No one else was coming forward saying they were loyal to the government and wished to help her escape from these people.

"Very well, if I hear anything of importance, I shall be sure to tell you, Mr. Merrick. Is that even your real name?"

"My real name is Philip McDowell. But let us keep that between ourselves."

She nodded, and he pressed his ear against the door. A few moments later, he opened it and slipped out.

***

Felicity sat at her desk looking over her Chinese language book, but several minutes had gone by and she had not even seen what was on the page. So she took out a sheet of paper and started to write the treatise she'd been planning in her head. She only wrote one sentence before her mind drifted away again.

The sooner Felicity and Mr. McDowell—no, she mustn't call him that, even in her thoughts—Mr. Merrick found the important information about the revolutionaries, the sooner Felicity could be free of this nightmare she'd been living the past two days.

"What was that?" Aunt Agnes looked up from the book she was reading as she sat by the window.

"What, Auntie?"

"I heard something, a loud sound. Did you not hear it?" She looked out the window, clutching her open book to her chest.

"I did hear, but it was probably just a servant who dropped something."

"Or it may have been a horse kicking the side of the stable."

"That's probably what it was. Nothing to worry about."

Poor Aunt Agnes. Felicity probably should have kept their situation a secret from her aunt. She had always been of a nervous constitution, and if there was anything upsetting in the papers, her parents were careful to conceal it from her. She'd even known her mother to shush her father at the dinner table when he was speaking of someone being hurt in a carriage accident, or seeing a street urchin beaten by a ruffian. And now poor Auntie startled at every loud noise or raised voice.

"There is a man out there, near the stables, who looks very much like your father. Do you think that is your father?"

Felicity stood and went to the window. "No, that man is much too thin to be Father."

"He has gone inside now, but his hair was very like your father's."

"It was probably one of the stable workers." Felicity laid her hand consolingly on Auntie's shoulder.

"Felicity, you did write to your father, did you not? He is coming to take us home, surely."

"Truthfully, Auntie . . ." How could she tell her aunt the truth? That she had written a letter and that Mr. Merrick had burned it? "The truth is, it is too dangerous to write a letter home. I am unsure how to get word to Father. But you must not worry about it. We are both safe." *For the moment.*

"Too dangerous to write a letter." Auntie's eyes had a glassy look. "What is to become of us?"

"Auntie, please do not fret. All will be well. You must just pray and expect that God will keep us safe." Should she tell her aunt that they had a champion in Mr. Merrick? Perhaps it was best to give Aunt Agnes as little information as possible.

"Would you not like to go for a walk in the garden to take our minds off things? Some fresh air will do us good."

Felicity closed her book and fetched Aunt Agnes's bonnet and brought it to her.

"Do you think it's safe?"

"Of course! No one will bother us in the garden. Besides, Mr. Ratley will not allow anything to happen to us. He's my fiancé, remember?" Felicity nearly burst into hysterical laughter at this asser-tion. She did not intend to marry a revolutionary, but if she could turn him from his insurrectionist beliefs and save him from joining in with the plans of Lady Blackstone and her group, would she want to marry him then?

Strangely, Mr. Merrick came into her thoughts. She could not feel any attraction to Mr. Ratley when Mr. Merrick was lurking in her mind. How fickle she was.

Her situation was making her addled.

"Come, Auntie. It is not terribly cold today. Tomorrow may be rainy. We should take our exercise while we can."

Auntie obediently put on her bonnet and heavy cloak, and Felicity did the same, and they went arm in arm down the stairs and out into the garden.

They took a turn around the first bend in the hedgerow, not seeing anyone else, and headed toward the less formal area, which was rather overgrown with bushes and vines.

"Look at that lovely mass of flowers there." Felicity pointed them out. "I predict there will be many more of them soon, when the weather gets warm. And there's a new bird's nest over there." She pointed again. "Shall I see if there are any birds inside?"

"If you wish." Auntie's voice was a bit distracted as she stared down at her boot. "My lace has come undone."

Aunt Agnes crouched to tie her lace. Mother sometimes needed Felicity's help to tie hers, as she had grown quite round in the middle in the last few years, but Auntie was small and delicate and as yet only thirty-five years old.

Felicity continued to the tall bush where she'd spotted the bird's nest. She was just standing on tiptoe to peek into it when Aunt Agnes screamed. Felicity spun around.

Auntie cried out again and then made a sound like an anguished moan.

Felicity ran to her aunt's side. She followed her aunt's gaze and saw a man's hand stretched out from beneath a bush. It was not moving.

Aunt Agnes's hands flailed about. Felicity touched her aunt's shoulder. "It's all right," she said, talking as much to herself as to Aunt Agnes. Felicity embraced Aunt Agnes and held her arms to her sides, but her hands continued to shake.

She stared at the lifeless hand on the ground. She should go get help. Her heart was pounding, and her breath seemed to stick in her throat. Someone should come and look closer at this man, whoever he was, to see if he was still alive.

Oh, good heavens. What if the man was Mr. Merrick? Had they somehow discovered he was a spy and killed him?

Felicity let go of her aunt and stepped forward, pushing aside some branches. She fought through the dense, prickly limbs until she found the man's face. He had dark-brown hair. It was not Mr. Merrick. But his eyes were open, his lips were ashen, and she was certain he was dead.

Auntie must have seen his face, as she screamed and then collapsed to the ground, moaning.

Felicity felt strangely calm, almost numb. She would have to leave her aunt and get help.

And quickly. Because someone or something was crashing through the bushes nearby, coming toward them.

***

As Philip was saddling his horse for a short ride, a scream erupted from the direction of the garden. He ran from the stable toward the sound. The scream was shrill and piercing, as if the person had just been attacked. Could it be Miss Mayson? Was she being murdered in the garden?

He ran faster, dodging small trees and crashing through a hedge until he heard another scream. He leapt over a two-foot-tall bush and saw Miss Mayson standing beside her aunt, who was lying on the ground.

"There's a man in the bushes," Miss Mayson said. "I think he might be dead."

Except for the pallor of her cheeks and her wide eyes, Miss Mayson seemed well.

Philip strode past her aunt and bent to push back the bushes where a hand lay outstretched. He did not recognize the man, and he did indeed look dead. He felt for the telltale throb in his neck but felt nothing. He examined the man's torso but saw no evidence of injury. Then he noticed the dark liquid seeping out on the ground next to him.

Nothing could be done for him now, so Philip turned and faced Miss Mayson and her aunt. Miss Mayson was kneeling beside Miss Appleby, who was wiping her face with a handkerchief and no longer moaning. She blew her nose as Miss Mayson spoke softly to her.

"Miss Appleby." Philip waited for her to look up and bent down to her. "Please allow me."

She nodded and gave him her hand. Philip lifted her by her elbow, and Felicity took her other arm.

"We should get you back to the house," he said as kindly as he could. "You have had a terrible scare." He looked now at Miss Mayson. "You both have."

Raised voices came from the direction of the house. Men hurried toward them.

"I shall take my aunt to our room." Miss Mayson put her arm around Miss Appleby, who was mumbling and visibly shaking.

Mr. Cartwright and several other guests, along with a stable worker, rushed toward them but allowed the two ladies to pass.

"We heard the screaming. What's amiss?" Cartwright asked.

"The ladies happened upon a dead body." He stood aside and pointed. "See for yourselves."

He watched their reactions as carefully as he could, mentally noting Mr. Cartwright's rush to see the body, then the shock on his face. He noted Mr. Sproles's wide eyes, Mr. Jones wiping a hand over his mouth and jaw as he stared down at the dead man, Mr. Renfroe's muttered, "Holy saints in heaven." No one appeared jaded or less than shocked.

"Does anyone recognize the man?"

"I think his name is Erickson," Cartwright said.

"Yes, that was it," Jones said.

"He was with us at the Black Boar Inn when we first began meeting and formed our reform group." Sproles shook his head.

"It is him," Renfroe said in a hushed voice. "Are you certain he's dead?"

Sproles pushed forward and lifted the man by one shoulder and hip, turning him over. A bloody hole, or more accurately a two-inch slit in his jacket in the middle of his back, gave proof to the cause of death.

"Should we bury the body?" Mr. Cartwright asked.

"We should ask Lady Blackstone."

"Or Mr. Ratley."

But the two leaders were conspicuously absent.

CHAPTER TEN

Felicity walked with Aunt Agnes back to their room as her aunt mumbled to herself.

How would her poor aunt survive this shock? She'd become nearly comatose after her sometime suitor, a Mr. Turner, had jilted her and married someone else. That had been years ago, and her disposition had never been strong since. Even if she was able to weather the shock of finding a dead man in Lady Blackmore's garden, how could Felicity protect her from future blows? Would she survive hearing of the other guests here becoming murderers, killing Members of Parliament, and even the king?

In their room, Felicity sat her aunt down in a chair and covered her lap with a shawl.

"Shall I go to the kitchen and get you some warm milk?"

"Who was that man, Felicity? Why was he dead in Lady Blackstone's garden? Are we to be murdered in our sleep?"

"Of course not. No one would want to murder us."

Felicity smiled, but it was wasted, as Aunt Agnes did not even look at her. She stared down at her lap and pulled at the fringe on the shawl.

"Shall I fetch your book, then? What were you reading? Perhaps something by Hannah More would make you feel better."

"You know I cannot attend to Hannah More's writings."

"Well, then, I shall bring you your favorite, *The Mysteries of Udolpho*. That always transports your mind." She hurried away to fetch it before her aunt should protest that as well.

When Felicity handed her the book, Aunt Agnes opened it and seemed to be reading. Felicity poured her a glass of water and brought it to her.

Aunt Agnes suddenly closed the book. "I keep seeing that man's face." She burst into tears.

Tears pricked Felicity's own eyes. "It was very frightening to see that man there, but we cannot let fear overwhelm us."

How noble and brave and capable Mr. Merrick had looked when he had leapt over that bush to get to them, and how kind and gentle he had been with Aunt Agnes. Truly, he must be a very capable man for the Home Secretary to trust him enough to infiltrate this dangerous group alone.

"And in truth, we are not without a friend here, Auntie. God has not left us friendless." That was a verse in the Bible, was it not?

"Yes, of course. Mr. Ratley." Aunt Agnes lifted her head and pulled out her handkerchief with shaking hands and wiped her face and nose. "Mr. Ratley will not allow anything bad to happen to us."

She refrained from telling her aunt that she was not talking about Mr. Ratley.

A light knock came at the door.

"I'll be back in a moment."

Felicity went to the door and opened it. Mr. Merrick quickly stepped inside and closed the door behind him.

Startled, but mesmerized by the intense look in his blue eyes, she held her breath as he began to speak in a hushed voice.

"Can you meet me in an hour?"

"I . . . I think so."

"In one hour, go to the library. On the left wall is a door to a small room. Will you meet me there?"

"Yes."

"How is Miss Appleby?" He glanced in Auntie's direction.

"She is very upset. I was just about to go get her some warm milk."

"Allow me. I shall find a servant to bring it up to her."

"You are very kind."

"I will meet you in an hour."

He left as quickly as he had come.

***

Felicity tried not to appear anxious, but her heart was beating fast as she made her way down the stairs. She had her answer ready in case anyone saw her—she was going to the library to get a book for her aunt.

She made it to the library without anyone seeing her. She walked to the left, pretending to look at the books on the shelves, moving rather slowly, listening for other people in the room. But when she found the door Mr. Merrick had told her about, she had not seen or heard anyone.

She turned the knob and stepped inside.

The room was completely dark except for the candle that Mr. Merrick was holding. He reached behind her and quietly closed the door, his arm brushing her shoulder in the small room.

Old books lined the walls and filled the air with a musty smell. But her gaze was arrested by Mr. Merrick's face. Truly, in the dim candlelight and shadows, he seemed even more handsome, and she noticed that he was quite tall.

She was endangering her reputation by meeting a man alone at a house party, but she felt safer in this moment than she had in days.

"Forgive me for asking you to meet me like this," Mr. Merrick began, his voice low and gravelly. "But I need to know anything that might help me discover who killed Mr. Erickson. Did Miss Appleby see anyone before she found the body?"

Mr. Merrick leaned toward her, and she was very aware of his being only inches away.

"Neither of us saw anyone else in the garden. I went to look into a bird's nest, and Aunt Agnes screamed. When I returned to where she was, she was hysterical, and I saw a hand lying on the ground. I pushed back the bush then, and we could see the man's face. A puddle of blood seemed to be coming from beneath him."

"Did you know him? Had you seen him before?"

"No, never."

"And you saw no one else in or around the garden?"

"No. Who was the man?"

"He was a reformer, but he favored peaceful means of reform. After Lady Blackstone's gang made it clear that they intended to seize the government through violent means, he may have opposed them and may have tried to turn some of the other members of the group against Lady Blackstone and the others who favored violence."

"I see." She shivered, then found herself leaning toward Mr. Merrick's tall, muscular frame. Would he keep her and her aunt safe? The look in his eyes was compassionate while his jaw was hard and unflinching.

"Lady Blackstone and Mr. Ratley were nowhere to be found as everyone was trying to figure out what to do. Do you know where they were? Did they mention going on some errand today?"

"No, but it would be unusual to go an entire day without Mr. Ratley asking me to go for a walk with him or escorting me down to the drawing rooms to talk." She wasn't sure why she was blushing. There was nothing strange about a man spending time with his fiancée. Perhaps she was embarrassed about agreeing to marry a revolutionary.

"You have no idea where he was this afternoon?"

"None at all."

His forehead creased, forming a *V* between his eyes. Serious and sober or friendly and smiling, he stole her breath a little bit. But at the moment, she needed to be thinking about more important things.

"Mr. Merrick, I would do anything to get my aunt out of this house and away from these nefarious people."

"Miss Mayson, please forgive me, but I have no way at present of getting a message back to the Home Office without exposing myself and my motives."

A twinge of guilt pricked her chest. She seemed to be only thinking of herself and her aunt.

"It is imperative that I stay here and find as much information as I can about these insurrectionists' plans. Believe me." He suddenly took hold of her hand while holding the candle in his other hand. "Nothing would please me more than to assist you by taking you and your aunt back to your family, to deliver you from danger, but—"

"No, no, I understand. There is much at stake here—our country's survival and many other lives besides my own. And though I would be happy to be home with my family, I am willing to stay and do my best to help, to discover what information I can."

"Thank you, Miss Mayson. I appreciate and admire that more than you know."

She felt a strange flutter in her heart at his words. She swallowed, forcing herself to ignore it. "I am a loyal subject to the king. I will do the best I can."

"Again, I thank you." He was still holding her hand, and now he squeezed it and let go. "I think this is a good meeting place. If you have anything you wish to tell me, anything at all that might be pertinent, just say something about the sky or the clouds, and I will understand it to mean you will meet me here as soon as possible."

"The sky or the clouds. Very good." Felicity nodded.

"Now, we should probably get back. How is your aunt feeling?"

"She is resting. She drank the warm milk—thank you for having that sent up for her—and seemed calmer when I left."

"And you? Were you able to bear the shock?"

"Yes, very well. The more excitable others are, the more calm I seem to be."

"That is a good trait."

"I suppose I should go before anyone comes looking for me."

"I shall wait for you to go before exiting."

"Thank you for your kindness, Mr. Merrick."

She stared into his eyes, wondering how to take her leave. But the concern in the blue depths shook her more than seeing the dead body in the garden.

She turned and fled the room.

***

Philip searched the faces around the table that evening at dinner. Lady Blackstone and Mr. Ratley had returned from wherever they had disappeared to. Mr. Ratley looked rather grim, which was not his usual demeanor. Lady Blackstone's eyes were bright, but so they often were.

Who amongst them had murdered Mr. Erickson? No one looked particularly altered, except perhaps Mr. Ratley. But anyone capable of stabbing someone in the back would be coldhearted enough not to appear remorseful.

Miss Mayson looked appropriately subdued as yet another guest asked her if she was the person who had discovered the dead man's body.

"It was actually my aunt, Miss Appleby. She is now quite distraught and doesn't wish to leave our room. I shall leave when dinner is finished to go and sit with her."

"You will be missed, my dear," Lady Blackstone said.

"I hope your aunt will be feeling better very soon," someone else said.

"I can hardly blame her," Mrs. Cartwright, the young wife, said. "I am sure I would have screamed for a full ten minutes if I had seen him lying there. Mr. Cartwright said it made his blood go cold to see him with his eyes staring straight up."

"A dead man!" Lady Blackstone clutched her table knife and fork so tightly her knuckles were white. "Is there nothing else we might speak of?" Her lips were turned up at the corners, but her eyes were steely.

Mr. Ratley wiped his face with his handkerchief and tucked it back inside his jacket pocket.

"Will we still have the ball tomorrow night?" Miss Mayson spoke up, evoking surprised looks from several guests as they turned toward her.

Lady Blackstone's smile seemed calmer as she said, "Yes, we will. Thank you for asking, Miss Mayson. A newly engaged couple should be afforded the opportunity to dance with each other."

Mr. Ratley smiled at his fiancée, and Philip's stomach turned. Was Miss Mayson having the same reaction? She couldn't possibly want to marry him, even though she had only just accepted his proposal a few days ago. Did a woman fall in and out of love so quickly? But perhaps she had not been in love with him at all. Marriages so often were based not on love but on money and position.

Or perhaps she was more in love with Ratley than he knew. Would she prove more loyal to her country or to her fiancé? He should remember that her loyalty might well be divided when she was forced to choose. Would she betray him, revealing his identity as a spy to her fiancé and Lady Blackstone? But, no, Miss Mayson was obviously frightened of these people. *God, please let me be able to protect her, should she ever need protection.*

When Lady Blackstone announced it was time for the ladies to retire to the drawing room, Miss Mayson took her leave.

The men spoke of the dead body, but then the conversation turned to the fact that they would be waging war soon and it was no time to be faint of heart. And the more they talked of it, the more they all drank.

Philip made an excuse to go to bed early, and no one even seemed to notice. But instead of going to his own room, he went to Mr. Ratley's.

Mr. Ratley's room was down the corridor from his own. He moved quickly but quietly until he was standing in front of it. He tried the knob. It turned, and he slipped inside.

Philip let his eyes adjust to the dark room, but it was a cloudy, moonless night, so if he hoped to find any important documents or written information, he'd have to light a candle.

He pulled out the small candle he carried in his pocket along with some matches. When the candle was lit, he began looking through the papers on the small desk.

He found costs and estimates for supplies that the insurrectionists would need. Philip needed to find written plans, locations of weapon stockpiles, names of people and places. If he did not find something useful and concrete, his supervisors might not even believe his tales of a large gang of insurgents and their plans to kill Members of Parliament and the royal family. So far, he had no proof besides what he had heard. And his wounded pride would be nothing compared to the consequences to the entire country if he did not stop them.

But now he had the added worry of Miss Mayson and Miss Appleby. They were innocent, but he was the only person who knew they were. And if he was caught and killed, the authorities would believe they were as guilty as the others. Nor would they have anyone to help them escape from Lady Blackstone and Ratley.

But the way Miss Mayson had gazed up at him in the library closet, so trusting, so vulnerable . . . so lovely . . . His chest ached.

He shook his head to clear his thoughts as he scanned one paper after another.

When he'd glanced over every paper in the desk drawer, he placed them back in the same order he'd found them. There was nothing here of particular significance.

Suddenly, he heard voices. Were they coming from the corridor? He blew out the candle and darted to the door. He listened, plastering himself against the wall. His heart thumped, and he kept his mind alert and clear as the footsteps and voices neared . . . then continued down the corridor.

His heart slowed. The men should linger downstairs for quite a while longer, at least an hour. But most of them were already drunk when dinner ended. Lady Blackstone might order them to bed sooner, especially if any more fights broke out.

He didn't want to leave this room without something of relevance, so he went back to the desk to continue searching.

After at least ten more minutes, he found two receipts—one from a gun shop in London and the other from a gun shop in Birmingham. And since the receipts were underneath several other papers, he decided to fold them and shove them into his pocket. They might not help him locate the arms stash, but they could at least serve as evidence against Ratley.

Perhaps Philip should not push his luck any longer. He turned from the desk and strode to the door. The knob turned silently, but when he pushed the door open, it made a creaking noise.

Philip hurried to close the door again, then heard footsteps. Someone was coming.

CHAPTER ELEVEN

Felicity went to her room and looked in on Auntie. She'd taken a small dose of laudanum before Felicity went downstairs to dinner, and now she was in bed.

Felicity tiptoed to her side. Aunt Agnes's breathing was heavy and regular, so Felicity blew out her candle and went back to the door.

Did she dare go and trespass on her hostess's room? The thought of Lady Blackstone finding her was so terrifying her blood pounded in her temples and she felt a little faint. But how else would she find out the important information Mr. Merrick—and her country—needed?

Felicity turned the knob as quietly as possible, mentally preparing an excuse for where she was going and why. She heard only silence as she stepped out into the corridor.

Lady Blackstone's bedroom was in another wing of the house. She followed the meandering corridor until she came to the correct door. She turned the knob, and it opened. Felicity went inside and shut the door.

Her hands were shaking as she gazed across the room. A single candle lit the room.

Where should she search? A small chest of drawers stood on a low table. A key protruded from the bottom drawer. She crossed to it, turned the key, and opened the drawer. Inside was a small pistol and a knife.

Felicity's breaths came faster as she stared at the weapons. Shrinking away from touching them, she shut the drawer and opened another. Inside were papers. Felicity pulled one out and tried to examine it, but the light was so dim she could barely see the words written on it.

There were still some glowing embers in the fireplace, and the candle was on a table near it. She picked up the stack of papers and took them closer to the light.

At the very top were the words *Lancashire/Manchester* and below that was a list of men's names and then *The Red Lion* and *54 West Clover Street, Manchester.*

Felicity looked at the next paper. At the top was written *Yorkshire* and below that was another list of names and then *29 Bleecker Street, Bridlington.*

The other papers followed a similar pattern: a place name at the top, then a list of men's names, then sometimes the name of an inn, and then a street address.

O God, help me memorize something from these lists.

She scanned the one titled "Lancashire/Manchester" and read over each of the names on the paper, the name of the inn, and the street address. She read them again and again until she was fairly certain she had memorized everything. Her hand was shaking so badly she had to brace her forearm against the side of the fireplace mantel.

There. She closed her eyes for a few moments to imprint the words on her memory. Then she went back across the room and put the papers carefully back into the drawer and closed it.

A female servant entered the room through a side door.

Felicity froze, not daring to move. The servant had walked beyond Felicity's line of vision. Had she seen Felicity?

The servant seemed to be at the fireplace that Felicity had just left based on the sounds of someone putting more wood on the fire and using a poker to stoke up the hot embers.

Felicity's mind raced. What would she do if the servant saw her? How would she answer if the girl asked her what she was doing there? She would surely tell Lady Blackstone.

The maidservant's back would be to Felicity while she tended to the fire. Should she try to hide, risking that she would make a noise and draw attention to herself?

Before she could consider the option further, the maidservant walked back to the side door, went through it, and was gone.

Could it be that she had not seen Felicity standing there? Of course, the servant had not been expecting anyone to be in the room, it was rather dark, and Felicity had not moved while the servant was there. And after stoking the fire, her eyes would have been somewhat blinded by the flames.

Weak-kneed and atremble, Felicity turned and walked to the door leading to the corridor. She opened the door, and with only the barest sound, walked out into the hallway.

Her heart was beating so hard it made her feel sick. Her breath was shallow, but she quickened her step, hurrying out of that section of the house and into the corridor where her own bedroom was located. She could see it ahead of her, even as her vision was spinning and going dark.

Suddenly, someone was running toward her from the opposite end of the corridor. Had the servant girl reported her? Were they coming after her?

O God! Help me get to my room! She tried to hurry, but her knees were so weak. *Don't let me faint.*

Just as she reached her door, the figure emerged from the dark corridor.

"Mr. Merrick." She sighed.

But why was he running toward her? Her hand slipped off the knob as all the strength ebbed from her limbs. Everything was going black.

***

Philip could hear the heavy footfalls behind him, the heels of a man's shoes clicking on the polished floor. He ran as quietly as he could down the dark corridor, until he saw the slight figure of Felicity Mayson approaching her bedroom door.

She seemed to catch sight of him, and just as he reached her, her eyes closed and she started to crumple.

He held her up with one hand on her waist and opened her door with his other hand. He swept her up in his arms, carried her into the room, and closed the door behind them.

He stood still, holding her against his chest. Had the person seen him go into Felicity's room? Would they knock on the door?

The steps came to within a few feet of the door and stopped. Three seconds went by, four, five, then the steps started back the way they had come, and soon the sound disappeared.

"Miss Mayson, forgive me," he whispered. "Are you injured? Are you well?"

She had not moved since he'd lifted her. Then she drew in a labored breath, her head lolling on his shoulder. "I think I just fainted."

He carried her to the nearest bed and laid her down with her head on the pillow. He'd never carried a woman before, and he was trying not to think how pleasant it had been as he took a step away from her. He found a stool and sat beside her.

Miss Mayson brought her hand to her head. "Thank you, Mr. Merrick. I don't know what caused me to do something so foolish and dangerous as to faint outside my room."

Her voice was still weak, but at least her eyes were open now.

"Please don't trouble yourself, Miss Mayson. All's well that ends well, and it seems the man, whoever he was, who was following behind me has given up his pursuit."

"Was a man chasing you?"

"I don't know if he was chasing me, but he was curious who I was and where I was going, at the very least."

"Oh dear, I hope I didn't forget!" She sat straight up, then sank back. "Please, will you fetch a piece of paper from my writing desk, and a pen. I need to write down what I saw in Lady Blackstone's room."

Philip went and fetched her traveling desk from the table. "Tell me, and I'll write."

She held a hand to her temple and closed her eyes. She began to say names, one after the other, and he wrote as quickly as she spoke, scratching out the names on the paper.

When she finished speaking and he finished writing, she said, "There were many sheets of paper with the same type of information, with a different place name at the top. What could these lists be?" she asked. "I should think it was a list of supporters in each area, although it could be a list of enemies or people to stay away from."

"I think you are right with your first idea. She's listing their supporters, the inn where they hold their meetings, and the street address is—and this might just be wishful thinking—but it could be where they are storing their weapons. Where did you say you found these papers?"

She told him, then said, "But I was nearly discovered. In fact, I'm not completely sure I wasn't discovered."

"What do you mean?" If she had been discovered, they would kill her as they had killed that man in the garden. How could he bear it if he got her killed doing *his job*? He was the spy, the informer. He was the one employed by the Home Office to discover the plans of this group of rebels.

"I had just put the papers back in the drawer when a maidservant entered the room from a side door. She went and stoked up the fire, then left. It was very dark in the room, so I don't think she saw me, but I cannot be sure. It frightened me so much I left. Then when I was almost to my room, I saw you running toward me, and . . . I'm sorry. I know it was foolish to faint."

A vision flashed before his eyes of Lady Blackstone plunging a knife in Miss Mayson's back. He ran a hand over his jaw, his throat suddenly dry.

"I—I will do better in the future. I can be brave, I promise. I don't want you to think you can't count on me. Tomorrow when she goes for a walk in the garden or is out of her room, I'll bring some paper with me and I'll write down the rest of the information in those papers and—"

"No. It's much too dangerous. I never intended for you to search Lady Blackstone's room, only that you would inform me if you heard something important. Please. I will steal the papers and copy them myself."

"You don't trust me because I was nearly caught." She lay back and covered her face with her hands. He imagined her cheeks blushing a pretty pink.

"That's not true. I am greatly impressed with your spying skills. But . . . I don't want you to endanger yourself anymore. It's my job to spy on these people, not yours."

"But I can help you. I know I am only a woman, but—"

"Why do you say that? Only a woman?" It was the same as his saying he was "only a fourth son." That was a painful way of thinking . . . and he should know.

"Because I fainted. Men don't faint."

"Nonsense. You faced more dangers today than many men do in a lifetime. I think you're very brave. Besides, I should imagine fainting has more to do with involuntary impulses and biological factors than with courage."

She was silent for a few moments. "You are very kind to say so. But I will try very hard not to let it happen again."

"You have discovered some very important information. And the sooner I can retrieve the rest of it, the sooner we can leave this place. However, it is extremely dangerous for you to go into Lady Blackstone's room. You must not attempt it again."

"I nearly forgot. I also found a small gun and a knife in Lady Blackstone's bureau."

It was an interesting discovery, but it was not unusual for a wealthy woman to have a gun in her room. The knife was no great surprise either, although he couldn't help wondering if it was the murder weapon. Even if it was, it would be difficult to prove. However . . .

"That's another reason it would be dangerous for you to go back into her room. We must accept that it was either Lady Blackstone or Mr. Ratley who murdered that man in the garden."

A sudden noise from the bed beside Miss Mayson made him jump. Philip reached for the dagger in his coat pocket. But it was only Miss Appleby as she drew in a loud, snoring breath.

"I should get back to my room before someone comes to look in on you," he said.

"Yes, please do not endanger unnecessarily." She was so gentle.

He folded up the paper he'd written her information on and shoved it into a hidden pocket in the lining of his coat.

"I shall let you know if I find out anything new—or I shall give you our 'sky' signal and meet you in our secret meeting place in the library."

Was it his imagination, or was she smiling?

"Miss Mayson, I hope you have not forgotten how dangerous this is."

"I am as loyal to my country as anyone—I have a brother in the army. I grew tired of always waiting for . . . That is, I rather thought I would become a missionary. But I am pleased to help, Mr. Merrick, to save our king and Parliament."

Again, he shook his head, this time at Miss Mayson. "I am glad, since you are risking your life, that you are able to do it wholeheartedly."

"We women are able to do many things wholeheartedly."

***

Felicity could not convince her aunt to take a walk in the garden with her the next day, but she could not bear to stay in the house all day, so she took her walk alone.

The sky was dark and threatening, but at least it was not terribly cold. Spring was well underway, producing more color. But the flowers were hardly a distraction, as she could think of little besides the drawer in Lady Blackstone's room where she'd found the papers with the counties and cities where Lady Blackstone's fellow rebels lurked, waiting to betray their government with violent overthrow. If only Felicity had stayed longer and memorized more or had been brave enough to steal them outright. She could have copied them in her own room and then returned the originals before Lady Blackstone was aware they were gone.

Or she could have gotten caught.

Would Lady Blackstone truly murder Felicity if she discovered she was spying on her? The dead body was proof enough of the danger, but Lady Blackstone professed to love her and Mr. Ratley. Would her fiancé defend her? She said a quick prayer that she never had to find out.

She examined the new leaves sprouting on a tree in the less-formal section of the garden. Her cheeks heated as she remembered fainting in Mr. Merrick's arms. When she had come to her senses again, he was placing her on her bed. Thankfully, Mr. Merrick was a gentlemanly sort of man and did not tease or berate her. And she did not even want to think about the impropriety of him carrying her to her bed.

But she was doing something important—something very important—for her country. All of those men who had refused to dance with her at balls because she had no fortune, would they not be surprised to see her now? All those times she had secretly sobbed into her pillow at night because someone at a party had looked down on her, or because a gentleman she fancied had become engaged to someone else, she had felt helpless. Now she felt strangely empowered, even though her life was in danger. But at least her life did not depend upon marriage. It depended on how well she could conduct herself.

But she had nearly forgotten: she was engaged to be married to Mr. Ratley. Such a foolish, impulsive thing to do, accepting that man's proposal. It was as if it was another person who had decided it was a good idea to marry a man because Lady Blackstone influenced her, because that man was cheerful and polite, and simply because he had a fortune with which to make her life comfortable.

But she had no mental energy to waste on regret and rumination. She had to think of how to get those papers from Lady Blackstone's room, even though Mr. Merrick had asked her not to endanger herself. If she were able to, why shouldn't she steal the papers? But if she tried to search Lady Blackstone's room during the ball, she might be missed. She would keep her ears and eyes open for Lady Blackstone's and Mr. Ratley's whereabouts and plans.

And thinking of Mr. Ratley, he'd seemed so distracted the night before at dinner. Tonight was the ball, and she'd be forced not only to talk to him but also to dance with him. She only hoped she'd be able to dance at least once with Mr. Merrick.

Foolish thought. They should stay away from each other, lest anyone get the idea that they were anything more than passing acquaintances. But she couldn't help thinking how much more handsome he was than Mr. Ratley. What had made her think Mr. Ratley was handsome at all? Mr. Merrick's blue eyes were so arresting, and his red hair and gentle features made her heart flutter even now. There was a certain deep look in his eyes, a solidness and honesty that she rarely noticed in a man so young as Mr. Merrick, who must be around twenty-four or twenty-five.

But she should not be thinking of him. She had to stay alert and clearheaded.

After her morning exercise, she walked back to the house. She opened the door and found Lady Blackstone and Mr. Ratley standing in front of her, as if waiting for her to come in.

CHAPTER TWELVE

Felicity's heart leapt to her throat. Had Lady Blackstone heard from her maidservant that she had been in her room the night before?

"Darling," Mr. Ratley said, reaching out for her hand. She let him take it, and he kissed her knuckles.

His lips were cool and moist. How many times had she dreamed of a man falling in love with her, kissing her hand whenever he saw her because he could not help himself? But his kiss did not make her heart pound. Perhaps that was because she was too worried these two people might kill her.

But they were both smiling at her with ingratiating looks, so her breaths started to come easier.

"Mr. Ratley. Lady Blackstone. I hope you are both well this morning."

"Yes," they answered. "We want to speak with you, sweet Felicity," Lady Blackstone said in her most winsome voice. "Won't you come with us someplace comfortable?"

"Of course." Felicity followed them to a small sitting room nearby.

Felicity and Lady Blackstone sat together on a sofa while Mr. Ratley pulled a chair close to them.

"Felicity, my dulcet niece," Lady Blackstone began, leaning close and speaking in a low voice. "I know you were surprised when you learned of our plans and purpose here, our mission to make our country a better place with a better government more representative of our nation's people and their desires and interests. But from your own sentiments, spoken to me on more than one occasion, I know you, too, believe in doing what is right and good for others, not trampling anyone underfoot, and upholding the democratic ideals of such leaders as the ones in America. I am not wrong about that, am I?"

Felicity swallowed, resolving to be as wily as the situation called for. "I was surprised, it is true. But you are correct in thinking that I believe in the democratic principle that all men—and women—deserve fair treatment. Whatever is right and noble, that is what I wish to support."

"Yes, exactly!" Lady Blackstone's eyes were still shrewdly trained on Felicity's face. "I am so pleased you are wont to see things as Mr. Ratley and I do. I only wanted to make certain that you are aware of all the ways this country's government needs to be reformed and the impossibility of that happening without extreme intervention."

"Of course. I believe I do, Aunt. I am not ignorant of the mistreatment of cotton factory workers, the plight of the weavers who are nearly starving and being treated most cruelly, as well as the farmers who have been unfairly injured by the Corn Law. Our government has made it nearly impossible for the small farmer to survive, and the cost of bread is beyond the means of many of our nation's people."

She searched her mind for newspaper stories she had read or heard about, events and political rumblings her father had discussed with her brothers. She did her best to say what Lady Blackstone and Mr. Ratley would want to hear.

"I do not think most of the Members of Parliament care for anyone but themselves and their privileged friends and family, and therefore, since you and Mr. Ratley have planned such an organized uprising, and since I trust you both to do what is just and good for all the people, I am with you. In fact, I relish the idea of change." She was able to make this latter statement with conviction since she certainly did see the need for the change, just not in the same way as these two insurrectionists.

Mr. Ratley was beaming at her. He took her hand and squeezed it, then kissed it again. "I knew you would see things our way. Did I not tell you so?" He turned to Lady Blackstone and then back to Felicity.

"The two of you are so well suited, both so reasonable and earnest." Her mouth twisted just enough to show her sardonic meaning.

"But Felicity, my dear," Lady Blackstone said, "if you have any reservations about what might take place in our fight for a better government, please know that you will not be expected to be involved in anything that is the least distasteful to you."

"That is very true, darling," Mr. Ratley said. "When we are married, you may stay at our home away from London, out of the . . . Well, there are many things that must be done, and you shall be shielded from . . . such things as go on during a revolution. You understand."

Yes, she understood. Murder, treachery. Perhaps they'd even get their own guillotine for the beheading of those who did not agree with their idea of good government.

Felicity forced a smile. "Thank you, my dear, for thinking of my comfort. You are so good to me." She lowered her eyes, hoping she would appear overcome with gratitude, rather than as if she was trying to hide her true feelings by not looking him in the eye.

"I haven't noticed you sending any letters lately," Lady Blackstone said. "You received a letter from your mother, did you not?"

"Oh yes, but Mother doesn't expect me to write her that often. She is not much of a correspondent herself, as she has so many children."

"Well, you must have friends you'd want to write to tell them about your engagement." She was eyeing her suspiciously now.

"Oh yes, I should write my friends." But she did not want Lady Blackstone to know that her two best friends were Mrs. Julia Langdon, whose husband had worked with the government to thwart a traitor to the Crown, and Lady Withinghall, whose husband was a member of the House of Lords and would no doubt be a target of execution. "I shall write them soon."

"I hope you will remember what I have told you. The important thing," Lady Blackstone said, "is that you are never disloyal to us or to the cause. We need your support." She stared straight into Felicity's eyes, as if pinning her to the spot. "Every person's support is important and necessary, but especially the wife of someone as high in authority as Mr. Ratley is and will be. You will be closely watched."

"For your own safety, as much as for any other reason," Mr. Ratley hastened to add.

"Oh. Of course." It was not difficult to muster a frightened look.

"Well, I shall leave you two alone," Lady Blackstone said as she stood and left the room.

As shaken as Lady Blackstone's words had made her feel, Felicity wished the woman had told her where she was going. Would she be away from Doverton Hall today?

Mr. Ratley moved from the chair to the sofa beside Felicity. "I hope you know I would never let anyone harm you, Felicity."

Her name sounded strange on his lips, as if he found the four syllables difficult to string together.

"Thank you . . . Oliver." She did not want to address him by his given name, but he might find it suspicious if she allowed him to address her as Felicity and she did not reciprocate. Truly, she was thinking too much about this. A trickle of sweat was forming between her shoulder blades, and another on her sides under her arms. She had to relax—

He was leaning toward her, his obvious goal to kiss her lips. She didn't want to let him kiss her. But what else could she do?

She let him press his lips to hers, then pulled away. She put her arms around him and pressed her face to his shoulder to keep him from kissing her again.

"Oh, darling." He caressed her back.

She forced herself not to shudder as he continued to stroke her back. Then she pulled away.

"I should probably go look in on my aunt. She gets nervous when I am away too long. Please forgive me."

He sighed. "I understand, of course. You must see to your aunt. But tonight . . ." He gave her a knowing smile. "I shall expect to dance with you at least four dances. And perhaps we can sneak away for"—he ran his finger over her cheek—"half an hour . . . to be alone."

"That doesn't sound very proper." She gave her best reproachful expression. "Some of the men here do not seem to respect the rules of propriety, and we do not want to set them a bad example. Society will be looking to us to show them the guidelines for proper behavior."

He frowned and shook his head. "I think you just do not want to be caught kissing me. You would be embarrassed. Very well, very well." He smiled and tapped a finger under her chin. "We will be married soon enough, and you will not have to worry about such things." He squeezed her shoulder. "Then I can kiss you all I want."

She caught herself, realizing he had not meant the words to sound sinister, so she smiled back at him. "You are so considerate and kind. I'm not sure what I ever did to deserve such a wonderful fiancé as you."

"My dear." His gaze settled on her lips.

"I must go. Aunt Agnes will become anxious about me."

"Of course. I hope you can persuade her to come down to the ball."

"I shall try. Perhaps she will come for a portion of it."

She took his arm and let him walk her to her room. All the while, he held her close and squeezed her hand. She let him kiss her on the cheek and, as quickly as she could, extricated herself from him and slipped into her room.

Once inside, she shuddered and wiped her lips and cheek with her handkerchief.

I can do this, I can do this, she chanted to herself. She had to steel herself against all shudders and harden herself to his touch. She must.

***

After assuring herself that Aunt Agnes was well and occupied with a book, and after half an hour for Felicity to compose herself, she ventured downstairs again. Perhaps she could discover if Lady Blackstone was away from home.

As she was entering the drawing room, she nearly collided with Mr. Merrick. He was wearing a dark-blue coat and waistcoat that made his eyes seem even bluer. Though she hadn't thought that possible.

"Good afternoon, Mr. Merrick."

"Good afternoon, Miss Mayson. I trust Miss Appleby is well."

"She slept rather fitfully last night, but she is well, I thank you." Should she let him know that she wished to meet with him in their secret meeting place? She could tell him about her conversation with Lady Blackstone and Mr. Ratley.

"The sky is quite overcast today." She looked him in the eye.

"Yes. It could rain in about five or ten minutes."

"Yes, well, I should go . . . up to my room. Good day, Mr. Merrick."

"Good day."

Her heart fluttered as she went back up the stairs to wait for him to make his way to the library closet. For the next five minutes she kept glancing at the clock while assuring Auntie that all was well.

Felicity went back down to the library, praying she looked calm and would not meet anyone on her way. She did meet two of the men, but they barely glanced at her and only mumbled a quick greeting before continuing toward the billiard room.

She slipped into the library, wandering around a few moments, as there were some chairs situated at the back of the library in a rather hidden corner behind some bookshelves. Thankfully, no one was there. Then she went in through the side door and shut it behind her.

"Have you learned something new?" he asked her.

Her face stung as she realized he might think she had not truly learned anything and was only trying to be alone with him. What they were doing was highly improper, besides being dangerous. She probably should not have risked it. But she was here now, so she might as well tell him.

"Lady Blackstone and Mr. Ratley pulled me into a sitting room to question me about my loyalty to them and their cause. I believe I was able to assure them that I am supportive of everything they wish to do. They told me that they will make it possible for me not to be too involved. Mr. Ratley said I may stay far away from London when the actual revolutionary events take place. But that is a bit of a problem."

"What do you mean?"

"I believe he expects us to be married by then. And I . . . I cannot marry him." The very thought of marriage to Mr. Ratley was horrifying. "But I don't know how I can avoid it. I suppose it depends on how long it takes us to get the necessary information to your people at the Home Office."

"Yes." He rubbed a hand over his mouth and chin, drawing her attention to his masculine, square jaw with just a hint of reddish-brown stubble. "That is a quandary."

If she had met Mr. Merrick sooner, perhaps she would not have engaged herself to Mr. Ratley. But she had engaged herself. Shouldn't she be willing to sacrifice in this way to save the lives of her countrymen and her king? In a time like this, she could not be self-centered.

The story of Esther came suddenly to her mind. That woman had married a pagan king she hardly knew to save her people. Could Felicity marry Mr. Ratley? Her stomach twisted.

***

Philip looked Miss Mayson in the eye and said again, "It is a quandary. But you are right. We must get the information quickly and get it back to my superior."

"Yes, but if we make a mistake in our haste . . ." She bit her lip, a crease forming between her eyes. "It may come down to me having to marry him." She pressed a hand to her eyes.

He longed to comfort her, to put an arm around her and tell her everything would be well, that he would protect her, but not only would that not be wise, but he couldn't in all honesty promise her that. And he could not afford to think sentimentally. If she was willing to sacrifice herself, he should let her. The Home Secretary, Lord Sidmouth, would not want him to jeopardize the mission for one woman, no matter how beautiful, gentle, and innocent.

"We shall assume the best and hope we don't come to such drastic measures." The thought of Miss Mayson marrying Mr. Ratley made his stomach sick.

"Yes, of course." She took her hand away from her face and nodded, suddenly brave again. "Forgive me. I am sure all will turn out well. Do we have a plan for tonight at the ball?"

"I will get those papers in Lady Blackstone's room, but it will be too dangerous tonight. Lady Blackstone is quite clever. She would notice if someone was missing—especially you."

"Yes, you are probably right."

"The men are becoming more comfortable with me, so I have managed to get some bits of information. But the problem is that none of them know very much."

"It all comes down to those papers."

"Yes." He thought for a moment and said, "If you happen to discover Lady Blackstone plans to leave the house for any reason, or that she has left, you must get word to me."

"Will you take them, copy them, and then return them?"

"That seems the best plan. Since you were cleverly able to memorize the paper on the top, we can replace Lady Blackstone's papers with blank pages but leave the top sheet. That way she wouldn't notice we'd taken them unless she looked very closely."

"That sounds very good."

It was the first genuine smile he'd seen on her face all day. How pretty she was, with her pale, red-blonde hair, her gentle green eyes, and her pink lips. Her features were as delicate and appealing as early-morning sunshine on a dewy meadow.

He was becoming a poet. His brothers would laugh him to scorn over such sentimentality.

Philip rarely made time to see his brothers anymore. He had grown tired of their pranks and tricks a few years past, and their conversations had become strained. But they would have to respect him after he saved the country and the monarchy.

"Well, I suppose we should go before we are missed." She was looking at him quizzically.

He nodded. He wanted to say that he hoped he might get to dance with her. Would her fiancé see something in the way they looked at each other—after all, they had such a huge secret between them—to make him suspicious?

Still, the opportunity to dance together could present itself. Wouldn't it be more suspicious if he avoided her?

"I should like to dance with you," he found himself saying, "if it does not attract attention to do so."

"I would like that." She smiled again, and he felt a not-unpleasant ache in chest.

He could not allow himself tender feelings. His mission was to save the monarchy and Members of Parliament, to preserve the lives of many, not concern himself with this woman who had created her own dangerous situation by associating with revolutionaries and engaging herself to be married to one of them.

She may have done a foolish thing by becoming engaged to Mr. Ratley, but by spying on him and the other conspirators, she had proven herself both courageous and clever.

The fact that she was a woman made things more difficult—he would feel protective of her, more so than he would of a male colleague—and the fact that she was lovely and . . .

"I shall see you tonight." He nodded as she moved to the door.

"Till tonight, then."

CHAPTER THIRTEEN

Felicity dressed carefully for the ball. Her mother was unable to spare a lady's maid to send with her, after sending one with Elizabeth, so Camille, Lady Blackstone's maid, came in to prepare Felicity's hair.

"Miss Mayson, you look a bit pale. You should not be nervous. You are not trying to find a husband. And your shoulders are so stiff and tense. Are you well?"

Some maidservants never said a word, but Camille was rather talkative.

"I am very well. I suppose I am simply trying too hard to impress."

"You are very impressive without trying. Beautiful and pleasant."

"You are too kind." She thought for a moment, then said, "You know Lady Blackstone very well, do you not?"

"Oh yes, better than anyone. I've been with Lady Blackstone for many years, since she was married to the baron. When her sister died, it did things to her." She scrunched her face and sighed, pausing in her work to get Felicity's hair to curl on top of her head. "It is a pain she will never overcome, I think. It made her determined to never be poor again. But . . . it also created some frightening things in her. I do believe . . . But she has never mistreated me, so I shall say no more."

"Is she planning any trips in the next fortnight? I was only wondering because I need some ribbon to match my blue dress, and I thought she might visit some shops."

"Bless you, I do not know of any plans for visiting any shops, but perhaps she would send a manservant to get what you need. I shall speak to her, if you wish."

"Oh no, don't trouble her. It is not important. I only thought if Lady Blackstone were planning to travel somewhere she might—but I would not wish to ask her for such a trivial thing."

Soon they were talking of other subjects.

Felicity could not persuade Aunt Agnes to go down to the ball with her, but then, she might be able to use that as an excuse to leave the festivities.

Camille had been right; she was nervous. Her hand shook as she touched the banister. And when she saw her fiancé speaking with Lady Blackstone in the ballroom, then glance up and give her an eager look, her stomach sank.

He took her hand and kissed it, then took the liberty of kissing her cheek. Felicity forced herself not to cringe at his affection.

"Darling. You will be the prettiest woman here."

That would not be too difficult, as there were not many women there at all. But then she remembered Lady Blackstone had said she was inviting several other ladies from the county. If only Felicity or Mr. Merrick knew one of the women and could trust them to take a letter. But that was not likely.

More people began arriving. Lady Blackstone was smiling, greeting her guests. Finally, she seemed to notice Felicity and Mr. Ratley, and she came over to embrace them.

"Drink some sherry, my dear Felicity. You are as good as married, and you may as well enjoy yourself."

Felicity had the same opinion of spirits as her most beloved author, Hannah More. But she smiled and said, "Thank you, Lady Blackstone. I shall enjoy my evening. I am with Mr. Ratley, after all."

Perhaps she should not have said anything quite so facetious. Her words caused Mr. Ratley to stick out his chest and draw her closer to his side.

Lady Blackstone nodded knowingly. "Of course you shall. Dancing is just the activity for an engaged couple." She winked at Mr. Ratley, then turned to greet more guests.

Just then, her eyes were drawn to Mr. Merrick as he entered the room. He was dressed very stylishly in a dark-green coat and tall black boots. His red hair was thick and well groomed, and he appeared relaxed but alert. If only she could feel that way. Instead, her hands were sweaty, and her thoughts were so jumbled she felt as if she were in a fog.

What would Mr. Ratley attempt tonight? Would he try to get her alone? She had heard tales of house parties where men would take women into darkened side rooms and take liberties with them. What sort of liberties, she was not sure, but certainly kissing. The thought of kissing Mr. Ratley again was not appealing. Now, she could no longer remember when, or if, it ever was.

Felicity was obliged to greet and speak with several more people before the music finally started.

She danced the first and second dances with Mr. Ratley. She noticed Mr. Merrick dancing as well, though Felicity did not know his partners. One was quite pretty, and she smiled at him a great deal.

"Darling, are you looking for someone?" Mr. Ratley said as they waited for their turn in the reel.

"Oh, I was just wondering who that pretty woman is who is dancing with Mr. Merrick."

"I believe that is Miss Catherine Watson. I shall make sure you are introduced."

She must be more careful not to stare at Mr. Merrick or his partners. It was a foolish mistake.

Everyone around her seemed to have forgotten the dead man they'd found in the garden. They were smiling and laughing and drinking sherry. Everyone was relatively young—there were no old men or women—and it might have been her imagination, but everyone seemed to have a sort of reckless look on their faces.

How did I end up here? Had she really wanted to go to China and become a missionary? That girl seemed so naïve now. Everyone had warned her of how dangerous it would be to go there, but England had proven to be quite dangerous itself.

The song ended, and Mr. Ratley led Felicity over to Mr. Merrick and his partner. He greeted Mr. Merrick and introduced her to Miss Catherine Watson.

Miss Watson smiled and said, "Very pleased to make your acquaintance." But the woman could hardly keep her eyes off Mr. Merrick. Finally, she tore her gaze from him and said, "I am afraid I have promised to dance with a Mr. Webster next. If you will excuse me."

Lady Blackstone came over and said something very quietly in Mr. Ratley's ear.

"Oh, darling Felicity," Mr. Ratley said, "I must go and speak with Lady Blackstone. Why don't you dance with Mr. Merrick?"

Mr. Ratley moved away and left her standing with Mr. Merrick. The gentleman's eyes followed Lady Blackstone and Mr. Ratley.

"Where do you think they are going?" Felicity asked him as discreetly and quietly as she could.

"I would follow if I thought they wouldn't see me." Instead, he took her hand, and they joined the others on the dance floor.

As they waited in the round, Mr. Merrick said, "You look quite lovely tonight."

"The maid said I looked pale and nervous."

"You did seem a bit stiff when I first saw you, but no one would think anything was amiss now. You are doing very well."

"Thank you."

They danced all the steps competently. Mr. Merrick was a good dancer. He smiled at her occasionally when he had to take her hand, but she also noticed him glancing about the room. Of course, he had to try and keep up with who was there and who was doing what and was probably also looking for Lady Blackstone and Mr. Ratley to return. And he couldn't look as intently into her eyes as he did when they met secretly in the library closet.

But she allowed herself to look at him. He was handsome. She'd always thought so, absently, but now that she truly examined him, she imagined how easy it would be to look at this man every day.

But her feelings were only a consequence of the fact that he'd likely saved her life when he snatched her letter and burned it—and she was still relying on him as their only real friend in this place.

He, on the other hand, had no reason to have tender feelings for her. Yes, she had found the crucial papers in Lady Blackstone's room, but he'd have found them himself soon. But perhaps she might prove even more useful to him and to his mission.

"Thank you for the dance, Miss Mayson." His eyes were back on her as several people happened to be pressing close to them as they left the dance floor.

"My pleasure."

His eyes were already back on the door Mr. Ratley and Lady Blackstone had exited by. He excused himself and headed in that direction, perhaps to see if he could eavesdrop on them.

Her mind flitted to Lady Blackstone's room and those papers in her drawer. Is that where Mr. Merrick had gone, to try to steal the papers?

She wandered over to the refreshment table set up in an adjoining sitting room and took a cup of lemonade. When she walked closer to the doorway, she caught a glimpse of Mr. Merrick walking toward the stairs.

Now might be a good time to go check on Aunt Agnes.

Felicity put her cup down and headed to the stairs. Mr. Merrick was just disappearing at the top as he rounded a corner toward the wing of the house where Lady Blackstone's room was located. Might she not prove helpful as his lookout?

She walked quietly up the steps and stopped at the top. If she went left, she would seem to be going to her room to look in on Aunt Agnes. If she went right, she would be following Mr. Merrick toward Lady Blackstone's room.

No one seemed to be around, so she turned right.

She walked slowly until she was in sight of Lady Blackstone's door. Was Mr. Merrick inside? She continued on. Lady Blackstone's door was slightly ajar. She pushed it open. Mr. Merrick was hunched over the small bureau where she had found the papers.

Felicity heard footsteps coming up behind her. Her heart lurched. If she were to call out to Mr. Merrick, whoever was walking toward her would hear.

She turned and walked down the darkened corridor to await who-ever would appear. *Let it not be Lady Blackstone or Mr. Ratley.*

It was a man. He appeared at the top of the stairs and turned right. *Oh dear.* It was Mr. Ratley.

He was walking toward her. She hurried toward him. "Mr. Ratley!" she called out, a bit louder than necessary.

O God, please let Mr. Merrick get away before he is seen.

***

Philip found the papers. He was just picking them up when he heard Miss Mayson's voice: "Mr. Ratley!"

His blood pounded in his temples. For a moment he debated—should he take them? Did he have time to replace them with the dummy papers and secure the real papers inside his waistcoat? He clenched his teeth and left them, closing the drawer and turning to leave.

He tried the side door, which might lead him to the back stairs. It was locked. There was no escape except through the door he had come in. He hurried to it and peeked out.

"What are you doing on this corridor?" Mr. Ratley asked, pulling Miss Mayson into his arms.

Philip felt sick.

"I was looking for Lady Blackstone. I wanted to ask her something."

"I was just going to take something to her room."

Energy surged through his veins. He glanced the opposite way down the hall. He saw only shadows. Perhaps if he went that way he'd come to the back stairs. It was risky, as he'd probably be seen by the servants coming from this corridor, and they'd tell Lady Blackstone, but if Mr. Ratley saw him, he was a dead man.

He glanced back toward Miss Mayson and Mr. Ratley. Miss Mayson leaned in and kissed the man.

Philip's stomach churned, but he ignored it and darted from the room, to his left, hurrying through the shadowy corridor. Soon he came to the narrow wooden back stairs and rushed down. Miraculously, he did not encounter any servants, even as he reached the bottom, near the kitchen. He dashed into the ground-floor corridor between the vestibule and the large drawing room. Soon he was back in the ballroom.

**

Felicity was glad it was dark. Her hands trembled where she held Mr. Ratley's shoulders, and she suddenly felt light-headed and faint. Had Mr. Merrick had time to escape?

When the kiss ended, she whispered, "My darling," hoping to distract Mr. Ratley further. She kissed him again, inwardly cringing at her own deception—and at his wet, flaccid lips.

She pulled away, trusting Mr. Merrick to have escaped by now.

"Darling." There was a note of pleasant surprise in Mr. Ratley's voice. He was smiling. "If you wanted to be alone with me, you should have said so."

"Oh no." She laughed, the sound coming out as breathless. "I came up here to look in on my aunt, then thought I would see if Lady Blackstone was in her room. But when I saw you . . . forgive me. It was very impulsive of me."

"But not at all unwelcome." He bent to kiss her again.

Her insides squirmed, but she allowed it for a couple of moments, then pulled away. "We shouldn't. I . . . I don't want anyone to see us. Come. Let us go join the party. I wish to dance and dance with my future husband." She tried to sound merry and enthusiastic.

"Just a moment. I need to put something away in Lady Blackstone's room."

"Won't she mind?"

"No, no. She sent me to do it. It will only take a moment." He removed his arms from around her, tucked her hand in the crook of his arm, and strode toward Lady Blackstone's room.

He did not seem too surprised that the door wasn't completely shut. Felicity removed her hand from his arm and strode inside to Lady Blackstone's small desk.

Felicity glanced around the room but did not see Mr. Merrick. She allowed herself to relax and concentrate on being the madly-in-love but piously modest fiancée of Mr. Ratley.

Mr. Ratley turned to come back toward her, then stopped, as if remembering something. He went to the small bureau and opened the very drawer where Felicity knew the incriminating papers were kept.

Her heart crashed against her chest. Had Mr. Merrick taken them? Would Mr. Ratley see that they were missing?

He seemed to sift quickly through them, then he shut the drawer and headed toward her.

"Is everything well?"

"Yes, of course." He reached the door and shut it closed behind him, then took a key from his pocket and locked the door. She watched as he slipped the key into his coat pocket.

"Does Lady Blackstone always have you lock her door for her?"

"So many questions." Mr. Ratley smiled down at her and shook his head. He looked as if he might kiss her again.

She pretended not to notice and took his hand in hers and started toward the staircase. "Come. Let us go. We've probably missed at least two dances."

"So eager to dance with me?"

"Of course! You are such a good dancer. I don't always have such a wonderful partner." It was true. She often had no partner at all.

Mr. Ratley beamed. "I have been told, on occasion, that I am a good dancer." They started down the stairs. "I would imagine we make a very handsome couple."

Felicity smiled up at him.

How could she have fancied herself in love with this man? She couldn't help hoping that Mr. Merrick realized she did not wish to kiss Mr. Ratley, that she had done it for Mr. Merrick's sake. Tears welled in her eyes, but she resolutely blinked them away. So much depended on her strength of will. *God, give me strength.* She clenched her teeth and kept smiling.

CHAPTER FOURTEEN

Philip was on his way up the stairs when he met Miss Mayson and Mr. Ratley coming down. Her smile was rigid.

"Mr. Merrick. Are you well?" Mr. Ratley asked.

"Oh, someone spilled brandy on my coat. I'm going up to change."

"My valet is a wonder at removing stains, if you need his assistance."

"Thank you. I shall let you know."

He did not allow himself to even look at Miss Mayson.

He continued up as they went down.

He went back to Lady Blackstone's room, but this time the door was locked. Ratley must have locked it. He hurried to his own room, changed his coat, even though he'd lied about the spill, and went back downstairs.

Miss Mayson and Mr. Ratley were dancing, smiling at each other and drawing the gazes of several people. Philip's stomach churned to see the way she looked at her fiancé. Of course, she was only pretending. He knew it, but it brought back the memory of her leaning into Mr. Ratley and kissing him.

Philip's stomach sank at the thought of her kissing the man in order to help him escape. He had to get those papers before Mr. Ratley took advantage of her, for it was surely only a matter of time before the man wanted more than just a kiss in a corridor.

Philip asked a young lady to dance and wondered if she had any idea that she was dancing amongst the top leaders of a dangerous and capable group of revolutionaries. But she could speak only about the most inane things—the latest fashions, men's neckcloths, women's gowns, and whether it was more socially fashionable to curtsy or shake hands. He was so bored he had to stifle a yawn. As soon as it was polite to do so, he excused himself.

Philip asked another young lady to dance, then another and another. He danced every dance that Mr. Ratley and Miss Mayson did. Meanwhile, Lady Blackstone seemed to have been absent for more than an hour. Was she out somewhere hiding the dead body from her garden?

Lady Blackstone finally reappeared to host the supper, during which Philip flirted with every young lady who came near him, and soon he had three of them around him, each trying to get in more words with him than the other two. Meanwhile, Miss Mayson stayed by her fiancé's side, talking and smiling.

Would Mr. Ratley and Lady Blackstone convince Miss Mayson that their cause was noble? That the violence and upheaval they would wreak would be justified? Seeing her now with Mr. Ratley, he could believe it was possible. Or was she as nauseated at the thought of kissing Ratley as Philip had been to see her do it?

He wished this night would end.

***

Felicity's thoughts were focused on the key in Mr. Ratley's pocket. Unfortunately, he was not much of a drinker, not enough for her to hope he would drink until his senses were dulled so that she could take the key from his pocket without his being aware. But if she could get that key . . .

She wanted this to end, to get out of this house, out of this engagement, and out of this revolutionary plot. She was not bold and courageous like her friends Julia and Leorah. She was nervous and emotional, and yet, she did not think she was doing too badly at pretending.

Perhaps if she could get Mr. Ratley to walk her to her door she could get close enough to him to steal the key.

Her stomach twisted at how she was manipulating this man, deceiving him with kisses when she had no intention of marrying him. But was it justified if she was doing it to save people's lives?

By the time the guests began to leave, Felicity's eyelids were heavy and so were her feet. But she was aware that she had led Mr. Ratley to believe that she enjoyed kissing him. Extricating herself from him might prove a challenge. She needed her wits about her.

When Lady Blackstone was saying good night to the last of the guests, Mr. Ratley looked down at her rather meaningfully. "Shall I walk you to your door?"

"Oh yes, I am so very tired. And poor Auntie. Sometimes she does not sleep well at all. I hope she is not worried that I stayed up so late."

She held on to his arm as they made their way up the stairs.

When Felicity and Mr. Ratley arrived at her door, he brought her around to face him.

"I hope you enjoyed the ball."

"Of course. I danced with you all night." She smiled and let him draw her close, meanwhile keeping her hand at the level of his pocket. She buried her face in his chest, as if she thought he merely wanted to embrace her. But wouldn't he feel her hand inside his pocket?

She could not avoid it. She lifted her face and let him kiss her while she fished into his pocket, caught hold of the key, and drew it out. Clutching it in her fist, she ended the kiss and quickly turned the knob on her door.

"Good night, Mr.—that is, Oliver."

He did not try to detain her, only looked slightly disappointed as she closed the door behind her, gripping the key so tightly it dug into her palm.

***

The next day, Felicity rose earlier than she thought it would be likely for Lady Blackstone to be up. She tried not to look suspicious as she prowled around downstairs, praying she would see Lady Blackstone leave her room. She was rather surprised not to see Mr. Merrick anywhere, but that was a good thing. She didn't want to be tempted to tell him she had the key. Then he might insist on using it to go in Lady Blackstone's room, and Felicity wanted to do it herself. She could get the papers, copy them, and be able to hand them over to Mr. Merrick to get them safely to the officials in the Home Office. Then this whole thing would be over. She could escape, somehow, to her home in London and have her father break her engagement with Mr. Ratley, who would then be arrested and . . .

Mr. Ratley might be hanged for his involvement in this plot. And Lady Blackstone as well. But of course they would be hanged. They were plotting high treason, planning to murder Members of Parliament and even the royal family.

She could not be missish about Mr. Ratley. Besides, she had only to do what was right. She was not responsible for the final outcome. Mr. Ratley and Lady Blackstone had only themselves to blame for whatever trouble they found themselves in.

Still, a pain stabbed her chest at the thought of Mr. Ratley being hanged. After all, she had planned to marry him and love him for the rest of her life. She'd had tender feelings in her heart when she told him yes, and pity and compassion lurked there still. She would not escape pain for her poor decision to form an attachment to Mr. Ratley.

Someone was coming down the stairs. Felicity waited in the empty sitting room, her hands shaking as she silently prayed for calm.

As the steps came closer, she casually exited the room and pretended surprise as the person turned out to be Lady Blackstone herself.

"Good morning, my lady."

"Felicity. You are up early. I would have thought you'd still be sleeping."

"I'm not a late sleeper. I like to get dressed early. Are you going somewhere?"

Lady Blackstone was dressed for riding.

"I like my solitary rides in the morning." She smiled, but it was a tight smile.

"I am not much of a rider, but I hope you have a good ride."

Lady Blackstone thanked her and went out through the back door toward the stable.

Felicity's heart pounded hard against her chest as she started up the stairs. At the top, she turned toward Lady Blackstone's door.

"Felicity?"

She spun around and pressed a hand to her heart and swallowed. "Mr. Ratley. You are up early." He'd nearly caught her! What if he'd followed her and seen her using the key she'd stolen from him to unlock Lady Blackstone's door?

How foolish of her to try to do everything herself. She should have informed Mr. Merrick that she had the key. She was not a spy. She would get herself and Mr. Merrick killed.

He walked to her and put his arms around her. "How is my darling this morning? Did you sleep well?"

She avoided his lips by turning her head when she embraced him. "I did, I thank you. Did you?"

"Yes. But where were you going just now?" He pulled away and gazed into her face.

"I—I thought I heard something, Lady Blackstone's voice, but I suppose I was wrong."

"Good morning."

Felicity pulled out of Mr. Ratley's embrace as Mr. Merrick's voice came from down the corridor.

"Mr. Merrick," Mr. Ratley greeted. "You are also an early riser, I see."

"I don't like to sleep my day away."

"I was just about to ask Miss Mayson to take a walk in the garden with me."

"I would not intrude on you. I was on my way to practice billiards."

"The sky is very lovely," Felicity hastened to say. "I hope you will take the time, later, to enjoy the mild weather and pretty clouds."

"Thank you, I shall," Mr. Merrick said. He met Mr. Ratley's eye. "Enjoy your walk."

Felicity accompanied Mr. Ratley out into the garden, trying to attend to what he was saying about the ball the night before. Once they were outside, she was glad the sky was indeed lovely—she had said the first thing about the sky that came to her mind. Equal portions of blue sky and white clouds mingled, a milder-than-usual day.

Soon Mr. Ratley had led her to the back of the garden to a hidden spot between a wall and a very tall hedge and seated her on a bench and sat beside her. He pulled her close and started to kiss her.

Felicity pushed him away. "I'm not comfortable with so much kissing before our wedding." She was looking down when she said it, then up at him through her lashes. "Please don't be angry with me."

He sighed. "I do not know what to think. Sometimes you are eager to kiss me. What is the meaning behind your disposition—hot one moment and cold the next?" He gave her a disapproving scowl.

"You would not want to marry a woman of loose morals." She gave him a half smile, hoping he would see the humor in the situation. But her insides were trembling, and she might become desperate enough to scream for help, or even fight him, if he tried to kiss her again. She just couldn't bear his lips on hers, not right now.

"But you know we will be married very soon. Why do you object to a simple kiss when no one is looking?"

"I am impulsive sometimes, but someone might come along and see us. And you have not spoken to my father yet, so my reputation is at stake."

"But you have already agreed to marry me. This is carrying modesty to an extreme. Do you not think so?"

"Darling." She took his hand in hers. "Please grant me this tiny request. You may kiss me once or twice a day. Is that not enough? As you said, we shall be married soon, and then it shall not matter. We shall not be obliged to sneak out to the garden to kiss each other then."

He sighed again. "I will honor your request. But it is very hard. A great hardship." He looked at her as a parent might as they scolded a small child.

"Thank you, my dear. You are extremely forbearing."

"I flatter myself I am." He gave her another scolding half smile.

Being meek and afraid of his temper was probably not the best tactic. She should have straightened her spine, raised her chin, and asserted in an insulted tone that she was not married to him yet and he was not to kiss her at all. Too late for that now.

"Let us walk a bit." She took his arm, and they wandered through the garden.

"Did you hear what the Parker twins said to me?" Mr. Ratley smiled and then proceeded to tell her about some flattering statement made about his approachable manners at the ball the night before. Someone else had complimented how well looking the two of them were together, and yet another guest had praised their dancing.

It was the sort of flattery commonly spoken at such parties, but Mr. Ratley seemed to think the guests had truly thought him and Felicity exceptionally gifted.

"Forgive me, Oliver, but I believe the sun is giving me a headache. I should probably go inside."

"Of course. Come." He led her inside and walked her up to her room.

"What will you do the rest of the day?" Felicity hoped he would not be wandering the corridors while she went to her rendezvous with Mr. Merrick.

"I think I will go and see Lady Blackstone's falcons. She is quite a good falconer."

"I hope you enjoy yourself. I may go and find myself a book to read after I've lain down for a few minutes."

They were standing at her door. He leaned toward her, but stopped short of kissing her. He straightened. "Am I permitted to kiss you here?"

"Only on the cheek." She smiled and offered her cheek.

He frowned, then kissed her on the cheek. She quickly went inside her room.

Aunt Agnes was breaking her fast by the window.

"Auntie, are you well?"

"Yes, but I have been wondering when we might go back to London."

"Soon. I hope. But I do not know exactly when." Felicity walked to her bed and lay across it.

How many times had she lied to Mr. Ratley today alone? She was not a spy. Would guilt overtake her and cause her to make a mistake? *God, forgive me for the lies. I know liars have their place in the lake of fire.* Was there justification based on motive and situation? She couldn't recall reading anything in the Bible about such a thing. Although . . . God often commanded the Israelites to kill during wars with other nations. If killing was permissible in wartime, wouldn't lying be also?

She waited until she felt Mr. Ratley must be safely outside the house. She could go and try to get into Lady Blackstone's room with the key, but her hands shook at the mere thought. What if Lady Blackstone came back from her ride and caught her?

If she were as bold and fearless as Lady Withinghall, she would take the risk, but she decided it was best to go and meet with Mr. Merrick, as he would be waiting for her in the library closet. Besides, she was bound to make a mistake sooner or later, and a mistake could cost her life as well as Mr. Merrick's. No, as she had decided earlier, she would give him the key.

"Auntie, I'll be back soon. Do you need anything?"

"You might pick out another book for me, if you are going near the library."

"Of course. I will."

Felicity hurried down the stairs, then reminded herself not to look suspicious and slowed her pace. She entered the library, picked a book from one of the shelves, and went inside the closet door. Mr. Merrick stood waiting for her in the tiny room.

He had brought two small stools into the room. He indicated one with his hand. "Would you like to sit?"

"Thank you." She perched on the small stool and handed him the key that, embarrassingly, had become damp from her sweaty palm.

"What's this?"

"It's the key to Lady Blackstone's room. I took it from Mr. Ratley's pocket."

He stared at the key, then at her, from his perch on the stool. He was only two feet in front of her, and the closet was quite dim, having no windows and being lit by only one candle.

"Very well done, Miss Mayson. Truly, you are a great spy."

A giggle suddenly escaped her throat. She pressed a hand to her lips and shook her head. If he only knew how afraid she had been, how her hands had hardly stopped shaking.

But his bright-blue eyes continued to gaze at her. "Truly, I am very impressed."

She had to blink away tears. "Don't be. If I were not so afraid, I might have stolen the papers by now. Lady Blackstone went riding this morning, and Mr. Ratley said he was going to look in on her falcons, but I was too afraid Lady Blackstone would return while I was in her room. I am not a spy, Mr. Merrick."

She took a deep breath to try and force back the threatening tears.

"Well, I do appreciate what you had to do to get the key, Miss Mayson."

She shook her head again. "I had to let him kiss me. I hated myself for doing it." The words made the tears come back. One slipped from her eye, and she wiped it with her fingers.

Mr. Merrick quickly pulled out a handkerchief and handed it to her.

"I am pretending to be his fiancée—I am his fiancée. But I have no intention of marrying him." She wiped her eyes and nose. "I am not that kind of girl. I have never kissed a man before, Mr. Merrick, and I do not even like it." A tiny sob escaped her.

"Miss Mayson, you don't have to tell me—"

"And I have lied to him over and over. I don't lie, Mr. Merrick. I never lie."

Why was she telling him all this? What must he think of her? She had to stop.

She covered her face with his handkerchief and forced herself to think only about breathing. *Breathe in. Breathe out.* But it was no use. She couldn't stop her thoughts.

"You must believe me. I had no idea they were revolutionaries when they invited me here or I never would have come. I thought Mr. Ratley truly loved me. But now the thought of marrying him makes me feel sick. Kissing him is repulsive, but I know I am doing it not only to save my own life and that of my aunt but to save my country. Still, I wish it was over." She pressed the handkerchief to her face again to catch the tears that fell.

"Please do not cry, Miss Mayson."

She felt his warm hand on her shoulder, just resting there, comforting.

"You don't know how grateful I am that you distracted Mr. Ratley when I was in Lady Blackstone's room. If not for you, I might have been killed, and all might have been lost. You are a hero, Miss Mayson."

She tried to sniff discreetly and wipe her nose. She didn't want to blow into his handkerchief. How mortifying.

"How you must scorn me for crying." She did her best to wipe her face and clear her throat, determined not to cry any more. "I am not fearless like you."

"Not at all. I think you are much braver than any woman I know."

She let out a short laugh at that.

"Truly, most women—even most men I know—would not have agreed to help spy on such dangerous people. And I am not fearless, only motivated. Truthfully, I don't enjoy lying and pretending either. I thought I wanted to be a spy, that it would be exciting, but . . . You will think me foolish and immature."

She looked up, forgetting about how red and puffy her face must appear. "I won't. Tell me."

"I wanted to prove to my brothers that I could do something they had never done. You see, I am the youngest, and my older brothers always did everything before I was able to—they climbed the highest trees while I fell and broke my leg. They went hunting with Father while I was left at home. My oldest brother will inherit my father's estate, and my next oldest brother is a rector, while my third brother is an officer in the army. I thought I could impress them if I did something important."

He half frowned, half smiled at himself. His eyes held such a vulnerable light.

"You see? I am not so brave. I began only to impress my brothers. But now . . . I am serving England and the Crown."

"Yes, of course. You are doing something very noble and good. Your brothers *would* be impressed. Will be impressed."

His shoulders were wide and seemed to fill the tiny room. But it was the vulnerable, self-deprecating expression in his eyes and on his face that made him even more appealing. Truly, she wondered how different it might be to kiss Mr. Merrick's lips than Mr. Ratley's. She wished she could find out.

Felicity ducked her head, unable to look Mr. Merrick in the eye. How could she think such a thing? All this kissing and duplicity was addling her mind.

"I wish I had tried to get the papers earlier, after Mr. Ratley left."

"No, you did the right thing. It is best to be cautious, especially now that we have this." He held up the key. "When we get out of here and get back to London, I shall make sure Lord Sidmouth knows what you've done, stealing this key and helping to find those papers, memorizing information. Your help has been very valuable."

"That is kind of you to say."

"It is the truth."

The longer she stayed in this room with him, the more she realized how improper it was. But propriety seemed the least of her worries. England, as she knew it, could cease to exist if she and Mr. Merrick did not succeed in stopping Lady Blackstone.

CHAPTER FIFTEEN

Philip couldn't help admiring Miss Mayson's determination to do what was right even when she was terrified. What an admirable girl she was. Mr. Ratley didn't deserve her even on his best day—even if he weren't an easily led, lawless insurrectionist.

She was also quite lovely, her eyes shining with residual tears. Every instinct urged him to protect her, but so much was at stake. Protecting her could lead to mistakes, and a mistake could cost him his mission, the respect of his colleagues, and public humiliation, not to mention his life and the lives of others.

And yet, he owed her so much.

"Thank you for this key. Since Lady Blackstone's rides are usually of short duration, and she'll probably not be with her falcons for long, I'll wait until another time to use it. But I do want to thank you for saving me from getting caught in Lady Blackstone's room last night. I owe you my life."

"Well, you saved me when I fainted and carried me into my room. Thank you for being a gentleman."

"It was my pleasure. I mean . . ." It *was* his pleasure, but he shouldn't say that. "What I mean is, I am glad I was there to help."

She smiled. "I don't know what I would have done if you had not been here to find my letter and destroy it. What would they have done if they had read it?"

"Probably locked you in your room or at least forbade you from leaving the house. You would have probably been subjected to constant indoctrination of their beliefs." Or they would have killed her.

She nodded.

"But now we must concentrate on getting this information before their revolution begins. We probably only have three or four weeks."

The look on her face said that a few weeks seemed like a long time—too long. And he agreed. They needed to work fast, before Ratley forced her to marry him.

"With your permission," Philip said, "I shall hide the key until there is a good opportunity to use it."

"Of course."

Some of the tension seemed to leave her shoulders. She looked down at his wadded handkerchief in her hands.

"You would not want your fiancé to find my handkerchief in your possession."

"Oh." Her cheeks flushed a pretty pink. She handed the wet handkerchief back to him. "Forgive me for crying and soiling it."

"No harm done. It can be washed." He smiled as he shoved it into his pocket. "My sister embroidered my initials on it, which also match my assumed name."

"That was very clever." She clasped hands and rose from her stool. "I should go back to my room. I told Mr. Ratley I had a headache and that I might come down to retrieve a book."

He stood. "Of course. I hope you are not having too much trouble fending off that gentleman's advances." It was a delicate subject, and he probably should not ask, but . . . he wanted to know.

"I . . . no, not too much trouble. But I am glad I have hope—that this will all be over soon." She seemed to shake her thoughts away and smiled, meeting his eye. "But the answer to your question is no. Mr. Ratley is not as much of an ogre as he might be."

She was trying to put on a brave face. As she put her hand on the doorknob, he touched her shoulder. She turned to look at him.

What could he say? *Be careful? Don't be afraid to scream if he refuses to listen to protest?*

"I will be careful not to betray myself or you," she said, mistaking his thoughts. "Please let me know if I can assist you in any way."

"Thank you, Miss Mayson."

As he stared into her determined but vulnerable face, Philip ached to promise that he would protect her. But he couldn't do anything that would endanger the mission. Those words sickened him, even as he left them unsaid.

She gave him a slight smile and left the room.

***

Felicity was taking her morning walk the next day when she decided to change into her riding clothes.

She came back out of the house and walked toward the stable, thinking she might ask one of the grooms to accompany her on a short ride. If she could develop a habit of riding every day, she might figure out a way to escape, or at least ride to a nearby town to send a letter.

She was just entering the stable when she heard voices coming from farther in. Lady Blackstone said something, then Mr. Ratley answered.

Felicity slipped into the first stall, which happened to be empty, and listened, concentrating to make out the words.

"Don't you think we can trust her?" she heard Mr. Ratley ask.

"Felicity?" Lady Blackstone said. "Trust is something we can't afford. You know that."

Felicity's breath came fast and shallow upon hearing her name.

"But do I still think you should marry her? Yes," Lady Blackstone continued. "She can't testify against you if she's married to you. Besides, she's such a timid little thing, afraid to speak up or own an opinion. She'll make you a good wife, and she won't make any trouble. That is easy enough to see."

Felicity's cheeks burned. Did people really have such thoughts about her? She clenched her fists.

She reminded herself to keep listening.

Mr. Ratley said something that Felicity couldn't quite make out. Then Lady Blackstone said, "Sooner is better. You don't want her deciding she doesn't want to marry you. Then things will get very messy."

"She says she can't marry unless her father approves. She wants me to go meet with him."

"No. Out of the question. You cannot leave, and there is no time. She wants her father's approval, then we will give it to her, in a letter."

Felicity flushed even hotter. She tried to force herself to keep listening, but Mr. Ratley's voice was too low. She thought she heard Lady Blackstone say, ". . . in a week."

Then, more clearly, she said, "I wish to go on my ride."

"I will go find Felicity."

"I saw her in the garden earlier, but then she went inside."

They mumbled a few more words, and Felicity stepped up on a bucket in the corner of the stall so no one walking by would see her feet under the door. She crouched down, making herself as small as possible.

Footsteps came nearer, then passed by. As she waited for Lady Blackstone to leave with her horse, Felicity felt herself fuming at the things she and Mr. Ratley had said about her. *Timid. Afraid to speak up or have an opinion. Would never make trouble.* They might just be surprised at how much trouble she could make.

But then again . . . she had not yet done anything of much merit. They had not even been able to get what information they did have to the Home Office.

Finally, she heard sounds of a horse passing by her stall. She waited another minute or two, just to be sure Lady Blackstone was gone, and she opened the door and came out. No one seemed to be around, so she walked through, looking at the horses in their stalls. Most of them observed her placidly from giant brown eyes.

Felicity had never been much of a rider. She was rather afraid of horses, but she remembered Lady Blackstone's words about her and straightened her spine.

A groom came in carrying tack and a saddle. He hung them up and greeted her.

"Would you saddle a horse for me?" Felicity said. "I'd like to go for a short ride."

"Sorry, miss." He shook his head. "Lady Blackstone don't allow anyone to ride without her express permission. The lady's orders."

She might have known. How else could she keep anyone from leaving and passing unauthorized letters and messages to the outside world?

The groom exited the stable, leaving her alone with her swirling thoughts.

A minute or two later, Mr. Merrick entered the stable. He stopped, fixing his gaze on her.

"I was hoping to go for a ride, but I was informed I must get permission from Lady Blackstone."

"Yes, that is one of her rules."

"I don't suppose she will give me her permission."

"Probably not, not without her or Mr. Ratley going along on the ride. I have permission only to exercise my horse. I'm not allowed to go far." He was looking very rugged in his riding clothes, his buckskins and black riding boots. His bright-blue eyes sparkled even while they maintained a serious expression.

She stepped closer to him and said in a low voice, "I heard them talking about me."

He focused an intense look on her face.

"They don't particularly trust me, but they intend for me to marry him quickly. I cannot testify against Mr. Ratley if we are married."

"You must put him off. Don't agree to the marriage." He took a step toward her, now only about a foot away. "Think of excuses to postpone the wedding until later."

"Believe me, I shall try." But what would she do if they refused to accept her excuses? If they pressed her to marry him or even threatened her? She refrained from asking those questions of Mr. Merrick. After all, she was not his responsibility. Besides that, she didn't want to sound . . . desperate? Afraid? Timid?

No, she would not prove them right about her.

Mr. Merrick had already seen her faint and had seen her cry. He might think her even more weak and incapable than Mr. Ratley and Lady Blackstone thought her. And yet . . . Mr. Merrick had told her she was brave.

"I should let you saddle your horse." She took a step back, suddenly very aware of how close they were standing.

"Miss Mayson," he said, but then someone entered through the door of the stable, and he took a step back and turned.

Mr. Ratley stopped just inside. Staring at them.

"It looks as though I am interrupting . . ."

"Mr. Ratley," Mr. Merrick said, not seeming the least bit alarmed, though Felicity's heart was beating at double its normal pace.

Without bothering to explain, Mr. Merrick stepped toward a saddle on the wall nearby.

"I came into the stable," Felicity said, "to look at the horses. I thought I might also go for a ride, but the groom informed me that I need Lady Blackstone's permission. And then Mr. Merrick came in, and I was asking him about the good riding trails nearby, thinking after Lady Blackstone gives her permission, you and I might go for a ride."

She bit her lip, wishing she had not suggested that. Her fiancé's kisses were hard enough to fend off in the house. How much worse would it be if they took a ride together unaccompanied? Not to mention the fact that it was all a lie. She was becoming skilled at thinking up a good lie.

Mr. Ratley's expression changed as a smile spread over his face. "I don't think we need ask Lady Blackstone's permission if you go with me. But I thought you didn't like horses."

"I like them well enough. I feel the need for some fresh air."

Mr. Ratley went to get a groom to saddle their horses while Mr. Merrick was nearly finished saddling his. Felicity watched as a bit of sun broke through the clouds and warmed Mr. Merrick's hair while he tightened the horse's cinch strap. He then patted the gelding's neck and spoke softly to him.

Mr. Ratley came back with two stable workers who began saddling their horses. Meanwhile, Mr. Merrick mounted his horse and rode away.

If Mr. Ratley did not like her objections to his kisses, Felicity could use the excuse that Lady Blackstone and Mr. Merrick were also out riding. They wouldn't be entirely alone.

She asked a groom for his assistance getting onto her horse while Mr. Ratley was distracted. He seemed disappointed when he looked around and saw her already in the saddle.

"Let us go, then." He mounted, and they started off onto a trail that led away from the garden.

Her horse, a mare that Mr. Ratley promised was gentle, balked and pulled to the right. She pulled on the reins gently, but the mare shook her head and kept going right.

Felicity's brother had told her once, *You don't like horses because you're too timid to show them you are the master. You have to take a firm hand with them. Then they'll respect you.*

Fear rose in her throat, but she clenched her teeth and pulled harder on the reins, just as Mr. Ratley called over his shoulder, "Are you coming?"

The mare finally obeyed her and pointed her nose toward the trail, following behind Mr. Ratley's gelding.

***

Philip pushed Felicity Mayson from his thoughts yet again and tried to concentrate. The other men had told him a stash of guns was nearby, in an underground grotto between Doverton Hall and the sea. They said it was a strange cave Lady Blackstone had showed them. The walls were all covered in colorful shells that had been deliberately placed to form flowers and sunbursts and other decorative patterns.

Not only did Philip need to know the location of the weapons, but he was curious to see the place.

He made his way through the trees and the scrubby bushes, leaving the riding trail behind. He came upon some grazing pastureland and, giving his horse a running start, had him leap the fence.

He dismounted and looked all around the field. It was well grazed, and he had to watch his step to avoid the sheep dung. Finally, he spotted a broad, flat board lying on the ground with a footpath leading up to it before ending abruptly. Could this be the entrance to the cave?

He heard voices, one female and one male, coming from the riding trail he had just left.

He took his horse's reins and hurried back toward the trees.

***

Felicity had to pull harder on the reins than she wanted to, more than once, as she followed Mr. Ratley along the trail. Why had she suggested going for a ride? She could barely get the horse to do what she wanted. Still, she tried to sound confident and comfortable as she engaged her fiancé in a conversation that might serve some purpose.

"So, Oliver, when will our revolution begin?" She was proud of herself for thinking to call it "our" revolution.

"You are not worrying about me, are you?" He glanced back at her with an amused smile.

"No, I'd just like to know, so that I'm not caught by surprise."

"I don't suppose there's any harm in telling you." He swayed with the movements of his horse as they ambled slowly—at least she could be thankful for their slow gait.

"In May, we will distribute in all the major cities the leaflets we've been printing, to as many people as we can."

"Leaflets?"

"Yes, and some longer pamphlets too. Mr. Cartwright is quite good at writing essays that motivate and inspire. And we have our own printing press in the outbuilding beside the gardener's shed, where Lady Blackstone has some servants employed in printing them. They've been working twelve hours a day for weeks now."

Mr. Merrick probably knew this, but she needed to be sure and tell him in case he didn't.

"I see. And then what?"

"Then, probably in May, we will target the army and the home guards, convince them that the government is so corrupt they need no longer feel any allegiance to it or to the king. After all, a king whose government is so unfair and unjust has forfeited his right to rule. If we can get the army and militia on our side, we shall be unstoppable."

Felicity smiled as though the idea was a happy one.

"Meanwhile, we shall join with our supporters in London, who will assassinate the Members of Parliament, the king's advisors, and . . . well, you probably don't want to hear these particulars."

"And this will happen in May?"

"Yes. We plan to act fast once we begin. Better to strike quickly."

"When will you and the others have to leave here?"

"Probably the first of May. Lady Blackstone wants us all in place ahead of time. We'll be so spread out, the authorities won't possibly know where all of us are. And frankly, I don't think anyone outside our group has any idea what is about to happen. Lady Blackstone is so clever, she has made sure to keep our activities very quiet."

"Yes, Lady Blackstone is quite clever."

"She is indeed. But it could be dangerous. It is likely we could even lose a few men."

She should probably pretend more interest in Mr. Ratley's welfare and ask where he would be and his role in the revolution. Instead, she rode on in silence, turning her attention to staying on the horse's back.

"Here is a romantic spot I've been wanting to show you, but I had to wait for Lady Blackstone's approval." He had stopped to open the gate to a sheep pasture, then led his horse on foot while she and her horse followed. He halted in front of a large rectangle-shaped piece of wood lying on the ground.

Mr. Ratley came to stand beside her. "I have brought you to the shell grotto."

"The shell grotto?"

"Yes. Wouldn't you like to get down from your horse and explore it with me?"

She did not like the look in his eye. *O God, cannot you help me avoid kissing him? I do not think I can bear it.* "Won't it be dark inside?"

"I think it will be light enough." He bent and took hold of the large piece of wood and shoved. He seemed to have some difficulty with it but slowly pushed it several feet, uncovering a hole. Next, he walked several feet away and removed a tree branch, revealing another smaller hole. Were those holes to be the only light? Although she was quite curious to see the shell grotto, being in a dark, close space alone with Mr. Ratley did not appeal to her.

"I would prefer to come back another time with a group of people," she said.

"But we are here now, and we don't know when we might be able to gather a group to come with us. And we can't go home now. We have not been riding more than fifteen minutes. Come." He reached for her.

"I'm afraid my horse might run away. Besides, we are all alone out here. If someone were to come along and see that we were in the grotto, they might think we were improper."

"Darling, the horse will not run away, and we are engaged to be married. What does it matter if someone thinks we've been improper?"

She could think of no other excuses, so she let him help her off the horse.

CHAPTER SIXTEEN

Felicity kept her head down, watching her feet, as if she didn't know her fiancé was waiting to kiss her. When he did not let go of her waist, she looked up and let him press his lips to hers. But she quickly pulled away.

"Did I do something wrong?"

"No, of course not. I just . . . well, my mother taught me that kissing was only for marriage. I feel uncomfortable, as if we should wait until our wedding night."

"My darling. You are far too modest and chaste."

She pulled all the way away from him and took a step toward the grotto entrance. "I cannot help it. I am a deep and ardent admirer of Miss Hannah More, and I invariably ask myself, in any situation, 'What would Miss More say?'"

She was being facetious, knowing he was not astute enough to catch on, but she did very much respect Miss Hannah More's opinions on matters of morality. And yet, if she felt in her heart that she was truly going to marry Mr. Ratley, she would not object to kissing him, either on moral or any other grounds.

Mr. Ratley caught up with her and pulled her hand through the crook of his elbow. "You need not concern yourself with other people's opinions. Henceforth I shall tell you what to think."

She drew in a deep breath, her teeth starting to clench. If she were not pretending to be in love with the man, she might tell him some things he would not find pleasant.

He walked her to the edge of the hole in the ground, and she saw that there were some rudimentary steps leading down.

"It looks quite dark down there." Felicity stopped as he put his foot on the top step. "Likely it will be dirty."

"Felicity, my love, I brought you out here so you would not feel uncomfortable being alone with me."

No, you brought me out here so you could take liberties and no one would see.

"Do you not enjoy kissing your future husband?"

"Darling, I told you. I would prefer to save kissing for after our wedding." An uneasiness came over her. She should think of some way to placate him. "But we will have the rest of our lives together. You don't mind being patient, just for a little while, do you, darling?"

He was not looking at her. "Perhaps you have changed your mind about marrying me."

"Of course not."

"Oh, good morning. Or should I say, good afternoon?" Mr. Merrick was standing behind them in the clearing. "I did not realize you had taken the same trail."

"Good afternoon, Mr. Merrick." Mr. Ratley's voice was tight, but he smiled anyway.

"Were you about to show Miss Mayson the shell grotto? I was hoping to see it myself. Shall we go inside?" He moved toward them as if he didn't realize he was interrupting their conversation, and he actually started down the steps.

Felicity took Mr. Ratley's arm, and they started down after him.

"It will take a few minutes for our eyes to adjust to the dark," Mr. Merrick said. "Mr. Ratley? Is there a lantern we could light?"

Mr. Ratley bent and picked something up off the ground that squeaked like a metal handle. "Here is a lantern, but we have no matches."

"I just happen to carry some." Mr. Merrick came close and struck a match. They soon had the lantern lighted, and Felicity gasped.

Seashells covered every inch of space on the walls. Someone had attached them in beautiful patterns and shapes, and the shells were of many different colors—various shades of yellow, pink, and even blue. They were arranged into sunbursts, swirls, and flowers, decorative borders and arches.

"This place is incredible," Felicity breathed.

Mr. Merrick was holding the lantern close to the walls, examining them. "I've never seen anything like it. Shall we explore further?"

They came to two arched openings, one on the left and one on the right. Mr. Merrick went left, and Mr. Ratley pulled Felicity toward the right one.

"But Mr. Merrick has the lantern," Felicity protested.

"They both lead to the same place," Mr. Ratley said.

She let him lead her into the dark passageway, and then he pulled her close and tried to kiss her, but in the dark his lips landed on her cheek.

"Come," Felicity whispered, "let us catch up with Mr. Merrick. I want to see the rest of the cave." She wrenched herself out of his arms, annoyed that he was causing her to miss seeing what Mr. Merrick was viewing with his lantern. She took Mr. Ratley's arm and hurried in the direction they had been walking, keeping her other hand on the wall so she wouldn't lose her way, the edges of the shells dancing on her fingertips.

A glow of light shone just ahead, and soon they reached the end of the tunnel and a large rectangular room. She drank in the fantastical and intricate mosaics someone had meticulously created on the walls, visible by Mr. Merrick's lantern, but more so by the light coming in through a hole high above them in the ceiling, letting in the sunlight.

"Look at this," Mr. Ratley said.

Felicity and Mr. Merrick both came over to see a small shell-covered table against the wall, almost like an altar.

"Lady Blackstone said it looked like a place where someone had performed pagan rituals," Mr. Ratley said.

"Or maybe it's where they placed their tea things." Mr. Merrick didn't smile, but the corner of his mouth twitched.

Felicity couldn't stop turning her head, trying to take in every beautiful inch of the shell-covered walls and ceiling. "Who could have created such a magical-looking place? It's so well done, so artistic. The walls, even the floors, everything is perfectly straight and level and symmetrical."

"Lady Blackstone doesn't know who created it," Mr. Ratley said. "She said one of her shepherds discovered it and told her about it. He was afraid it was a pagan cave and said he didn't want anything to do with it. He advised Lady Blackstone to cover the entrance and never go inside."

"And no one in the village knows about it?" Mr. Merrick asked. "There are no stories or legends about it?"

"Not that we know of. It seems to be completely forgotten."

"It is such a mysterious place," Felicity said. "I wish we could find a diary telling how it came about, who built it, and why. Perhaps there is a hidden compartment somewhere."

"That doesn't seem likely," Mr. Ratley said. "And it hardly matters. Those who carved it out of the ground and decorated it must be long dead, and now it's a perfect storage room for our weapons, as we have a large delivery of guns and ammunition coming soon."

Felicity sighed. So much beauty. So much mystery. "I hope you will not damage it."

"It should be about time for tea." Mr. Ratley did not seem very interested in looking at the walls and held out his arm to Felicity.

"Indeed," Mr. Merrick said cheerily. "I could do for some tea. Thank you for showing us the shell grotto, Mr. Ratley."

Mr. Ratley gave a half smile as he faced Mr. Merrick. "Of course."

They all walked toward the entrance with Felicity following Mr. Merrick as if she did not notice Mr. Ratley hanging back, probably hoping to take the other tunnel so he could try to kiss her again.

Once they were out of the grotto, Felicity allowed herself a deep breath and let it out. She was careful not to look at Mr. Merrick. Her gratitude for his interruption of Mr. Ratley's intentions would show on her face.

Mr. Ratley helped her onto her horse, and the two men also mounted and led the way back onto the trail.

Mr. Merrick stayed with them, engaging Mr. Ratley in conversation all the way back to the stable. He seemed to be purposely flattering her fiancé, paying him several compliments, making him smile, and putting him into a better mood. *May God bless you, Mr. Merrick.*

They went inside and took their tea together. Just as they were finished, Felicity walked to the window in the sitting room and looked up.

"It looks as if the clouds are clearing. We may get some more sun later."

When she spun around, she caught Mr. Merrick looking at her. He quickly glanced away.

"I believe I will go up to look in on my Aunt Agnes."

"I shall accompany you," Mr. Ratley said.

"There is no need. Please, stay and talk to Mr. Merrick." She hurried away as fast as was socially acceptable, before Mr. Ratley could insist.

Once in her room, she talked with her aunt, who was sipping tea. She had never required very much food, and since she seemed to be eating as much as she ever did, Felicity decided she would not suffer any ill effects from her recent moments of shock and nerves.

Felicity changed out of her riding clothes and into a white muslin dress with tiny blue flowers embroidered on the bodice. By the time

Auntie had finished helping her on with her dress, more than fifteen minutes had passed, so she hurried away.

She smiled at the few people she encountered on the stairs and in the corridor but did not pause to chat. As usual, she browsed through the library, pretending to look through the books, grabbed one to take back to her aunt, and slipped into the closet and shut the door.

Mr. Merrick greeted her.

"Thank you for meeting me, Mr. Merrick. I wanted to tell you what I learned from Mr. Ratley today." She proceeded to tell him about how the insurrectionists all planned to scatter and carry out their plans from different places around the country, and she told him especially about the leaflets and pamphlets.

"Did you know," she said, focusing on his blue eyes, "that they have a printing press here?"

"Yes. It's in a building next to the gardener's shed. They use it to print leaflets with their violent reform rhetoric."

Mr. Merrick's brows drew down in that now-familiar wrinkle above his nose, and he tapped the fingers of his right hand against his leg, another little habit of his.

"I have been considering whether I should destroy it so they can't print any more of their insurrectionist propaganda. It might even delay their revolution if they don't have enough leaflets."

"But wouldn't that be dangerous? They might realize a traitor lurked in their midst."

"I could make it seem as if it broke on its own."

"We could do it tonight, then, after everyone is asleep. They run the printing press twelve hours a day, Mr. Ratley said. No one will be running it tonight."

"You should let me take care of it. If they see us . . ."

"If they see you, they will kill you, but they probably would not kill me. Besides, I want to help."

"There is no need for you to risk your safety. I will take care of it." He was leaning toward her with that intense look in his eyes.

Felicity realized she'd been holding her breath. She let it out. "Very well."

He seemed to realize he'd been leaning in, and he took a step back and straightened. She saw him take a breath to steady himself. "Forgive me if I sounded . . . harsh."

"Not at all. You wish to do your job. I respect that." *Although you could accept my help with no extra risk to yourself—or your silly pride.* But, to be fair, there would be less danger of getting caught if one should sabotage the printing press rather than two.

"I am grateful to have you for an ally, Miss Mayson. I am only sorry . . ." He tapped his fingertips on his leg again.

When he did not continue, she asked, "Sorry? For what?"

"Sorry that you must continue to suffer Mr. Ratley's attentions."

Her stomach churned. He'd probably heard their argument about kissing. Her cheeks heated.

"Hopefully it will be over soon."

"I—yes." Her face was burning. "I am keeping him at arm's length as much as I can. I've told him we cannot get married until he asks my father's blessing, and since he isn't likely to go to London for that purpose . . ."

An awkward silence followed. If their situation was not so important to so many people other than themselves, Mr. Merrick would certainly come to her aid. But the thought stirred an ache in her chest, so she pushed it away. She didn't want to cry and make him any more uncomfortable than he already was. He was obviously a gentleman, so of course he wished to save her this indignity of having to fight off Mr. Ratley's kisses. Only because he was a gentleman. He did not care specifically for her. And she shouldn't wish he did. She shouldn't. But she did.

***

Philip felt the gut-wrenching pain of Miss Mayson's embarrassment and relived seeing Oliver Ratley looming over her by the entrance to the shell grotto trying to intimidate her into letting him kiss her. Philip imagined grabbing Ratley's shoulder, spinning him around, and slamming his fist in his cowardly face. The thought of Ratley's nose spurting blood was the only thing that kept Philip from doing something that might jeopardize his mission.

He should change their topic of conversation.

"Today I got a letter saying my mother's illness has worsened, and the doctors do not expect her to recover."

"Oh, I'm very sorry." Felicity gasped and pressed a hand to her chest.

"No, not *my* mother. It is a ploy. A colleague from the Home Office sent the letter, as per our plan, in case I needed a distraction at this point in my investigation. I shall tell Lady Blackstone of the letter—she no doubt already knows, for they open every letter that arrives—and then tonight after dinner I shall use it as an excuse to leave the company early and go up to my room to be alone and pen some letters to my family. I'll sneak out to the printing press, disable it, and be back inside before anyone misses me."

He would also use that time to go into Lady Blackstone's room and steal the papers, but there was no need to divulge that information. He didn't want her to worry.

"Very well." She seemed disappointed that she would not be helping him.

"Your information has been invaluable, Miss Mayson. I cannot thank you enough."

"I am happy for anything I can do. Although I would prefer to have these people apprehended sooner rather than later so that my Aunt Agnes and I can go home." She smiled, her lips curving symmetrically, her pink cheeks and green eyes delicately enhancing her beauty, and her pale-red-blonde hair framing perfectly arched brows and thick lashes.

But he should not be staring at her so blatantly, admiring her beauty.

"Thank you. Of course. You and your aunt shall be back home with the rest of your family very soon."

***

Philip did his best to keep up with the whereabouts of as many of the houseguests as he could but especially those of Lady Blackstone and her almost-constant shadow, Mr. Ratley.

That evening at dinner, Philip informed the latter two of the dire situation of his mother, saying that she was in an unconscious state and could die at any time, or she might linger for many months. However, he felt his first duty was to make her beloved country a better place, rather than sitting by her bedside.

Lady Blackstone commended his zeal. "You are a true son of England," she said. "Your mother would be very proud of you."

Mr. Ratley actually clapped him on the shoulder. "It is hard to lose one's mother. Let Lady Blackstone and me be your support. We are all a family here, of sorts, fighting for a common cause."

"Thank you. You are good friends." Philip endeavored to look humble.

Dinner was the same lingering affair, and everyone seemed to be drinking a bit more than usual. As the meal was drawing to a close, one of the women suggested a game.

"Mr. Ratley says he and Miss Mayson are engaged, but let us see if he is willing to pay for her hand with compliments. He must pay fifteen compliments or we shall lock her away from him until he does."

Miss Mayson's porcelain skin turned bright red as a hearty "Huzzah!" went around the table, and all eyes turned to her and her fiancé.

***

Felicity listened with self-conscious embarrassment as her friend Josephine Cartwright suggested Mr. Ratley pay compliments to his bride-to-be, "Or we will lock her away from him until he does."

Josephine laughed and clapped her hands as the rest of the guests shouted, "Pay up!"

Mr. Ratley beamed, obviously delighted to have so much attention directed toward him.

Felicity tried to smile good-naturedly. But she wished she could sink through the floor at finding herself the object of the raucous crowd's attention.

Mr. Ratley stood as the crowd began to chant, "Pay up! Pay up!"

"Very well, very well." He motioned for them to quiet down. "I am a man in love, so I have no objections."

"I will count for you!" someone shouted.

Mr. Ratley cleared his throat, then announced loudly, "My Miss Mayson is as lovely as any girl in England."

"Lovely! That's one!"

He paused, as if he could not think of any other compliments. Her stomach twisted. Everyone was staring, waiting, their faces fastened on her fiancé with caustic grins.

Finally, Mr. Ratley said, "Miss Mayson is the girl I have dreamed of my whole life."

"That's two! What makes you want to marry her? Come on, man!"

"She is an ornament on my arm, my brightest jewel."

"A bright jewel," Mr. Cartwright said. "That's three."

She pressed the back of her hand to her burning cheek.

"No, no, that's the same thing!" someone shouted. "Lovely, a dream, and a jewel. Something else, something else!"

"She is beautiful, handsome, lovely," Mr. Ratley listed, still smiling broadly.

"Those are all the same!"

Felicity tried to force an amused smile while she prayed he would think of some other compliment, something appropriate—or, better yet, put a stop to this "game." When she glanced up, she noticed Mr. Merrick's hands were clenched into fists as he glared at Mr. Ratley. But when he looked at Felicity . . . She couldn't meet his look of compassion.

"Think of something else," another man shouted, "or we will take her now and lock her away." He even went so far as to stand up from his chair, motioning to Mr. Sproles to join him.

O God, please don't let this escalate any further. Why did Mr. Ratley not put a stop to this? Instead, he wore a ridiculous smile.

"Oh, my Miss Mayson is the loveliest of women. She is the apple of my eye . . . my comfort . . . the mother of my future children."

Everyone roared with laughter. Felicity could not even lift her eyes from her lap. How humiliating to see and hear her fiancé unable to come up with anything he loved about her besides her physical appearance and usefulness to himself. Thanks be to God that she did not intend to actually marry him, that she was not trusting in Mr. Oliver Ratley to love her for the rest of her life. How could she have ever pledged herself to a man so shallow that he did not value her mind or her heart?

The men who had just been guffawing at Mr. Ratley's words now took a few steps toward her.

***

Philip gritted his teeth as he stared at the man who was humiliating his fiancée and himself and was too doltish to even realize it.

Could the blockhead not think of anything else to love about Miss Mayson? Philip was sickened. Was he too blind to see that she was clever, kind, and intelligent? That she was gentle and always found the good in others? Did he not see that behind that quiet voice was a steely conviction, a courage to always do what was right?

The man was a vile caricature, an utter failure at appreciating this glorious woman, not to mention that he did not even see how he was humiliating her in front of these rough men. Philip's blood boiled.

When a few of the men got up, focused on Miss Mayson, and stepped toward her, Philip rose from his chair.

"That is enough," he shouted, his hands clenched into fists. "You are embarrassing the lady."

Everyone stared at him as his heart pounded with the same intensity he longed to apply with his fists to their faces.

He went on in an even tone, forcing a calm he did not feel. "There is no need to throw decency to the winds in this undignified manner."

"Mr. Merrick is right," Lady Blackstone said in a hard tone of voice. "Ladies, let us adjourn to the parlor. And if the men can control their bawdiness, they may join us later."

Philip suddenly remembered. In all the chaos, he'd forgotten his plan for the evening. "Lady Blackstone, if I may . . ."

She stopped and turned steely eyes on him.

"Please excuse me and allow me to go to my room. I . . . after the news I have received about my mother, I feel I should write some letters to my family and—"

"Yes, of course, Mr. Merrick. You are excused." She turned and left, leading the other ladies with her.

He couldn't help glancing at Miss Mayson. He caught her eye, but only for a moment. Her cheeks still blushed red. She looked away and followed the other ladies out. Philip left with them, then went up to his room.

He took off his blue coat and replaced it with the black one that had Lady Blackstone's room key sewn into the lining. He grabbed a stack of blank papers off his desk and carefully placed them inside his waistcoat, then hurried back out his door.

In the corridor, he pressed himself against the wall and listened. He looked to the right and to the left. No one seemed to be around. He walked slowly and carefully toward the wing of the house where Lady Blackstone's room was located while ripping out the stitching in the coat lining one stitch at a time until he was able to extricate the key.

He paused in front of her door, inserted the key, and went inside, shutting the door behind him.

He quickly went to the drawer where the papers were located. He opened it and found them just where they had been before. He took them out and replaced them with the blank pages from inside his waistcoat—laying the first page of Lady Blackstone's papers on top—and stuffed the rest inside his waistcoat.

He looked all around, trying to spot anything he might have left out of place. Satisfied, he moved to the door, listened carefully, opened it, listened again, then slipped out. He locked it back with the key, then hurried back to his own room.

Inside, he went to his trunk and lifted it off the floor, tilting it onto its lid. On the bottom was a tiny latch. He turned it to reveal a compartment large enough for the papers and the key. He put them inside, closed and latched it, and put it back down on the floor.

He then moved as quietly as possible back out of his room, down the stairs, and out the door to the nighttime garden, all without encountering anyone, praise be to God.

Silently, he crept toward the building that housed the printing press.

CHAPTER SEVENTEEN

Felicity's stomach turned as she and the other ladies retired to the drawing room. But how relieved she had been when Mr. Merrick had raised his voice and halted the humiliating debacle. Tears rose behind her eyes as she recalled how he had stood up for her, but she blinked them away.

It doesn't matter. Why did she care? She wouldn't marry Mr. Ratley, but it still stung. She had thought him disinterested because he did not care that she did not possess a fortune, but that did not necessarily mean that he liked her for herself. As it turned out, he only cared about her beauty and her childbearing capabilities. And it made her cheeks sting all over again that she could have been so fooled as to think him worthy of her love, admiration, and hand in marriage.

But she could not dwell on that now. She had to stuff it down, down with the humiliation of everyone laughing at her buffoonish fiancé trying to come up with compliments for her—and failing miserably.

The few ladies in the room had paired up and were talking amongst themselves. Lady Blackstone seemed distracted. She even got up and looked out the window, then went back to her seat.

"Felicity." Lady Blackstone turned to her, startling her out of her reverie. "I hope you are not upset at what happened at dinner.

Mr. Ratley is not especially good with words or compliments. It does not mean he doesn't wish to marry you as much as any man might wish to."

"Oh, I never assign any worth to compliments." Felicity tried for a light and airy laugh, but it came out sounding hollow.

Lady Blackstone patted her hand. "Mr. Ratley adores you, and he is a good man. You two shall be very happy."

I shall be very happy as soon as I leave this place.

"Lady Blackstone." A man appeared in the doorway, a stranger to Felicity. "The delivery has arrived."

Her hostess stood quickly. "Ladies, I regret I must part from you early this evening. And I will borrow your husbands for a little while. Our task may take a couple of hours."

The ladies all expressed their regrets, but briefly, as it was evident that Lady Blackstone was eager to go.

The other ladies began talking together. As they were all ignoring her, Felicity slipped out without excusing herself.

Lady Blackstone was talking in a low voice in the corridor with three men.

". . . take the weapons to the grotto . . . With all the men helping, it should only take a couple of hours."

Felicity's heart crashed against her chest. Mr. Merrick! If they were all outside, they might see him as he came out of the shed after damaging the printing press.

"Tell all the men to change their clothes if they do not wish to get them dirty and meet us in ten minutes at the head of the trail that leads to the grotto."

Felicity ducked inside the nearest room—a small sitting room. She held her breath as Lady Blackstone walked past.

She waited only a few seconds, then headed for the back door.

With her white dress, she was like a lantern walking in the moonlight, but there had been no time to go to her room and change. Her heart thundered as she glanced around, seeing no one, and ran to the shed where the printing press was stored. She tried the door. It wasn't locked. She hurried inside.

It was dark and smelled of ink. She waited for her eyes to grow accustomed, and she saw a hulking shape, like a large machine. "Is anyone here?" she whispered loudly.

No answer.

"Mr. Merrick?"

The door opened. She gasped as a dark figured rushed in, then closed the door behind him. He turned to face her and put a finger over his lips.

She took a step back, and her foot hit something hard and round. She flailed her arms as she began to fall, and the man grabbed her and pulled her toward him.

She found herself pressed against Mr. Merrick's chest.

"Don't make a sound," he whispered gruffly, his lips next to her ear.

She froze, her forearms trapped between them. He had one arm around her, holding her up, as she still didn't have her footing. One foot rested on something like a log or a heavy metal cylinder.

Then she heard male voices outside the little shed. They grew louder, along with the sounds of a carriage or wagon being pulled by horses.

Mr. Merrick's chest rose and fell with hard breaths, which soon slowed to normal. Pressed so close to him, her cheeks heated for the second time that night.

"Are they coming here?" she whispered softly.

No, no. She remembered. "It's a delivery of weapons. I heard Lady Blackstone say"—she paused to listen—"that they were taking them to the grotto."

He gave a small nod to let her know he'd heard her.

The voices continued, some close, some farther away. Felicity thought she heard Lady Blackstone's voice amidst those of the men's.

And Mr. Merrick continued to stand perfectly still, his arm around her like an iron band.

Finally, the voices grew fainter and then ceased to be heard altogether.

"Forgive me," he said, stepping back. He kept hold of her, and she held on to him, until she was able to stumble forward and get her feet under her again.

She took the liberty, now that they were not so close, of looking up into his face. His expression was not quite visible in the bit of moonlight shining through the one small window, which was higher than her head. He was staring down at her too. Was he angry at her for coming here when she had agreed to let him take care of it?

"I—I came out here to warn you," she said quickly. "I heard Lady Blackstone saying that the delivery of arms had arrived. I was afraid they would see you, so I ran out here . . . I didn't want you to get caught."

"I was stealing the papers from Lady Blackstone's room."

"Oh. You got them?" Her heart expanded, and she could not help clasping her hands together and sighing with joy. "That is wonderful."

"Now I must copy and return them. I was coming out here to sabotage the printing press when I saw you running across the yard. You might as well have been a beacon of light darting across the yard. What if someone had seen you and followed you here?"

"I'm glad it was only you."

He exhaled rather loudly.

She still couldn't be sure if he was more angry or relieved. Perhaps it was better she didn't know. "Now, how do we wreak havoc on this machine?" Felicity was careful not to step backward again. Instead, she turned in place and looked at the large printing press the revolutionaries were using to generate rhetoric intended to deceive and inflame the masses to revolt against the government and do Lady Blackstone's bidding.

"Be careful," he said, resting a hand on her shoulder. "Have you ever seen a printing press before?"

"Never. Do you have any idea how it works?"

He leaned over part of it. "I have some idea, but . . . it should be simple. I should be able to find some tiny but important part, take it out, and bury it in the ground so they'll never find it."

"Sounds reasonable." She stood back and let him prowl around the machine, examining it. He stepped slowly, probably trying not to make any noise. She heard more voices outside. Apparently a lot of people were getting involved in the unloading of the guns.

"I should try to leave as soon as possible," Felicity whispered. "To get back to the house while everyone is busy."

"If someone were to see you . . . In the morning, the servants who do the printing work will find that the press is no longer working. If anyone saw you coming from here, they will assume you tampered with it."

"That is true, of course. And, if someone sees me leaving, they might be curious enough to come here and find you. I suppose we had better both stay where we are until no one is lurking outside who might see us."

"Yes, that would be safest. Please," he said, and she imagined that he was looking at her, although she could not see him well enough to know, as he was on the back side of the printing press now. "You may as well make yourself comfortable."

She found a stool and sat down.

She heard some slight sounds coming from the printing press, metal on metal. Voices could be heard outside, but it was difficult to tell how far away they were. More metallic noises, then a whispered word from Mr. Merrick that she could not make out. He must have been talking to himself.

Many minutes later, she leaned her back against the wall of the building and closed her eyes. Why was she so exhausted? Perhaps because she'd been tense and afraid and fending off the advances of Mr. Ratley for days and slept very little the night before.

"Miss Mayson?"

Felicity jerked awake, lifting herself off the wall and nearly falling off the stool she was sitting on. Mr. Merrick grabbed her arms to steady her.

"Forgive me. I didn't mean to startle you." He squatted in front of her.

"I must have fallen asleep."

"I took out a bolt and used a vise to break it, then put it back in. That will slow them down for a few days at least, and hopefully it will seem as if the bolt broke on its own."

"That's very clever." She stretched her back.

Loud laughter exploded from just outside the wall where Felicity was sitting. She caught her breath with a high-pitched, strangled sound in her throat.

Mr. Merrick pressed two fingers to her lips. He quickly took them away, but her lips tingled strangely, as if she could still feel his touch.

They both stayed perfectly still as people talked and laughed just a few feet away. After a few minutes, the raucous voices moved a little farther away.

"I think I hear Mr. Ratley's voice," Mr. Merrick said.

Felicity heard it too. He was speaking very loudly—he'd obviously had too much to drink. She sighed, remembering her humiliation.

"I haven't thanked you," she whispered.

Mr. Merrick brought another stool a couple of feet in front of her and sat down. "For what?"

"For coming to my defense tonight at dinner."

"Mr. Ratley is a toad."

Felicity covered her mouth, but her heart was still too heavy to laugh.

"What kind of man speaks that way about his fiancée?" Mr. Merrick's voice was tight, his whisper gruff. "And he's too half-witted to realize he was being disrespectful."

Felicity felt the sting of embarrassment all over again. It seemed so much more humiliating knowing Mr. Merrick had seen her kissing the man.

"You probably should not have done it," Felicity said, "as it might throw suspicion on us and jeopardize your mission."

"Please know, Miss Mayson, I wish I could have done more, and I certainly would have said much more . . . were we not in the situation we are. Please forgive me."

Her heart leapt inside her. But then it crashed back down. This was the kind of man she'd always hoped to marry. But . . . there was still the same issue that made all the handsome, eligible gentlemen reject her—she had no fortune.

***

Philip's chest tightened again at the awful, helpless feeling of not being able to properly defend Miss Mayson's honor. And yet, she was right. He shouldn't have even said what he did, as little as it was.

"There is nothing to forgive, and I thank you for your words, for they were decent and kind. You are a man of noble character, Mr. Merrick."

Was it noble to be glad she was here at this house party, because he might never have gotten to know her otherwise? Somehow, knowing she was in the world made him feel less cynical.

"I had seen you somewhere before," she said. "I realized it the day you arrived."

"Yes, and I had seen you before."

"I think it was at a ball."

"You were talking with Mrs. Langdon and Lady Withinghall, before she married the viscount."

"And probably not dancing."

"I saw you dance once or twice. You were wearing a blue dress. I remember you very distinctly."

Her lips were parted as she stared at him. A moonbeam streamed through the window and lit her face enough that he could see her expression. His breath stuttered in his chest at how ethereally beautiful and delicate she looked. To think that she was forced to let that oafish Mr. Ratley kiss her and touch her . . . If only he could save her from that. But he should be careful not to give Miss Mayson the impression that he was in love with her. She was far too beautiful to want him. And as the fourth son, he had no fortune to keep her in the style to which she seemed accustomed—not to mention that her two close friends Lady Withinghall and Mrs. Langdon were quite wealthy. She would not want to marry so far beneath them. And a man who had yet to distinguish himself, who was little more than a clerk at the Home Office, was certainly far beneath them.

"Were you a spy then, when you were at the ball?"

"I've been working at the Home Office for four years now, but I have not done a lot of spying. When I was able to infiltrate Lady Blackstone's group of revolutionaries, they gave me this assignment."

"How did you infiltrate it? Did you know Oliver Ratley?"

"I did not. The Home Office had been informed by someone who frequented the Black Boar Inn that a group was meeting there and taking illegal oaths. Lord Sidmouth sent me to investigate. I hid behind a partition in the back room where they were meeting and discovered Lady Blackstone and Mr. Ratley were the leaders. I wrote up a seditious tract and had it printed, then a few days later I tracked Mr. Ratley and struck up a conversation with him. Before long, I began talking of the injustices in our country, then I gave him my tract. He invited me into the group, introducing me to the other members. I promised to buy weapons for the revolution, and they asked me to be one of the leaders."

"That was a very clever strategy."

He shrugged. "Lord Sidmouth never believed that this group was as dangerous and well established as they are. We certainly had no idea they were so organized and had operatives all over the country, or stashes of weapons in at least fifteen locations. When I am able to give them this information . . . well, let's just say, I'm hoping for a promotion."

"Oh."

"But of course, the main thing is that we will have saved our country's government."

"And many Members of Parliament—my dear friend Lady Withinghall's husband is in the House of Lords. How horrible if he should be assassinated. And the poor royal family."

"Yes, exactly. And how would you like a buffoon such as Ratley running the country?"

"I should not like it at all." She couldn't help smiling. But her smile only lasted a moment. "I'm so ashamed when I think how quickly I became engaged to him. Lady Blackstone spoke of him in such glowing terms, and she seemed to think our union was the most ideal thing in the world. And even though I knew little about her, I never suspected she was involved in illegal activities. And Mr. Ratley seemed a good sort of person. But when I think of how wrong I was about his character and motivations . . . I was so foolish."

"Do not be hard on yourself. It is enough that you learned of his unsavory plans and associations before you actually married him."

"Well, we still have much to do before I am free of him, and before we are sure to escape with our lives."

"I'm afraid that is so."

Her delicate brows drew together as she stared thoughtfully off to the side. "The truth is, I do think there is room for reform, for better treatment of our workers and the poor. I can hardly bear to think of anyone going hungry, much less of someone starving to death."

"Of course," Philip said. She was so softhearted—just as a lady should be—but also wise and strong.

"But . . . it cannot be good, the things they have planned—to murder and assassinate so many people. It's so barbaric. How can anyone do such things?" She pressed a hand to her forehead and eyes. "But when I think how I have been lying and deceiving and . . . it makes me physically sick."

He wished he could comfort her, but he didn't want to seem as if he, too, was taking liberties.

"I remember you saying you have a mother and brothers." She must wish to talk of something else.

"I have a mother and father in Westmorland and three older brothers who were in London for the Season when I left. The oldest and heir to my father's estate is . . ." He couldn't say much about his brother that was positive. "He divides his time between the estate and London. Another brother is a clergyman in Sussex, and the third is distinguishing himself as an officer in the army."

"And you? Do you enjoy working in the Home Office?"

"I do. I think my father and brothers did not consider my choice"—how should he put it?—"distinguished enough for them. Their opinion is that I should be an officer fighting in foreign fields, or an orator or statesman, or at least a clergyman making sermons every week. But none of those things appealed to me particularly."

She was gazing at him, her eyes hardly blinking. She made him feel . . . admired. But perhaps he was only imagining things.

"What did appeal to you?" She leaned closer to him.

"I rather craved to be a spy. There is more of a need these days than you might think. So many reformers are tired of trying peaceful methods and think the French had the right idea—killing off the monarchy and those in Parliament and starting over."

"Not to mention the Americans, who revolted successfully."

"Yes, exactly. It should be interesting to see how their democratic government turns out."

She was smiling now. "I cannot help feeling some admiration for the Americans. If they were brave enough to sail across the ocean and start a new life in a wild and savage country, of course they do not wish to be governed by the country they vacated for a better one."

"Would you ever go to America?"

"I don't know. Perhaps. Would you?"

"If my prospects were good." He found himself smiling back at her. He imagined the two of them running away to America, escaping every unpleasant thing about their lives—pressure to impress his brothers, her engagement to Ratley, their lack of fortune and status.

But his thoughts once again were not headed in a direction likely to produce peace of mind or prudent decisions.

"You should get some sleep if you can. I will stay awake and listen for everyone to go back in the house."

A loud laugh came from several yards away, as if conjured up by his words, reminding her that as cozy and private as their conversation seemed, danger was near.

"That is generous of you," she said, leaning back against the wall. She stifled a yawn. "I am tired."

Philip's mind drifted to the false panel in his trunk and the papers and key he had hidden there. What terrible timing to be trapped here when he should be copying those papers. And yet, he didn't regret the time spent with Miss Mayson.

CHAPTER EIGHTEEN

Felicity awakened with a start. Someone was touching her shoulder.

A shadowy figure loomed over her.

"Miss Mayson?" Mr. Merrick's voice whispered. "I think now would be a good time to make a run for the house."

"Oh." How embarrassing to be sleeping sitting up, and in a gentleman's presence.

"I do not hear any more voices. I peeked through the door and saw several people enter the house some minutes ago. Soon it will be dawn."

Felicity stood and smoothed her skirt, taking a deep breath.

He said, "I shall wait a few minutes after you and then go in."

She walked to the door and took another deep breath. Would God keep her from being seen as she ran across the yard to the back door? Lately, she always felt that God must be upset with her, she was telling so many lies. But they were necessary lies to save herself and her aunt and even Mr. Merrick. Was God angry with her?

"God, please help me and forgive all my trespasses," she whispered, then pushed the door open.

She ran the whole way to the house and slipped inside. Keeping her head down, she stepped quickly but carefully, glad she was wearing her thin leather slippers so her footfalls were silent on the marble and stone floors. She went quickly up the stairs. *Thank you, God, that no one is around.* She made it to her door and let herself inside.

Auntie was sleeping, her breaths deep and even.

Felicity knelt by her own bed and clasped her hands. "God, forgive me of my many sins. I have lied and deceived, but I pray you will show me mercy and look at the motives of my heart and forgive me. And please cause these people in this house to repent of their wicked plans to murder your anointed rulers of our land, the Prince Regent and others. Let them be convicted and turn away from their plan. Please protect Mr. Merrick—Philip McDowell. Give him favor and help him. Keep Auntie and me safe and get us back to London. Thank you, God. May your name forever be hallowed in England and over the whole world. Amen."

She crawled into bed and felt at peace.

***

"Darling, a letter has come for you." Mr. Ratley carried the letter to her as she sat breaking her fast with Mrs. Cartwright in the breakfast room. "May I join you?"

"Yes, of course," Felicity said.

Felicity saw that the letter was from her family and tucked it away to read later.

"I heard a lot of voices last night," Felicity said as they were settled comfortably with their tea. "They sounded as if they were coming from the garden."

"Oh yes," her fiancé said. "We had some business to attend to, to get ready for our glorious revolution." He smiled sweetly. "I hope the noise did not upset you."

"It was a bit disconcerting, that is all," Felicity said.

"I'm so sorry you were bothered." He took the liberty to hold her hand and pat it. "We were storing some things, necessary things for the revolution. Nothing to worry about."

Felicity said no more on the subject and smiled and talked as though she thought nothing more about it. She did wonder if Lady Blackstone and Mr. Ratley knew of the broken printing press and whether or not they suspected it had been tampered with. The conspirators did not discuss the business of their revolutionary endeavors with Felicity, so it was not strange that they would not mention the broken printing press in her presence.

When she had eaten her breakfast, Mr. Ratley asked Felicity to take a walk with him. "You can read your letter while I look in on the progress with the garden."

She went with him, unsure how to refuse.

Mr. Ratley found a bench where she could sit with her letter, and he went in search of the gardeners.

Felicity opened her missive, already suspicious. But if she had not had reason to suspect the veracity of the letter, she might never have seen anything amiss in her mother's handwriting. But it spoke in such glowing terms, with such enthusiasm, she knew it had been forged.

My dearest daughter, Felicity,
I am writing to tell you that your father and I most heartily approve your marriage to Mr. Ratley. Your father gives his wholehearted consent for you to marry as soon as Mr. Ratley may like. We are satisfied that he is the most eligible, the most perfect, husband you could ever have found in the whole of Great Britain. You need not wait for anything, even your family's attendance on the ceremony, for we shall have plenty of time to visit you after the wedding.

Felicity's heart sank. So now, with her family's supposed eager consent to her quick marriage, they intended to pressure her to marry him before their rebellion began. What excuse was she to invent now?

She kept staring at the letter, pretending to read it.

She could feign sickness.

She could tell him she was not ready.

She could say she wanted more time with him for a honeymoon. If they married before the insurrection, they would have very little time.

Didn't special licenses take some time to get?

Mr. Ratley was walking back down the path toward her. The fraud. He knew exactly what was in that letter. He had not only read it, he had written it.

She pasted a smile on her face.

"Was it good news, my love?" He smiled just as sweetly as she'd ever seen him.

"It was. My father has given his permission for us to wed."

"That is very good news indeed."

"I suppose now you shall have to get a special license so that we may wed here instead of in London."

His smile widened. "I have already acquired the special license."

Her stomach sank lower.

"There is nothing stopping us from marrying this week, if I can arrange it with the rector."

"This week? Why so soon? Should we not wait until things are more settled, until we can be in our own estate without the seriousness of the revolution weighing on our minds?"

"Darling, there is nothing for you to worry about." He stroked her arm in a way that made her want to throw off his hand and rub every vestige of his touch from her skin.

"I am not worrying, but I would like the first few weeks and months of my marriage not to be marred by . . . by such upheaval as may—will—occur after your plans are enacted."

"Darling." Mr. Ratley gave her a look as one might give a small child who was crying over not getting her way—patronizing, with a pouty half frown. "Isn't it better to have a little time before I have to help with the revolution than to wait weeks, perhaps months?"

God, help me. She sent up the desperate prayer before turning on the bench to fully face him.

"Oliver, you are not so impatient as this. You wish us to have the best beginning possible, do you not? Now, think of how you will feel when the revolution starts. If all goes well, the crux of it will be over in a few days. We can get married in London with my family—or here, if you prefer—and begin our new life in the new republic. If the revolution takes longer than you plan, you would not wish to be thinking of your wife here at Doverton Hall, would you? Would it not be better to marry when everything is settled and there are no dangerous events to be planned and dealt with? We can start fresh after the revolution has been accomplished."

His face was immobile, his lips pressed together in a straight line. Finally, he spoke.

"I do not approve of your reticence, but I shall think about what you have said."

"Thank you, my dear. I appreciate your forbearance and wisdom. Also, I should feel very sad not to have my own dear parents at the wedding, as well as my most beloved sister, Elizabeth, and my other siblings." She looked down and sniffed, hoping he would think she was crying and be moved.

She took out her handkerchief and wiped her nose. But Mr. Ratley made no move to comfort her, and there was only silence for a full minute.

She glanced up, but Mr. Ratley was stone-faced.

"I know you want your own way in this matter, but I must give it some thought. I will decide what is best." His expression softened a bit. "Do not worry. All shall be well."

She was glad he got up and walked away then. How dare the man treat her as if her thoughts and opinions did not matter. A cold chunk of ice sank to the pit of her stomach. How awful it would be to be married to a man who had no empathy or tender feelings for his wife.

Of course, she had been trying to manipulate him with false tears. That was wrong, and she felt sorry for any man who had to live with a wife who feigned emotion in order to manipulate. But if they were married, would he care so little about her feelings and opinions and wishes? Could he watch his wife, the woman he professed to love, cry and feel nothing? She shivered.

She was tired of this spy game. She wanted to go home, to feel safe, and to be comforted by someone who cared about her. Aunt Agnes was sweet, but Felicity always had to be careful not to upset her nerves. Mr. Merrick seemed kind enough, but he had made it clear that his priority was the mission, not her. And he could not comfort her, being an unmarried young man wholly unrelated to her. It would not be proper.

"I want my mother," she whispered into the damp air. The clouds overhead were gray and threatening, and so were the very real tears damming behind her eyes.

God, help me. I don't want to be killed by these insurrectionists. But I'd rather die than marry Oliver Ratley.

***

Philip had finished copying all the papers he'd taken from Lady Blackstone's room by the time the sun was over the horizon. He hid the copies and the original papers in the false compartment in his trunk and managed to get a few hours of sleep. He had risen at ten, and now Lady Blackstone sat across from him in the breakfast room buttering a piece of bread.

"Did you write your letters last night, Mr. Merrick?"

"Yes."

"I only ask because I did not see them in the stack of mail going out."

He'd forgotten to write those letters. A stupid mistake. "I forgot to bring them down. I shall bring them later."

"You look as if you did not sleep very well."

"I did not, my lady. I was feeling . . . sad and restless, thinking of my mother."

"You poor dear." She clucked her tongue. "I'm so sorry we don't have any unmarried ladies here to distract you and make you think of other things."

"Thank you for your kindness. I find I prefer to be alone with my thoughts today."

Soon after, he hurried to his room to write the letters to his fake mother and brothers in London that he was supposed to have written the night before. Then he brought them down for the post, which had already gone for the day.

Now his focus had to be on getting those papers back into Lady Blackstone's room before she missed them. But as long as she stayed close to the house, he couldn't risk going into her room.

Later, he was discreetly trying to locate Lady Blackstone when he looked out a window and saw Miss Mayson and Mr. Ratley sitting on a bench talking. What was that boor saying to her? She looked distressed, possibly even crying.

He could not march out there and demand Ratley stop harassing Miss Mayson. He could not appear any more concerned about Miss Mayson than he already had. Ratley was her fiancé, and, like it or not, she had to continue with the charade for a while longer.

Mr. Ratley finally got up and left her. Just then, Philip heard someone approaching from behind him. He turned to see Lady Blackstone.

"Mr. Merrick. It's good to see you out of your room. I shall pay a little visit to Miss Mayson."

Mr. Ratley entered from outside. He and Lady Blackstone slipped into a small sitting room and talked in hushed voices, then Lady Blackstone left, striding out the door that led outdoors and to the garden.

Mr. Ratley now stood looking at him. "Merrick. I did not see you there. We should play a game of billiards. I have to go up to my room to take care of something, but perhaps later."

"Of course." Did Philip dare try to replace Lady Blackstone's papers while Ratley was upstairs?

If Lady Blackstone did not take any trips in the near future, he'd have no choice but to replace the papers while she was outside, or even just downstairs. Time was short—for himself, and even shorter for Miss Mayson.

He decided to risk it.

***

Felicity listened as calmly as possible while Lady Blackstone spoke.

"Dear Felicity, Mr. Ratley tells me that you are wishing to have your parents and sister at your wedding."

Felicity could see the disapproval in Lady Blackstone's lowered brows. "Oh. Well, I . . . I had hoped that they might be present."

"My dear, I understand, of course. But you must see that this is a time of war. We must do the things that are necessary for the good of all. Mr. Ratley is sacrificing his time and resources for the good of England, and you surely wish to honor that sacrifice."

"Of course, I will always wish to honor my husband. Mr. Ratley is not yet my husband, but I do wish to honor him. But does honoring my fiancé, or for that matter, honoring my husband, mean that I must do everything he wishes me to?" She had to be careful. She did not wish to speak too vehemently on the subject. Perhaps she was beginning to emulate her friend Leorah. But after all, God was the authority, first and foremost, even ahead of one's husband. Felicity could even imagine her favorite writer, Miss Hannah More, agreeing with such logic.

If only Mr. Ratley would change his mind about marrying her. Perhaps he would, if she was too outspoken.

Lady Blackstone's jawline was rigid. "Of course not. Do you think I did everything my husbands said?" Lady Blackstone laughed, but it was a cold, brittle sound. "But as I was saying before, this is a time of war. In wartime, brides must accept less time with their husbands, and they must seize the time that they do have, lest they have regrets later. Mr. Ratley is a good and a wealthy man. Even if he is killed in our rebellion, you shall be well taken care of. Imagine what you will inherit."

"I suppose I should think that way."

"But you are a kind and gentle person, so innocent and good, it had not occurred to you that it would be best to marry first, in case something happened to Mr. Ratley."

Felicity remembered what Lady Blackstone had said about her, that she was timid and afraid to speak her mind.

"You would never think of marrying a man only for his fortune," Lady Blackstone went on, patting Felicity's hand placatingly. "Of course, I know that, and Mr. Ratley knows that, which is why he wishes to make sure you are taken care of if the worst should happen."

"So he only wants to marry me quickly because he's afraid he might die, and he wants me to inherit his money if he does?" Felicity did her best to look wide-eyed and naïve.

"And why not? He cares so much for you." Lady Blackstone smiled with her lips, but her eyes seemed to be shrewdly searching, trying to read Felicity's thoughts.

"That is so incredibly kind and generous, I hardly know what to say. I would like to marry soon, just perhaps not quite as soon as Mr. Ratley would like."

"Why, what do you mean?"

Melanie Dickerson

"Oh, just that Mr. Ratley wishes us to marry in a few days, but I . . . I do not know if I am ready . . . just yet. Perhaps we could wait three or four weeks. I believe that would give me enough time to settle my nervousness about being married."

"Oh, I can tell you all about the marriage bed," Lady Blackstone said, waving her hand in the air and looking amused. "Having been married three times, I can prepare you for anything you might encounter, anything you might worry about—anything, in short, that you might be frightened or unsure about. Knowledge is power, my dear."

Felicity's stomach tied itself in a knot, even as heat infused her cheeks.

"Please, do not tell me anything until the night before the wedding, I beg you, my lady."

Lady Blackstone laughed, throwing her head back. But her sounds of mirth died away as she shook her head slowly back and forth. Then she took Felicity's hand. "You and our dear Oliver shall be very happy together, never fear."

"Thank you."

"You must not let fear stand in your way." Lady Blackstone curled her lip when she said the word *fear* and rolled her eyes, much as Felicity's friend Leorah often did. But she suspected Lady Blackstone was rolling her eyes at Felicity, something Leorah would never do.

"I only want to feel a bit more comfortable with my future husband, to know him better, his thoughts and feelings." Which was quite true. "Mr. Ratley and I—"

"You may drop the formalities, my dear. Call him by his given name. Call him Oliver."

"Very well. Oliver and I became engaged so quickly and suddenly, and I thought we might have a long engagement, to get to know one another better. You might remember that I had no notion that he was involved in a plan to revolt against the government when I agreed to marry him."

"Yes, exactly." Lady Blackstone's eyelids drooped, shading her gaze. "It makes me wonder if perhaps you have decided not to marry him after all."

"Lady Blackstone, please. Why would you say such a thing? I hope you do not say this to my dear Mr. Rat—to Oliver."

"I only wonder because of what you say—that you did not know of his sensibilities and political opinions when you became engaged to him. And now, when Oliver wishes to marry you and take care of you, you shun him."

"Shun him? I only asked for a bit more time. I see no reason to think that he will be killed—you make it sound as if he will almost surely be." Felicity allowed her true distress at being so questioned to bring up some quite real tears. "The thought of Oliver fighting and . . . and—"

She had to stop speaking and bite her lip to keep from crying.

"There, there, my dear. I am sorry I pressed you so, but I did want to know if your feelings for Oliver were true and deep, as true and deep as his are for you." Lady Blackstone rubbed her shoulder, and Felicity suppressed a shudder.

She took out her handkerchief and wiped her face and blew her nose.

"Now, then, how much time do you think you need?" Lady Blackstone asked.

Surely Mr. Merrick could have all the secret information copied within days—which would leave him free to leave, to escape to London to ensure the information reached the Home Office. Perhaps they would all run away in the middle of the night, even if Felicity had to saddle her own horse and Auntie's too and ride until she reached the safety of London. Oh, to be home! To see her mother's sweet face and wrap her arms around Elizabeth.

"Two weeks? Yes, I think two weeks would be enough time."

"In two weeks Oliver will be away leading the rebellion. One week seems ample time, with the two of you together every day. Then you will have a week together as man and wife."

"I don't want to interfere with his planning of strategies and meetings and the various duties he has."

Lady Blackstone clicked her tongue against her teeth. "Poor Oliver. He was hoping to wed at the end of this week. I shall try to placate him, but it might be difficult."

What did Lady Blackstone want her to say? Was she fishing for something? "I . . . I just love him so much. I don't want to disappoint him when we are married. I want to feel perfectly comfortable with him. You understand, don't you? As women, we cannot so easily enter into such a close physical relationship as men seem to be able to do. We need time and conversation." *God, please let her say she understands.*

Lady Blackstone stared up at the clouds. "I do believe you are correct. Do you know, you have a very wise understanding of human nature, especially for a girl of your age and so little experience." She smiled and touched Felicity's jawline. "But perhaps it is because you have so many brothers and sisters. Several of your siblings are married, I believe, and you were able to observe the characteristics of men versus women."

"Yes, I think that is so." Felicity let out the breath that had stuck in her throat.

"Very well, my dear. I shall request to our dear Oliver that he wait ten days. That is a little less time than you wanted but a little longer than he wished to wait. He may be disappointed, but as you insinuated, it is not good for men to always get their way." She winked. "He shall be the better for being forced to wait, I daresay."

Felicity had to hope that they would all be able to escape before ten days' time. "Thank you, my lady."

"By the by, do you know anything about what happened to the printing press last night?"

"The printing press?"

"Yes." Lady Blackstone was giving her that shuttered look again.

"I'm not even sure I knew there was a printing press. Where is it?"

"In that little building over there." Lady Blackstone waved her hand.

Felicity shook her head.

"It is very strange. The servants left it in the evening, and when they went back this morning, it was broken."

"Oh. I'm sorry. I hope it does not cause any serious problems."

"I daresay it shall not. I only ask you because you and Mr. Merrick were nearly the only ones who were not with us last night when we stowed away the weapons that arrived."

"Oh, I'm sorry, Lady Blackstone, I don't know anything—"

"No, I don't suppose you do. It is just as well. Oliver and I thought to spare you any of the details. Well, I hope you have a good afternoon. I must go now to my room and write some letters of business." And she kissed Felicity's cheek.

CHAPTER NINETEEN

As Lady Blackstone began talking with Felicity, Philip hurried upstairs to his room. He quickly opened the hidden compartment in his trunk and took out the original papers and the key hidden there. He tucked them in his waistcoat and stepped out into the corridor, closing his door behind him.

"Merrick!" Ratley stood three feet away. "I was just going to look for someone to play billiards. Won't you join me?"

"Oh, of course. Let me just . . . change my coat. I'll only be a minute." Philip ducked back in the room, carefully removed the papers from his waistcoat, placed them back inside the secret compartment, and changed his coat.

When Philip came out of his room, Ratley was waiting for him.

Philip did not exactly relish playing billiards with Ratley, but perhaps he could ask him some questions. The man was rather gullible for a revolutionary. And if there was one thing Philip had learned from his older brothers, it was not to be gullible.

They walked down to the billiard room together, and as they entered, Philip asked, "So, have you and Miss Mayson set a date for your nuptials?"

Ratley opened his mouth, then pressed his lips tightly together. "As a matter of fact, we have not." He took a deep breath and heaved a sigh. "I am for sooner, and she is for later, though I cannot understand why."

"My brother went through the exact same thing with his wife."

"He did?"

"Yes, and I shall explain it all to you and tell you exactly how to act."

Ratley turned wide eyes on him. "I would be grateful for your advice."

"You see, we men are always impatient to have the words said and the matter resolved, once we have made up our minds to wed. But women, well, they feel very differently."

"Oh?"

"Yes. You see, women feel so much more deeply than we men. Sometimes it is difficult for them to get their feelings and their thoughts moving together. Does that make sense?"

Ratley's forehead creased. "Do you mean, they want to get married . . . too much?"

"Yes! You understood me precisely." Philip was making this up as he went, but, *thank you, Lord*, he was selling it well enough for Ratley to buy. "The core of the matter is"—Philip put a hand on Ratley's shoulder—"Miss Mayson is quite attached to you. Anyone who sees the two of you together cannot help but believe that. But, as with all ladies, she needs a little time to get used to the idea of marriage."

"I suppose that makes sense. She is very devoted to me."

"Of *course*. And I saw Lady Blackstone talking with her in the garden just now. That is just the thing she needs—an older woman who has been married before, helping her to accustom herself to the ideas and duties of marriage." Philip clapped Ratley, hard, on the back. "Give her some time. Two or three weeks. You'll see. She will be as happy and anxious to marry as you are."

"I suppose it cannot hurt to wait a little longer, although I must leave in two weeks." Ratley's brow was still wrinkled. "I suppose I could wait . . . twelve days or so."

"Absolutely. Your union will be the stronger for it."

"You truly think so?"

"I know so. You cannot lose, for a woman of Miss Mayson's gentility cannot be expected to marry only a week or two after getting engaged. It's nearly unthinkable—for a woman of her refinement and sensibilities. You understand that, do you not?"

"Yes. Now that you explain it that way . . . it makes sense."

Mr. Ratley used his cue stick to make the first shot as he leaned over the table. In a few more minutes he was smiling and making jokes and in quite good humor.

Philip did not play very well and lost the billiard game, but he'd already played—and won—the important game.

***

Felicity trudged up the stairs to her room. Perhaps she could take a nap before dinner. She wasn't sure she could face anyone again without a respite.

When Felicity opened the door, Aunt Agnes crossed the room to meet her.

"Felicity, are you in some sort of danger?"

"Why do you ask that, Auntie?"

"I've been thinking about what you told me, that we could not write any letters home, and that our hosts were trying to revolt against the government."

"Oh, Auntie, I beg you not to worry." Felicity sank down on the edge of her bed and pulled out one particular hairpin that had been stabbing her scalp. "I shall get us out of this mess, I promise." But could she really promise that? She'd already fainted in a critical moment and otherwise proven that she was not much of a spy. So, she added, "God willing, *He* shall get us out of this."

"Is there anything I can do? Too frequently, I allow others to bear my burdens, but I don't want to leave you all alone in the matter." Auntie seemed more clear-eyed than usual.

"That is very kind of you, Auntie, truly." Felicity had never known her aunt to have such strength of mind and be so . . . aware—of herself and her circumstances. "But I don't know what you could do to help. And I don't want you to get hurt."

"I am not a child. I know I am sometimes nervous and fidgety, but I don't wish to be a silly old spinster who is a burden to her family. If there is anything I've learned from novels, it is that people can change, if they truly wish to. And they can be sensible, not silly. Consider Elizabeth Bennet from *Pride and Prejudice*. She does not allow herself to be intimidated. She would fight back against revolutionaries, not hide in her room. And I shall not hide either."

Aunt Agnes pursed her lips in a look of determination. Felicity could not recall ever seeing that look on her face before.

"Perhaps there is something you can do. I have been meeting with Mr.—with my friend who is employed by the Home Office to stop the revolution." It seemed unwise to trust Aunt Agnes with the knowledge that Mr. Merrick was a spy. But she would have to tell her if she was going to allow her to help. "That friend is Mr. Merrick, and if anything should ever happen to me, he is the one person you can trust. He and I have been meeting in a book closet just off the library. I have been pretending to go to the library to get a book for you, but you can go with me next time and be our lookout. If anyone comes into the library, you can warn us by speaking very loudly, or possibly by distracting them and getting them to leave with you."

"Oh yes, I would be able to do that." Auntie smiled, her eyes bright. "I could say that I was there to get a book, and then I could take their arm and ask them to walk me to my room."

"Excellent."

"Shall we try it today?"

"I don't think I have anything new to tell Mr. Merrick, but we can go downstairs and see if there is anything of pertinence afoot."

Aunt Agnes took a deep breath and lifted her shoulders. "Let us go."

***

Felicity felt refreshed after a fifteen-minute nap. With Aunt Agnes by her side, they prepared to leave their room.

Felicity warned her aunt, "You can trust Mr. Merrick, but we must not expect him to protect us. He has a very important job to do, and he cannot jeopardize it, even to save us from harm." Her voice hitched, but she played it off by clearing her throat. "We must be extremely careful not to inadvertently betray him."

Auntie's eyes were wide, but then she lowered her brows and pursed her lips. "I understand."

Once downstairs, they wandered past the billiard room, and, hearing voices inside, they strolled past it a second time. Felicity saw Mr. Ratley and Mr. Merrick, but thankfully Mr. Ratley's back was to the doorway.

Felicity led Aunt Agnes to the sitting room that was adjacent to the billiard room.

Aunt Agnes found a book and began to read, then whispered to Felicity, "No one will suspect me. They think all I do is read." She gave Felicity a wink.

"You are very clever, Auntie." Felicity winked back.

Felicity took up her embroidery while Aunt Agnes read her book. Finally, she heard footsteps. She peeked from where she sat, trying to make herself as small as possible. Mr. Ratley walked by, whistling softly.

A minute or two later, Mr. Merrick was walking by when Felicity said, rather loudly, "The clouds have become very threatening. What do you think, Auntie?" Her breath stuck in her throat. Why had she said that? She had nothing of importance to tell Mr. Merrick. But the thought of seeing him privately, talking with him in their secret meeting place, made her heart race.

Mr. Merrick paused and entered the room. "Miss Mayson. Miss Appleby." He walked to the window and looked out. "I believe you are correct, Miss Mayson. The sky does look rather like rain."

"Yes," Felicity said. "I believe it may rain any minute now."

"Yes, well, good afternoon." He nodded to them and left the room.

"That was rather abrupt, wasn't it?" Auntie whispered.

"'Sky' and 'clouds' are our signal. He has gone to the library," Felicity whispered back.

"Oh!" Auntie closed her book and stood.

"We must wait a minute or two," Felicity warned.

Aunt Agnes sat back down and opened her book again.

After a few more moments, Felicity motioned to her aunt to follow her, and they went to the library.

Inside they started browsing the shelves—or pretending to. Felicity's breath grew shallow the closer they wandered to the door where Mr. Merrick would be waiting. How foolish of her. He did not care for her, and how could she form an attachment to him when she was engaged to someone else? It was indecent.

But still her heart raced as she remembered the last time they had been alone, in the shed where he had sabotaged the printing press, when he had held her, a strong arm around her waist, and kept her from falling, his face just inches from hers.

Aunt Agnes was near the library entrance while Felicity opened the door and went inside.

Mr. Merrick looked up from the open book he was holding.

"Were you able to put the papers back while I was talking with Lady Blackstone?" Felicity said softly.

"No, unfortunately."

She rushed on. "I only have ten days. Mr. Ratley wanted to marry me at the end of this week, but I convinced Lady Blackstone to have him postpone it a few more days. But I only have ten days before the wedding."

He nodded slowly. "Mr. Ratley prevented me from returning the papers to Lady Blackstone's room and asked me to play a game of billiards with him. I did manage to convince him that he should not be upset about the fact that you wish for a longer engagement."

"Oh. That is most kind of you." Felicity's breath seemed to come faster. He must be concerned for her if he spoke to Mr. Ratley about postponing their marriage. Of course, she was his ally as they worked to thwart these revolutionaries, but did he feel more for her?

She was being silly. She should concentrate on the business at hand.

"Lady Blackstone is suspicious about the printing press breaking. She even asked me if I knew anything about it."

"Does she suspect you?"

"I don't know. But she was suspicious that someone may have broken it, and she mentioned that you and I were the only ones not helping store the weapons."

Mr. Merrick's brows lowered and his jaw flexed.

Felicity took a deep breath and said, "Mr. Merrick, you should leave. Escape this place. You have the papers with the information you need to capture all the leaders and confiscate their stockpiles of weapons. You can give me the key to Lady Blackstone's room, and I can return her papers."

His blue eyes stared intently into hers while she spoke, then he shook his head. "I don't want to leave you here. There is no way to know if they would spare you should they discover you were working against them. Besides, if we act too quickly, we might not discover all their plans. New leaders can rise up to take the place of the old ones. We need to find out every person involved."

"You can do that. After you leave, you and the Home Secretary—Lord Sidmouth, I believe?—can investigate the places and men in Lady Blackstone's papers."

"I suppose that is true. But . . . what about you and Miss Appleby?"

"I don't think they would kill us. They don't see us as a threat." She remembered Lady Blackstone's comments about Felicity being meek and quiet. "Besides, they believe I will marry Mr. Ratley and will be forever tied to them, unable to testify against my own husband."

The crease in Mr. Merrick's forehead deepened. "I can use my sick mother as an excuse to leave. But . . . I want to put the papers back before I go."

"I can help you. You could give me the key, and I can pretend to be sick at dinner tonight. I can go upstairs and put the papers back in her room."

"I don't like that plan. I don't want to endanger you."

"It is not so dangerous for me. And there is so much at stake. You must get that information back to your superiors."

"I hate to think of leaving you amongst these people." A muscle in his cheek twitched. He leaned down, staring into her eyes, then took her hand in his.

Felicity's heart beat hard and fast. "I shall be well. Just . . . say a little prayer for me." She smiled, hoping she looked brave.

"Yes, I will pray for you. Nothing is too hard for God, and I shall have to trust Him to watch over you."

Her heart skipped several beats at the gentle look on his face.

The door suddenly opened. Mr. Merrick let go of her hand. Josephine Cartwright stood in the doorway, her eyes wide and her mouth agape.

CHAPTER TWENTY

"I thought I heard voices in here." Mrs. Cartwright looked askance at Felicity, and a sly smile spread over her face.

"I was just looking for a book," Felicity said quickly.

Mr. Merrick took the book that he had tucked under his arm and held it up. "I have what I need, so I shall go. I hope you find the volume you were searching for, Miss Mayson." He nodded at Mrs. Cartwright.

Mr. Merrick moved to leave. Mrs. Cartwright stepped aside just as Aunt Agnes rushed up to the doorway.

"I did not see you," Aunt Agnes said breathlessly.

"Miss Appleby, isn't it?"

Mrs. Cartwright and Aunt Agnes moved aside to let Mr. Merrick pass, which he did quickly.

"Yes, this is my aunt, Miss Agnes Appleby. Auntie, this is Mrs. Josephine Cartwright."

Aunt Agnes said, "We were looking for books."

"I was sitting in the back doing my knitting. There are some uncommonly comfortable chairs in the back corner of this library. Have you ever tried them, Miss Mayson?"

So that was how they had failed to see her. Felicity bit the inside of her cheek. "I haven't. I do come to the library rather frequently to get books for Aunt Agnes, but she decided to come with me today to browse for herself. I happened to meet Mr. Merrick here as well. He was also looking for a book, but I believe he found his."

Mrs. Cartwright smiled and nodded.

"I hope you do not think there was anything untoward about Mr. Merrick and I being in there together," Felicity said in a low voice. "It was completely innocent—believe me—but I would be very grateful if you did not mention it to anyone."

"Of course not." Mrs. Cartwright waved her hand. "I understand. I would not wish to hurt your chances of marriage with Mr. Ratley."

"Thank you." Felicity did not know what else to say. If she weren't so terrified that Mrs. Cartwright might tell someone what she'd seen and cause suspicion to fall on Mr. Merrick, she might have felt even more embarrassed at her friend finding her in such a compromising situation.

"Well, I believe my aunt has found her book." Felicity indicated the book in Aunt Agnes's hand. "We should go. Come, Auntie."

They scuttled out of the library and up the stairs. As Felicity was just turning the knob to open her door, she heard someone clear his throat. She turned her head and saw Mr. Merrick looking at her. He was standing beside a small table that stood against the wall. On the table were a vase and other objects. He held up a key and a loose roll of papers. He put them on the table, behind the vase. Then he turned and went down the stairs, nodding as he passed them.

Felicity quickly fetched them, and she and Aunt Agnes went inside their room.

Auntie whispered, "I'm so sorry about Mrs. Cartwright. I don't understand how she got past me."

"It was not your fault. She must have already been in the room when we got there. I didn't check the back corner where she says she likes to do her knitting. It is my fault. I should have searched the room when we arrived."

Aunt Agnes placed a hand over her chest. "This is the same as a novel. My heart is racing even faster than it does when I read Mrs. Radcliffe's stories." Her eyes were bright and her face vibrant. "I am sorry now that I behaved so badly in the garden when we saw that dead man. I shall conduct myself better should it ever happen again. And I'm so sorry I failed you as a lookout in the library."

"No, no, it was not your fault. You are doing very well."

Indeed, Aunt Agnes was not plucking at her sleeves, and there was a slight smile on her lips.

Felicity went and hid the papers in her closet underneath her clothes. They only had to keep pretending for a few more days. After Mr. Merrick was able to get the papers to the Home Office, and the authorities were able to apprehend the people on the list, they would surely come and arrest Lady Blackstone and the others at Doverton Hall.

Only a few more days.

***

A knock came at Felicity's door. She had been sitting at her dressing table, finishing her hair, so she stood and opened the door.

"Felicity." Mr. Ratley was unsmiling, and he had not called her "darling" as he usually did.

"What is wrong—" She hastily added, "my darling?" though the words seemed to stick in her throat.

"I seem to have misplaced a key."

"A key?" Her voice went up unnaturally high.

"Yes, and Lady Blackstone will be very upset with me if she discovers I have lost it. Did you happen to see me with a key, or to see where I may have mislaid it? I have searched my entire room and cannot find it anywhere."

"It will turn up, in one of your pockets, perhaps."

"Yes, perhaps." He shook his head then held out his hand. "Let me escort you down to dinner."

Felicity ate her fill but did not even taste the food. Mr. Merrick was as friendly as usual, talking with those around him but avoiding eye contact with Felicity. Meanwhile, Mrs. Cartwright seemed to laugh more than usual, and whenever Felicity caught her eye, she quickly glanced away.

Mr. Ratley was as attentive as ever, remarking on what she ate, making weak jests, and talking rather loudly with those around him.

Soon Lady Blackstone stood and summoned the ladies to retire with her to the drawing room. They all followed her out.

Felicity caught up with her just outside the drawing room. "My lady, may I be excused? I fear I may be coming down with a head cold, as I have a sore throat and a terrible headache."

"Oh. You are not planning to meet Mr. Merrick again, I hope." Lady Blackstone fixed Felicity with a cold stare.

She heard a squeak behind her as Mr. Cartwright raced past, slipping by them into the drawing room.

Felicity's cheeks stung as her stomach sank. "No, of course not. Why would I meet Mr. Merrick?"

"I have heard of a certain private meeting you had with him in the library closet. Do you have any further business with this man?"

"No, of course not. It was not a private meeting at all. We were both looking at books. I hope Mrs. Cartwright did not insinuate that there was anything improper between us." Felicity widened her eyes and let her mouth hang open.

Lady Blackstone smiled. "Do not worry. I am sure if Mr. Ratley hears of it, he will be calm and reasonable. It will not be the first time an engaged lady did something to be gossiped about." She smiled and started to walk into the drawing room. "Are you coming in, my dear?"

"I thought I might go up to my room to rest, if it is all right with you."

Lady Blackstone made a pout with her lips. "I was looking forward to seeing you tonight. I have missed our walks. But very well." She waved her hand. "You may go. But I insist on a nice long walk in the garden tomorrow."

"Of course. If I am well enough."

Felicity hurried away, her knees shaking. Oh dear. And she had not even begun the frightening part of the night.

She climbed the stairs, her hand trembling on the railing. She went into her room, remembering that Auntie was still downstairs with Lady Blackstone and the other ladies.

She grabbed the papers and the key from inside her clothes closet and hurried back out, trying to keep her footsteps as soft as possible.

She could hear the sound of voices far below but none nearby. She walked down the corridor, finally reaching Lady Blackstone's room. The key shook in her hand as she held it up to the keyhole. *O merciful God, don't let me faint again.* She slipped it in and turned it. It made a loud metallic clicking sound. She cringed and pushed open the door.

She hurried over to the drawer and took out the stack of papers. Her hands fumbled as she tried to separate the blank pages from the originals, and three of the incriminating papers slipped from her hands and tumbled to the floor.

Her heart was pounding so hard it was like a roar in her ears. She quickly fell to her knees and gathered up the papers, putting them back in their stack. *Oh, dear heavens,* had she put them back in the correct order? She placed the blank sheets on the floor, then replaced the original papers. Then she shut the drawer. She stooped to retrieve the blank papers.

Oh dear. Only a few more steps. Her arms were trembling so badly she clutched the blank papers to her chest to keep from dropping them.

She yanked open the door and stepped outside. She fumbled with the key and managed to lock the door. She turned to hurry back to her room.

When she came in sight of the little table and vase, she took the key and placed it where she had seen Mr. Merrick put it, behind the vase. At least no one would find it in her room or on her person.

She reached her door just as she heard someone coming up the stairs behind her. She quickly rushed inside, dashed to her bed, and lay down, shoving the blank papers under the covers with her.

A knock came at the door.

"Come in," Felicity called.

Lady Blackstone opened the door and walked in. "My dear, I wanted to come and see if you were well. Mr. Ratley wanted to come and look in on you himself, but I told him I was sorry I had not acted more concerned for you." She made the same pout Felicity had seen her make earlier.

"I am well. I think it is only a passing headache. I get them sometimes. And my throat is a bit better as well. It is nothing, I hope."

Lady Blackstone walked over and picked up the only lighted lamp in the room, which was on the table beside Aunt Agnes's bed, and brought the lamp to Felicity's bedside.

"My dear, you look quite flushed. Are you sure you're all right?" She placed her cool hand against Felicity's forehead, then her cheek. "I will never forgive myself if you become ill while in my care. What would your dear parents say?"

"I daresay I shall be well in the morning. A good night's sleep always cures my headaches."

"But, my dear, you are still wearing your clothes. Shall I help you undress?"

"Oh no. I just wanted to lie down for a few minutes first. I shall get into my nightgown soon. Aunt Agnes can help me."

Lady Blackstone looked askance at her. "Very well. I shall leave you alone. Is there anything you need? Shall I send up a hot toddy for you? Some of my physician's nerve medicine?"

"No, thank you. I shall be well."

Lady Blackstone finally left, but the concerned look had been replaced by a blank expression.

Oh, thank you, dear God, that this is over. Her hand touched the papers under her covers. Was it safe to remove them and put them back in her desk? Her head truly was aching with the tension of the last few minutes. *God, please don't let Lady Blackstone suspect anything.*

Finally, when she was satisfied that Lady Blackstone had gone, she threw back the covers and got out of bed, snatched the papers up, and put them back in her desk.

There. It was done. But Felicity could not stop feeling uneasy. Had she left a paper on the floor? Would Lady Blackstone notice something out of place and realize someone had been in her room?

She lay back down and squeezed her eyes tightly shut. "God," she whispered, "send Mr. Merrick safely back to London, and allow this to all be over."

***

Felicity and Aunt Agnes were about to leave their room the next morning to go to breakfast when a knock sounded at the door.

"You may come in," Felicity called.

Mr. Ratley entered and shut the door behind him. "Felicity, I need you to tell me the truth. Do you know where Lady Blackstone's key is?"

"Lady Blackstone's key?" Felicity felt the breath rush out of her lungs. She shook her head as if she did not understand.

"I had it a few days ago, and now I can't find it." He took a step closer to her and took hold of her arm. "Come for a walk with me."

"Would you not rather break your fast first?"

He stared at the floor. Finally, he looked her in the eye again. "Very well. Let us go now, if you are ready."

"Auntie, are you ready?"

Aunt Agnes nodded and mumbled something indecipherable.

The three of them went down to the breakfast room where a few others were up early enough to partake. They ate rather quickly, as none of them seemed to have much appetite, and Mr. Ratley turned to Aunt Agnes.

"Please excuse us, Miss Appleby, but I wish to take Miss Mayson to the garden for a walk. You don't mind."

"Not at all," Aunt Agnes said, but she was looking questioningly at Felicity.

"We will not be terribly long, I think," Felicity reassured her. But she was far from feeling her own reassurance.

She took Mr. Ratley's arm and walked with him out into the garden.

The sky was completely overcast with heavy white clouds. Not a spot of blue was visible, and the air was quite cool, too cool for her light muslin dress, thin spencer, and flimsy bonnet. She did not complain, however, as they walked along until they were enclosed on two sides by hedges taller than they were. Mr. Ratley stopped and turned to face her.

"Forgive me for saying this, but Lady Blackstone thinks you may have stolen the key to her room."

Felicity tried to laugh. "Why would I do that?"

Mr. Ratley put a hand on the back of his neck and scowled. "She thinks you don't agree with our cause, that you are still loyal to the present government."

"But I am here, aren't I? Would I still want to marry you if I did not agree with the cause of revolution and reform?"

"You don't agree wholeheartedly. You practically said so yourself. And Lady Blackstone thinks you may have convinced one of the men to think the way you do, to turn against us."

Felicity folded her arms across her chest. "This is terribly unfair. Steal a key? Turn other people against you? Does that sound like something I would do?" But her stomach felt sick, as if she might lose the breakfast she had just eaten. *God, help me pretend I know nothing.*

Mr. Ratley removed his hand from the back of his neck, huffed, and took Felicity's hand. "I admit it does not. But Lady Blackstone . . . She does not take opposition lightly. And she is obsessed with finding who may have stolen that key."

"But it is probably only lost." Felicity allowed herself to smile. "Surely everyone here is very loyal to both Lady Blackstone and the cause. I am sure she will understand if you just tell her you lost the key."

He closed his eyes, his face crestfallen. "She means so much to me. And now she is so angry." He opened his eyes, suddenly looking Felicity directly in the eye, then glancing away. "She and I became very close after . . . We met after her husband died and I inherited my father's estate. I had been away at school for so long, and I knew nothing about how to run a business or a household. I hardly remembered my mother, she died so young. My father sent me away to school when I was only six years old, so I had been alone for a long time. Lady Blackstone, she . . . she was concerned for me. She was so helpful and gave me such good advice. She knows so much about everything. We would talk for hours about politics. She'd had such a sad life, so many hard things when she was a child . . . I would do anything for her, and I simply cannot bear to disappoint her."

Something about the passionate way he spoke of his attachment to Lady Blackstone made Felicity shudder inwardly. It was suddenly very obvious that Mr. Ratley had decided to marry her based solely on what Lady Blackstone had said to him. Was Felicity so desperate to marry, so desperate to feel loved, that she would engage herself to a man who neither knew her nor understood her? A man she neither knew nor understood? She'd imagined she saw love in a man who was so broken he was incapable of being a mature husband to her.

As someone who believed in God's Providence, shouldn't she have checked her impulsiveness long enough to pray and ask God to show her if this man was right for her? She did not have to make such an important decision in the same moment he asked her.

Obviously, Mr. Ratley had been so desperate to have a family, to have someone to lean on after being alone and losing his father, that he had allowed himself to be completely controlled and manipulated by Lady Blackstone, a woman old enough to be his mother, but who had many ulterior motives. No doubt she had seen him as a means to an end, a person who would do her bidding, and especially someone who would use his wealth to fund her revolution.

Felicity felt sorry for Mr. Ratley. But the thought of marrying him was as abhorrent as ever. If only she had told him no . . . but then she would not have been able to help Mr. Merrick.

"Do not worry," Felicity said. "Let us think about where you might have lost the key."

"If we do not find it, Lady Blackstone has threatened to search everyone's rooms."

Felicity's throat went dry. Mr. Merrick had copies of those incriminating papers in his room, hidden somewhere, and if Lady Blackstone were to find them . . . they would kill him.

Felicity swallowed down her panic and took a deep breath.

"Let us think. Where did you have the key last?"

"I think it must have been when I went into her room a few nights ago. You were with me. I locked the door, and then we . . . well, we kissed in the corridor. I don't recall seeing the key after that."

"Then let us go up to the corridor outside Lady Blackstone's room and look for it. Come." She took his arm and tugged gently.

"We can try, I suppose."

They went back into the house and immediately encountered Lady Blackstone and Mr. Merrick in conversation, standing at the bottom of the staircase.

As they passed near, they heard Lady Blackstone ask Mr. Merrick, "Do you have designs on Miss Mayson?"

CHAPTER TWENTY-ONE

Mr. Ratley's face went rigid as he stared intently at Mr. Merrick. Felicity held her breath, her blood turning to ice in her veins.

"No, Lady Blackstone," Mr. Merrick answered. He looked very convincing, so earnest and upright. "I am committed to our cause, and I would not betray Mr. Ratley in such a way. Besides that, there is a girl I have been pledged to marry since we were children, a Miss Geiger from my home county, a friend of the family."

Was that true? Did he have a sweetheart at home? She felt her heart plummet.

Mr. Ratley glanced at Felicity, and she gave him a tiny shrug and shake of her head.

"Well, one may be 'pledged to marry but plan to dally.' Is that your philosophy, Mr. Merrick?"

"No, it is not, Lady Blackstone. I intend to be completely faithful to my wife. Even Miss Hannah More could not fault my marital philosophies." Mr. Merrick twisted his lips in a wry smile.

Felicity's heart fluttered at the thought that he admired Hannah More as much as she did. But he could be lying about that as well.

"Well, one does not have to take it quite as far as Miss Hannah More, after all. It depends on the circumstances and the understanding one has with one's spouse."

Mr. Merrick cleared his throat. "Forgive me, my lady, but I cannot agree with you there."

Mr. Ratley stepped toward them. "Lady Blackstone, Miss Mayson wishes to help me search for the key upstairs."

"Mr. Ratley, Mr. Merrick here has decided he must go and say good-bye to his poor mother, who is deathly sick. But I am uncertain we should let him go. What do you think?" Lady Blackstone had that same narrow-eyed look of suspicion she had given Felicity earlier.

"Oh well . . . saying good-bye to one's dying mother . . ."

"But we are so close to setting our plan into motion. I suppose it will all be well." Lady Blackstone suddenly turned away from Ratley and faced Mr. Merrick. "You will not object to our examination of your things before you go, will you?"

"Examination?"

"Yes, to make certain you are not taking anything with you that you might use against us, to have us arrested."

The silence that ensued was so thick it seemed to roar inside Felicity's head.

Finally, Mr. Merrick said, "You may search my things, but I don't know what I might have done to make you think—"

Suddenly, Lady Blackstone said, "No. I cannot let you leave." She was staring Mr. Merrick in the eye, and he was staring back. "We need you too much. You have a task to do. We are all counting on you."

"I would come back in time to—"

"Would you? Would you come back in time? No, we cannot risk it. There is too much at stake. Sometimes, Mr. Merrick, we must think of the greater good. We must let the dead bury their own dead and carry on with what we know is right and necessary. We need you here, Mr. Merrick. Do you not understand that?"

"Of course, my lady. I do understand. But I would only be gone for one week."

"Your family would not understand. They would try to prevent you from leaving them and coming back here." Lady Blackstone's eyes were flashing with a strange light.

"Perhaps you are right." Mr. Merrick bowed to her. "I was selfish to pursue it. They might even become suspicious, and that is the last thing we need—suspicions to destroy all our plans. Perhaps I will be able to see her after the revolution is over."

"I am pleased that you are being so reasonable, Mr. Merrick."

Mr. Merrick sighed. "Perhaps it is best this way. I was never her favorite, and now they can be peaceful without me there. I will see her in heaven."

"Yes, yes, that is just the way I see it too," Lady Blackstone said briskly. "You would not wish to see her sick and wasting away. Better to remember her as she was when she was healthy. And they will not need you there. Much better to let them see that you had important business to be about, once the revolution is well underway."

She turned to Mr. Ratley and Felicity. "What are you two doing skulking there?"

"My lady," Mr. Ratley said, "as I was trying to tell you a few moments ago, we are on our way up the stairs to look for the misplaced key."

"You would not happen to know where the key is, would you, Felicity?"

"No, my lady."

"And you, Mr. Merrick? Have you seen a key lying around?"

"No, my lady. Is someone missing a key?"

"Yes, Mr. Ratley has lost a key of mine. Would you care to help us look for it?"

"I'd be happy to help."

They all started up the stairs. Mr. Merrick needed to get the papers he had copied to the Home Office. All would be lost if Lady Blackstone found them in his room.

He had trusted Felicity to return the original papers, but she had not yet had a chance to tell him that she had been successful. She would reassure him with a smile.

They walked slowly up the stairs. She kept trying to catch Mr. Merrick's eye, but he did not look at her. He probably was too afraid of exciting suspicion, and Lady Blackstone did keep looking over her shoulder at them.

Once they reached the top, Felicity said, "Mr. Ratley says he had the key near here."

"I had it at Lady Blackstone's room," Mr. Ratley said. "I locked her door after returning something for her. I should have put the key in my pocket, but I don't remember exactly what I did with it. I walked away with Miss Mayson."

They were all looking around the floor. Would it be too suspicious if Felicity looked on the table and pulled out the key from behind the vase? Mr. Merrick certainly couldn't risk it, not with the papers somewhere in his possession. *God, please let someone look behind the vase.*

"Perhaps one of the servants found it and didn't mention it to you," Felicity suggested as she bent and stared at the floor, inching along, looking from one side of the corridor to the other.

"I have already questioned the servants," Lady Blackstone said.

"It must be somewhere." Felicity peeked through her lashes and saw Mr. Merrick also examining the floor. He suddenly glanced up at her, and she winked. Then she kept her head down and her eyes on the floor, not daring to glance at him again.

Mr. Merrick gradually moved toward the little table with the vase.

She hadn't intended for him to reveal the hiding place of the key. She'd only meant to put him at ease that she had taken care of the papers. But he kept moving toward the table.

Meanwhile, Lady Blackstone seemed to look more at Felicity and Mr. Merrick than she did at the floor.

"Perhaps Mr. Ratley dropped it in his room," Felicity said.

"I have been over every inch of my room and haven't found it."

Mr. Merrick stooped and used his hand to feel all around the floor at the base of the table that held the vase.

Felicity looked away from him, forcing herself not to stare. She bent even lower as she moved farther away from the light. She heard the slight scrape of metal on wood. Then Mr. Merrick's voice said, "Is this your key?"

Felicity straightened and turned toward the others. Mr. Merrick was holding up the key.

Mr. Ratley stepped toward him and took it in his hand. "I believe it is."

"Let me see it." Lady Blackstone took it from him. "Where did you find it?"

"It was on the table there, behind the vase."

Lady Blackstone said, "I have another key, but now at least I won't be worried about the spare. Thank you, Mr. Merrick." But her eyes were full of suspicion as she stared at him.

"I am glad to be of service." Mr. Merrick smiled and gave her a slight bow.

"Truly, thank you," Mr. Ratley said, looking very humble as he clasped Mr. Merrick's hand. "I must have dropped it somehow, and it landed on this table."

"Or someone could have found it on the floor," Felicity said, "and put it on the table."

"That is probably exactly what happened," Mr. Ratley said. "I'm just so in love with my fiancée, Miss Mayson, that I lose my head sometimes. I'm sure that is what happened in this instance."

He stepped over to Felicity and put his arm around her, pulling her to his side. She forced her cringe into a stiff smile.

Mr. Merrick said, "When I am with my fiancée, I am the same way."

Why did those words feel like a knife to her heart? Foolish.

"Oliver," Lady Blackstone said, her voice sharp, "stop crushing the poor girl."

Mr. Ratley let go of Felicity. He laughed. "She doesn't mind."

There wasn't much Felicity could say to that, so she forced the smile to stay on her face. But her heart sank as Mr. Merrick avoided looking at her and excused himself.

"Thank you again," Mr. Ratley called after him.

When he was gone, Lady Blackstone hissed, "Do you really think you could have dropped the key and have it end up on that table?"

"Yes, I think so." Mr. Ratley's expression was slack. "After I locked your door, Felicity and I . . . well, we kissed while standing here. I probably just forgot to put it in my pocket, was distracted by our kissing, and dropped it. Then one of the servants—or one of the guests—saw it on the floor, picked it up, and put it on the table."

But Lady Blackstone still did not look satisfied with Mr. Ratley's explanation.

Felicity's cheeks flamed, and her stomach twisted at the memory of kissing Mr. Ratley simply to get the key from his pocket. She had done it for Mr. Merrick, and he would not condemn her for it.

But he also might not respect her. And she could hardly blame him.

***

The next morning, Aunt Agnes insisted on sitting downstairs with everyone else. "I can eavesdrop," she whispered while they were still in their room. "No one pays any attention to me."

Strangely, Felicity realized she had not seen Aunt Agnes plucking her sleeves lately.

So they went downstairs and sat in the parlor with Lady Blackstone, who was serving tea. Nearly everyone was there, and Mr. Ratley perched on the sofa next to Felicity. Mrs. Cartwright ignored Felicity and talked with her husband in the corner of the room.

"It is a rather fine day," Lady Blackstone remarked, glancing out the window. Then her face scrunched in a scowl. "It's the rector, Mr. Birtwistle, coming to call on us."

A man, rather short and dressed in black, was walking toward the front door. Soon, the servant came to Lady Blackstone and announced, "Mr. Birtwistle to see you."

"Show him in." Then she muttered under her breath, "Might as well see him now as later."

The balding rector entered the room with a rather solemn expression. He bowed to Lady Blackstone.

"Come in, Mr. Birtwistle. It is so good of you to visit." She was all smiles as she showed him to a seat near her. "Everyone, say good afternoon to Mr. Birtwistle, the parish rector."

Several people nodded to him, and he nodded and said, "Good afternoon to you all." He wiped his forehead with a handkerchief and stuffed it back into his waistcoat. "It is rather warm out."

"What brings you to see us today? Is everything all right with the church? No one is sick that I should know about, I trust?"

"No, everyone is well. That is, everyone who was formerly well is still well, that I know of. Mrs. Carter of Shrewsbury Lane has been in a decline for several months and is not expected to recover, and Mr. Loudon, as you probably know, is not at all well. But I came to look in on you, as I did not see you or any of your party at church the past two Sundays."

"That is very astute of you, Mr. Birtwistle, for, to own the truth, we were not there." She laughed a short, merry laugh. "We are enjoying each other's company so very much. Let me pour you some tea."

Lady Blackstone proceeded to serve Mr. Birtwistle tea and cake.

"Thank you, Lady Blackstone. Very kind." Mr. Birtwistle made eye contact with Aunt Agnes, as they were sitting very near each other. Aunt Agnes actually gave him a smile.

"Have you met my guests Miss Felicity Mayson and her aunt, Miss Appleby?"

"I don't believe I have. How do you do?" He smiled first at Felicity, then at Aunt Agnes. He seemed to notice the book in Aunt Agnes's hands. "Are you a great reader, Miss Appleby?"

Mr. Birtwistle looked to be about the same age as Aunt Agnes, who was thirty-five. Was the man married? By the look of his rumpled coat, crooked neckcloth, and the way the sides of his hair grew rather long over his ears, Felicity guessed that he was not.

Auntie blushed. "I do like to read, very much."

"She is very well read, Mr. Birtwistle," Felicity said. "She has read every book in my father's library."

"Do you reside with Miss Mayson, then?"

"Yes. Her mother is my sister."

"And have you been a guest of Lady Blackstone for long, Miss Appleby?"

"Nearly three weeks, I believe. And how long have you lived in Margate, sir?"

"I have been here these ten years, first as a curate, then as a rector."

"And you like being so near the sea?"

"I admit I rarely go near the water, but I have seen a sunrise or two over the ocean that was simply spectacular."

"Oh."

Felicity chimed in occasionally to praise her aunt's taste in music or how much she was beloved by various great-nieces and great-nephews—the children of Felicity's siblings—but mostly she listened, enthralled with how well her shy and reclusive aunt was able to converse and hold the rector's attention.

Fortunately, Mr. Ratley was talking with Mr. Smallwood about the various types of pheasant and grouse in the area and the best ways to shoot them, the best guns to use, et cetera.

"Lady Blackstone," Mr. Ratley said, suddenly standing, looking quite jovial. "Since it is not the season to be shooting but the weather is so dry and warm, may we all ride to the seashore soon, if the weather is still fine?"

Lady Blackstone smiled. "I don't see why not. Mr. Birtwistle, are you fond of riding?"

"No indeed, my lady. I am more of a man of letters myself. I prefer a carriage to horseback riding." He stood to take his leave as the room suddenly became more lively with discussions of their upcoming outing to the sea.

While everyone else—everyone except Felicity—was otherwise occupied with their separate conversations, Mr. Birtwistle bent toward Aunt Agnes and said quietly, "I should like to call on you again tomorrow, if that is all right with you, Miss Appleby."

"Oh." Aunt Agnes's eyes went wide, and she opened and closed her mouth a few times. Finally, she said, "I would like that. Thank you."

He smiled and gave her a quick bow before turning to Felicity. "Good day, Miss Mayson."

"Good day, Mr. Birtwistle."

As soon as he was gone, Felicity squeezed her aunt's arm. "Oh, Auntie," she whispered. "You have made a conquest!"

"Do you really think so?" Aunt Agnes plucked at her sleeves, her usual sign of nervousness, but something she had not done once while Mr. Birtwistle had been there.

"He said he wished to call on you—on *you*—tomorrow, did he not?"

"It is so very strange." Auntie chuckled. "No one has ever . . . Hmm. Mr. Birtwistle. Well. I never." She shook her head.

***

The next day, Mr. Birtwistle did come, and he brought a book for Aunt Agnes.

Aunt Agnes examined the book, then looked up at him. "You wrote it?"

"It is only a little novel, a morality tale of sorts, not too different from Miss Hannah More's allegorical works."

"Oh, how impressive! You simply must allow me to read it."

"But of course, Miss Appleby."

"It is such an honor to meet a published author."

Mr. Birtwistle grinned as Aunt Agnes gushed and made much of the fact that he had written a novel.

"I have two others. I can bring those later if you enjoy this one. I also have compiled all my sermons, but as of yet, I have not published those."

Felicity couldn't help smiling at the enthusiastic conversation between these two people who seemed to get on so well, having only just met the day before.

She only hoped her aunt would not end up in the type of situation in which Felicity presently found herself, engaged to a man who turned out to be involved in something nefarious. But how nefarious could a rector who spent his spare time writing moral allegories be?

Mr. Birtwistle ended his short visit by saying, "I understand that you are going on your seaside ride tomorrow, and I have some business at the parsonage that I must attend to, but I shall visit you the day after tomorrow? May I?"

"Yes, of course." Aunt Agnes smiled. She certainly seemed to know the appropriate amount of encouragement to offer an eligible gentleman.

Felicity was also glad to make Mr. Birtwistle's acquaintance, as his friendship might prove helpful to them, should they become desperate enough to risk telling the rector that the people at this house were plotting to overthrow the government. Besides the guests who had been present for the ball, the rector had been the only outside person Lady Blackstone had allowed in the house.

***

Philip stuffed the papers he had copied into the special pocket sewn into the inside of his shirt the next morning as he dressed for their ride to the seashore. In case he managed to slip away and escape the group, he wanted those all-important papers on his person.

The weather turned out to be fine again, with plenty of blue sky to accentuate the white clouds overhead. It was a rather big to-do to saddle all the horses for such a large group. Only Miss Appleby and two of the married women stayed behind with the house servants.

Miss Mayson, Philip noticed, was dressed in a pretty green riding habit and matching hat that brought out the vivid color in her eyes. He got close enough to her to tell her good morning before walking away to avoid more suspicion. Thanks to Mrs. Cartwright, Lady Blackstone now had her eye on them, and he often caught her looking at either him or Miss Mayson.

Miss Mayson was soon mounted on a rather skittish brown mare. He supposed Ratley had chosen this mount because she was thought to be gentle, and Miss Mayson was not very confident around horses.

Philip examined his horse's girth and bridle and assured himself all was in good order before mounting up. Soon they were all headed onto the trail that would lead them to the seashore.

Miss Mayson's horse kept wandering off the trail. She pulled on the reins, but the horse was not cooperating. Her dolt of a fiancé should have helped her, but he was too busy talking to one of the men to even notice what was happening. Philip clenched his teeth, forcing himself not to go over and take the reins and get her horse back in line.

Finally, she managed the task herself, and they all rode past the garden.

Miss Mayson's shoulders remained stiff the entire ride. Philip tried not to stare, but he was determined to keep an eye on her.

In half an hour, they had reached the sandy beach at the water's edge.

Mr. Ratley helped Miss Mayson down from her horse. Philip dismounted as well and took in the sight of the vast ocean and its crashing waves. He'd always liked the seaside, but now was not the time to enjoy it.

The men were passing around a few flasks of brandy. He wished Lady Blackstone would insist they put them away, especially with the ladies present. But he was also glad, because if they were all drunk, it might help him slip away unnoticed on the ride home, if he could manage to remain at the rear of the group.

Philip was careful not to attract attention to himself as they all sat on blankets to enjoy a small repast before heading back. Miss Mayson sat beside Mr. Ratley, although that man seemed to pay her little attention. And by the time they'd had their picnic and were preparing to get back on their horses, many of the men were laughing raucously and even stumbling about.

Miss Mayson's brows were drawn together.

The sooner they all returned to Doverton Hall, the better.

Finally, they were preparing to leave. Philip had to help two men onto their horses, as they were too inebriated to manage on their own.

Then Lady Blackstone said, "Let us take a more scenic route home. We shall see the cliffs to the south."

South was not his preferred direction, but he should still be able to slip away. He hoped.

Miss Mayson's horse was between Mr. Ratley's and Lady Blackstone's as they set out. At least that seemed to keep the skittish horse in line and moving in the right direction. Philip let several people go in front of him, and he and a couple of the drunkest fellows took up the rear.

They were going along at a slow pace. It was soon clear that Mr. Ratley was nearly as drunk as the worst of them. He kept reaching out and touching Miss Mayson's neck. She kept leaning away from him. Meanwhile, Ratley's black stallion, which he was inordinately proud of, kept nudging Miss Mayson's mare's neck, as if mimicking his master.

Their trail was winding rather near the edge of a white chalk cliff overlooking the ocean. Other riders kept moving in front of him and causing him to lose sight of Miss Mayson and her horse.

Suddenly, Miss Mayson's horse reared, screaming as if in pain. Ratley's horse danced and leapt, sending Ratley out of the saddle and onto the ground on the seat of his breeches. His stallion showed his teeth and bit Miss Mayson's horse in the rump.

Miss Mayson's mare screamed again and bolted, racing ahead.

"Go after her!" Lady Blackstone yelled at a groom.

Philip had already kicked his horse forward, sending him into a gallop. His horse surged past the others.

Miss Mayson was leaning forward, trying to hold on and stay in her sidesaddle. And what was worse, she appeared to have dropped the bridle. Her horse careened close to the edge of the cliff.

Philip never took his eyes off Miss Mayson. His heart pounded with the thundering of his horse's hooves as he drove him to reach her before she went off the edge.

CHAPTER TWENTY-TWO

Felicity had grown more and more uncomfortable the longer they had stayed on the beach. She had wanted to enjoy the beauty and magnificence of the place, but the men had all become more boisterous and showed less and less restraint, Mr. Ratley included.

When they had all gotten back on their horses, she was relieved, but she dreaded having to deal with her horse again. She'd never been very good with horses, and though this one seemed fairly gentle, she also startled at every little thing.

She explained the situation to Lady Blackstone, who kindly positioned her horse on Miss Mayson's left, while Mr. Ratley's horse was on her right. Riding between the two, her mare would have little choice but to stay on course.

But as they started on their way, Mr. Ratley reached out and touched the back of Felicity's neck. She flinched and leaned away from him. Heat rose inside her at the inappropriateness of his action. He was grinning.

"Please do not do that, Mr. Ratley."

"What do you mean?"

A moment later, she felt his hand on her neck again.

She jerked away from him, and he laughed, a throaty sound. Just then, Mr. Ratley's stallion used his head to nudge her mare's neck. Her mare snorted and tossed her head, edging closer to Lady Blackstone's horse. Felicity did her best to pull the horse back to the center of the trail.

Mr. Ratley's horse nudged Felicity's horse again, this time more aggressively. Felicity's horse reared, her front hooves lifting off the ground.

Felicity leaned forward, terrified she'd slide right off the sidesaddle. She scrambled to hang on, and the reins slipped from her fingers. The horse dropped back to all fours, jarring Felicity's teeth together so hard her vision went black for a moment.

As soon as the mare's front hooves were back on the ground, she bolted.

Felicity grabbed the horse's mane, holding on as tight as she could. The pommel of the saddle stabbed her stomach, making it hard to breathe.

She managed to glance to her left and saw blue ocean instead of green grass. At any moment the horse's hooves could slip right off, sending them both to their death.

Darkness started closing in on all sides. She was about to faint.

Something tightened around her ribs, a steel band, or perhaps someone's arm. She felt herself being lifted. She floated above the ground as everything went black.

***

Philip snatched Miss Mayson off her horse and let his own horse slow and stop. He was holding Miss Mayson's limp body rather awkwardly, so he pulled her upright in front of him, seating her in the front of his saddle and letting her upper body slump against his chest.

Thanks be to God, he had reached her in time. Her head rested on his shoulder, as she was obviously in a dead faint. Her horse had slowed her frantic run as soon as Philip had taken Miss Mayson off the mare's back, and the horse now stood fifty yards ahead, calmly grazing.

After carrying Miss Mayson into her room after she fainted, and holding her up after she nearly fell into the printing press, it was the third time Philip had held a woman in his arms. He had no sisters and no other experiences to compare it to, but holding Miss Mayson made him want to hold her forever.

"Oh, good heavens, Mr. Merrick." Lady Blackstone rode up beside him. Several more horses galloped up behind her.

Mr. Ratley galloped up, stopping his horse short, sending rocks and dust flying.

Miss Mayson began to rouse, her head lolling on his shoulder. He held her firmly to him so she wouldn't fall, but everyone was gathering around them now, staring.

"You are quite the heroic rider." Lady Blackstone looked almost amused. "What do you say, Mr. Ratley?" she called. "Mr. Merrick has saved your fiancée from falling over a cliff to her death."

Mr. Ratley scowled at Philip. "She would not have fallen over the cliff. Her horse is over there."

"Rather ungallant of you, Mr. Ratley," Lady Blackstone said, "not to at least thank him."

Ratley's drunken face was flushed, and he scowled and barely glanced at Miss Mayson.

Miss Mayson made a sound like a deep sigh, then said in a groggy voice, "What happened?" She lifted her head off his shoulder. "Did the horse fall?"

"No, my dear," Lady Blackstone said. "It is a miracle she did not, and that Mr. Merrick was able to rescue you."

"I could have rescued her," Mr. Ratley said loudly.

Several of the men laughed long and hard. Ratley glared all around.

Philip said softly, "Are you hurt, Miss Mayson?"

"No, I don't think so." She looked him in the eye. In her disheveled state—strands of hair falling against her cheeks—she was so pretty it took his breath away. "You saved me, didn't you?" Her voice was so soft, he barely heard her.

"I hope I didn't hurt you."

"I am very grateful."

And he was grateful too. Even though his chance of sneaking away was probably gone now, saving her had been worth it.

***

Felicity was comfortable sitting across Mr. Merrick's saddle, leaning against his chest. But then she realized how many people were staring at them.

"Mr. Ratley," Lady Blackstone snapped, "get over here and help your fiancée down from Mr. Merrick's horse."

Mr. Ratley appeared below her and reached out his arms.

Would her legs hold her? If only she could stay with Mr. Merrick. If only he were her fiancé instead of Mr. Ratley.

But she did not have the luxury of such a thought.

She placed her hands on Mr. Ratley's shoulders and let him help her down. Her knees wobbled, but they held.

"Miss Mayson," Lady Blackstone said, loudly enough for the entire party to hear, "are you capable of riding back to Doverton Hall, or should we hire you a carriage?"

The thought of getting back on the mare that had careened out of control and nearly killed her sent a shudder through her body. But she bit her lip. Everyone was watching her. No one else seemed to care that she was frightened, and somehow she could not bear to let them see her looking anything other than strong and brave. She squared her shoulders and clenched her fists as she neared the grazing mare.

"I am well enough to ride."

Steeling herself, she took hold of the saddle pommel and placed her foot in the stirrup as Mr. Ratley leaned down to help boost her up. But when he leaned, he stumbled and kept stumbling until he bumped into her horse's flank.

"I'm all right," he said, a smile on his face. He came near Felicity again, and the smell of brandy on his breath made her cough and lean away from him. He didn't seem to notice and stooped again, offering his hands as a stirrup. Felicity placed her foot in them and pulled herself into the saddle.

"Thank you, Mr. Ratley," she said, but he was already walking away, swaying as he went.

Lady Blackstone and Mr. Merrick had come alongside her with their own horses, and she heard Mr. Merrick address Lady Blackstone.

"Since it was Mr. Ratley's stallion that nipped Miss Mayson's horse, causing her to bolt, might I suggest that someone else ride beside Miss Mayson?"

"Mr. Ratley," Lady Blackstone called.

"One moment, please." Mr. Ratley was still trying to mount his horse, which was refusing to stand still.

A scowl crossed Lady Blackstone's face. She muttered, "A man who can't control his own horse and doesn't know when to stop drinking . . ." She raised her voice. "Mr. Ratley, Mr. Merrick will take your place beside Miss Mayson. You are not to ride behind her either. Her horse is too skittish to be anywhere near that beast of yours. You may ride at the rear. Now come along. I wish to get home before sunset."

Lady Blackstone set her horse into motion, and they were on their way once again.

Felicity's hands still trembled, but she was determined to make her horse mind her. She would not be timid this time.

Mr. Merrick sat very tall in his saddle, looking straight ahead, and Lady Blackstone was doing the same, but all Felicity could think was that she'd almost died ten minutes earlier, and everyone was so calm. Tears stung her eyes, but she refused to let them fall. She instead put her mind on Aunt Agnes. What might she be doing today? Undoubtedly, she had already finished reading Mr. Birtwistle's book.

A memory flashed before her eyes of the blue sea below her as her horse had skidded inches from the edge of the white chalk cliff. Her heart started to pound, so she pushed the memory away and replaced it with the image of Mr. Birtwistle talking with Aunt Agnes, the way his eyes fastened on Auntie's, and the way she smiled at him. Felicity had been so surprised to witness her aunt flirting.

But her mind kept switching back to her terrifying ordeal. How foolish had she looked, clutching her horse's neck after stupidly dropping the reins? And why did she have to faint again? Her face tingled in embarrassment. Once again, Mr. Merrick had saved her. The poor man. He knew he'd have to risk his life to infiltrate a gang of revolutionaries, but he could not have known he'd have to risk his life to save a girl who couldn't seem to stop fainting at the worst possible moments.

Tears rushed back into her eyes. She had to stop these thoughts.

She longed to start a conversation to take her mind off herself, but Lady Blackstone's expression was stony, and she probably should not attract attention to Mr. Merrick by speaking with him. He would not wish it, certainly.

But she couldn't help remembering the deep resonance of his whispered words, *Are you hurt, Miss Mayson?* And later, *I hope I didn't hurt you.* Her heart thumped hard against her chest. He must care about her, at least as much as any kindhearted man would. He'd even drawn attention to himself by suggesting to Lady Blackstone that he, instead of her fiancé, should ride beside Felicity. And how grateful she was to him for that! It was Mr. Ratley's uncontrolled stallion that had caused her mare to bolt, and Mr. Ratley was too full of brandy to save her. If she actually intended to marry the man, she would feel humiliated at his behavior.

But with Mr. Merrick beside her, she felt safe, even on her skittish mare.

Thank you, God, for Mr. Merrick. She couldn't help glancing over at him. How handsome and strong he was. He must have plucked her right out of the saddle of the galloping horse.

A bawdy drinking song broke out behind them. Mr. Merrick met her eye for the first time since they had remounted their horses. He gave her a sympathetic smile, then looked at the trail again.

Lady Blackstone's scowl deepened. She turned to Felicity. "Men are just overgrown boys. We have to be their mothers, even when they're grown and married. I hope you will take Mr. Ratley's brandy away from him when he starts drinking too much. You should take a firm hand with him, Felicity. He requires it."

"Yes, my lady. That sounds very wise." But she had no intention of taking any kind of hand with him, firm or otherwise. She was getting out of this nightmare, the sooner the better, and she would have to trust Providence to help her.

***

Philip sat down at the dinner table, the stiff folded papers jabbing his side.

It was the evening after their ride to the seaside, and the men were either still drunk or already feeling the effects from the morning's drinking. But Lady Blackstone insisted on dinner protocol, so they gathered and ate and talked. Most of them were quite subdued.

The men's headaches should work in Philip's favor. He could sneak out of the house after everyone had gone to bed, saddle his horse, and ride to London to deliver his evidence. The Home Office could arrest all the leaders before Lady Blackstone could warn them, and the revolution would be ended before it began. The public might never know how close they had come to being taken over by this band of would-be assassins and usurpers.

"Felicity," Lady Blackstone said rather loudly. "I still have not seen any of your letters in the outgoing post."

"Oh, I am not much of a correspondent, I'm afraid. My mother doesn't mind. She has so many children, she cannot write to me very often, so she doesn't expect many letters from me."

Philip wondered how much of it was true. But he could not fault her for not writing her mother, given their situation.

How might he and Miss Mayson have got on if they had not both had to practice so much deception? He might have danced with her at a ball and would have certainly found her very beautiful and alluring. He would have admired her smile and her easy way of conversing, her delicate laugh and the modesty in her expressions. He might have asked her for a second dance and even a third. He might have called upon her the next day.

No. Unfortunately, he probably wouldn't have. Miss Mayson possessed no fortune and neither did he. What did he have to offer her? He lived at his parents' town house in London and went to work every day at the Home Office at the Horse Guards in Whitehall. On the contrary, he would not have shown her undue attention. He was too much of a gentleman to sport with any girl's affections. But Miss Mayson . . . she made him hope . . . that he might make his fortune somehow, and that she might like him as himself, Philip McDowell, not Philip Merrick, the spy.

"Mr. Merrick, now that everyone is present, I have something to say."

The two footmen at the end of the room moved closer to the table, and two more footmen suddenly entered the room and stood by the two exits.

Every muscle in his body tensed.

CHAPTER TWENTY-THREE

Felicity felt the tension in the room. She had thought she was imagining that Lady Blackstone and Mr. Ratley were staring a great deal at Mr. Merrick. But now Lady Blackstone stood, placing her hands on the table in front of her. Her eyes glittered in the candlelight as she looked at the men around the table. Virtually all of them had droopy, bloodshot eyes, except for Mr. Merrick, who looked quite as handsome, and alert, as ever.

"We have been making plans while we've been here. We have trusted each other completely, have we not?"

The men mumbled their agreement and nodded their heads. Some were starting to take closer notice. Mr. Ratley's face was flushed, and perspiration beaded on his forehead.

"But we have a traitor in our midst."

A gasp and a few grunts went around the room.

"Ladies, if you are squeamish, you should leave the room immediately."

Mrs. Cartwright stood and cried out dramatically. The other women followed suit, and they all filed out of the room, but Felicity stayed in her seat. She wasn't sure why, but she couldn't seem to move.

"Felicity, you had better leave as well. I do not want you to see anything that will be too disturbing for you. Mr. Ratley, take her out."

Did they not suspect her, then? Mr. Merrick. *O God, please help him!*

She let Mr. Ratley take her arm, help her from her chair, and lead her into the next room.

She wanted to look back at Mr. Merrick, to assure him that she would risk her life to save his. Surely they would not kill him in the dining room.

She began to feel light-headed, the familiar sting in her forehead and cheeks that came when she was about to faint. *No. I won't. I can't. I must keep my wits. I must think of how I might help Mr. Merrick.*

"Are you all right?" Mr. Ratley asked, but there was no real concern or gentleness in his tone.

She had to take the focus off herself. "I am well, but what is happening? Do you know who the traitor is, Oliver?" She gazed up at him, still fighting the darkness that was creeping into her vision.

"Yes." He was quiet for a moment. "Do you not know who Lady Blackstone is about to expose?"

"How could I know?" Felicity sank down in a chair at the back of the drawing room to which the ladies had all withdrawn. No one spoke. She held her breath as she stared at Mr. Ratley's face, as if waiting to hear what he would say next, when in reality she was straining to hear any sound that might carry from the dining room.

A crash. Felicity jumped. The loud noise was followed by a thud and other scuffling sounds from the dining room. Would they murder Mr. Merrick as they had murdered that poor man in the garden?

She stood and ran toward the dining room.

***

Philip was very aware that he would have to go through two healthy young footmen before he could escape through either door. He might be able to accomplish that, but there were several other men in the room—although most were still suffering the effects of too much alcohol.

"Mr. Merrick, you aroused my suspicion some days ago. I cannot even put my finger on exactly what it was. Perhaps it was intuition, or the fact that I never heard you rage against the ruling class. There was always something about you."

She made eye contact with one of the footmen and nodded. The man stepped toward Philip.

Philip jumped from his chair, knocking it backward, and dashed for the other exit. He barreled through the first footman, using his shoulder to knock him aside, then cut the man's feet out from under him with his foot. The second footman slammed his fist into Philip's eye before he could even get his hands up.

Philip managed to stay on his feet, but another fist punched him in the stomach. He fought to draw in a breath, bent over and reeling.

The footman stepped aside. Philip's gaze fastened on the open doorway. He took one step, then felt the cold metal of a gun barrel jab the side of his neck.

Lady Blackstone pressed the gun hard into his skin. "Going somewhere, Mr. Merrick? I'm afraid I have to ask you to stay a bit longer."

His cheekbone throbbed, but he still very much wanted a chance to reciprocate the footman's blows. But when he calculated the odds of getting out of the room alive if he ignored the gun in his jugular, he decided they were not in his favor.

"Tie his hands," Lady Blackstone ordered.

Another footman produced some rope, and they tied his hands together behind his back, pulling the rope so tight it cut into his wrists.

"May I ask why you think I'm a traitor?" Perhaps he could yet talk his way out of it.

"Do not pretend, Mr. . . . . What is your name again?"

"You know my name. Philip Merrick." All the men were standing around him, flanking Lady Blackstone. Now, instead of looking weary, their eyes were alert and trained on him.

"There is no Philip Merrick of Yorkshire with a sick mother about to die."

"I am as real as you are, my lady. My name is different from my father and mother's. I was raised by an uncle, who adopted me and gave me the name Merrick. He was from Devonshire, but he died a few years ago. You may search it out. My father's name is Thomas Fitzhugh."

Lady Blackstone narrowed her eyes. "Perhaps you are telling the truth. We shall see. I have my butler and a manservant looking through your things in your room as we speak. I am sure they shall turn up evidence. But in the meantime, who will volunteer to search this traitor's person?"

"I will." Mr. Cartwright stepped forward. His wife must have told him of seeing Philip holding Miss Mayson's hand in the library closet.

"Take off his coat and shirt," Lady Blackstone said, her voice hard.

Philip pulled on his bonds, which rubbed harshly against his wrists, biting into his skin. How would he escape now?

A helpless, hollow feeling bloomed in his chest as Mr. Cartwright pulled off Philip's neckcloth, exposing his throat. Then the man jerked Philip's coat off his shoulders and yanked it down. The ropes binding his wrists kept it hanging from his elbows.

"Go through his coat pockets," Lady Blackstone ordered.

He felt them rifling through his pockets while Cartwright tore the buttons from his shirt and exposed his chest, pushing the shirt off his shoulders. And there were the folded-up papers, like hot coals against his side.

Lady Blackstone's eyes fastened on the papers. She stepped forward and snatched them from where they were tucked at the top of his trousers.

She unfolded them, her eyes scanning them. She wadded them in her fist, looked Philip in the eye, then slapped him across the same cheek the footman had struck.

His ears rang with the stinging blow.

When he opened his eyes, Lady Blackstone was leaning toward him, her face only inches away from his. "Do you know what we do to traitors?"

He could easily imagine.

"Let's torture him," one man said.

"Yes, we should make him suffer."

"He planned to give us all up to be hanged."

Lady Blackstone raised her hand to silence them. "Since we cannot risk his escaping, we should kill him right away."

"He won't escape," someone said. "We'll make sure of that."

Wilmott, a tall, heavy man, lumbered up to Philip, shaking his own fist as if weighing it. "Let me take a shot at the little traitor."

Had it occurred to them that they were the actual traitors to England, not him? Philip braced himself for the blow.

Wilmott drew back his huge, meaty fist. This was it. Philip was going to die.

A scream split the air. Wilmott stopped and turned his head.

Felicity Mayson stood in the doorway, Ratley hurrying up behind her.

"What are you doing to that man?" Miss Mayson's voice was almost high enough to be called hysterical. "Are you savages? What are you doing?"

He did not want her to see him like this, stripped to the waist and hands tied behind his back, about to be beaten to death, but he was still grateful for the reprieve, no matter how short.

"Get her out of here," Lady Blackstone hissed.

"Please!" Miss Mayson's eyes were full of tears. "Please don't do this. He is a human being. Have you no conscience? Have you no fear of God?"

Ratley pulled on her arm, but she shook him off.

Lady Blackstone went toward her, talking in a mild, pleasant, low voice, blocking her view of the room, urging her away from the door.

"Is she gone?" Wilmott asked.

"I think so."

"Good." Wilmott drew back his fist and his knuckles connected with Philip's face.

Stars exploded in his head, and he hit the floor on his side. He couldn't move, couldn't feel, except for the explosion happening in his head.

"You killed him," someone said, but the voice seemed to drift from far away.

Miss Mayson cried out again. He lay still.

***

Felicity heard the words, "You killed him," and a strangled cry escaped her throat. She pushed her way past Lady Blackstone, who grabbed her arm and stopped her. Mr. Merrick lay on the floor, blood oozing from his mouth and nose. Her knees went weak. He couldn't be dead.

"Leave him alone!" Lady Blackstone was talking to the men, who all backed away.

Felicity broke free from Lady Blackstone's grip and started toward Mr. Merrick's motionless body, but someone caught her around the waist and held her fast. She struggled but couldn't get away.

"How could you?" Felicity screamed to the men all around. "You monsters! Send for a doctor, please," she said, turning to Lady Blackstone.

"Are you also a spy, working with this man?" Lady Blackstone's eyes bore into her.

"I am your niece. I am not a spy. And why do you think Mr. Merrick is a spy?" She was too frantic. She had to be careful if she had any hope of helping Mr. Merrick.

"He stole papers from my room. Here is the copy he made." Lady Blackstone held up the crumpled papers. "He was planning to have us all hanged."

Felicity stared at her hostess and blinked. "Oh." She had to be smart, had to pretend to be on Lady Blackstone's side. "That is . . . despicable. But surely you will not kill him. Not you, my lady."

"Why should we not?" Lady Blackstone's voice was calm and low. "He would have done the same to us. He planned to betray us, every one of us, including you." She sighed and crossed her arms over her chest. "Felicity, I had your room searched. I confess I believed you might be a spy as well, helping this man, whatever his name is, but the servants found nothing. The maidservants are cleaning it up and should have everything put back in its proper place."

"What about Aunt Agnes? You did not harm her, did you?"

"Of course not. She is well and ensconced in the library where I had the servants set up her dinner."

"Oh." Felicity's mind raced as she mentally thought over all the things in her possession. No, she had nothing that would incriminate her as a spy.

"I am sorry for my suspicions, Felicity, but you were seen with Mr. Merrick in the library closet."

"I have explained this many times—"

"Yes, yes, it was very innocent. Forgive us for our suspicions. We cannot be too careful. There is too much at stake, after all." Lady Blackstone actually smiled.

Felicity looked back at poor Mr. Merrick, his hands bound behind his back. Her stomach twisted. How badly was he hurt? She had to save him. *O God, help me save him!*

"What will you do with him?"

"I haven't decided."

"Please don't kill him, my lady." Felicity's lip trembled, and she did not try to stop the tears that flowed from her eyes. "Please. I beg you. I cannot bear it. I know you love me, you said so, as your own daughter, and Mr. Ratley and I will always be your family. Please do not allow these men to kill Mr. Merrick."

"What do you suggest we do?"

"You could lock him up somewhere until the revolution is over, treat him as a prisoner of war. You could give him a trial afterward, sentence him fairly. Then if he must be hanged for his crimes, at least it will be civilized. You don't want people to think the English as barbaric as the French, surely."

Lady Blackstone frowned out of one side her mouth. "Perhaps you are right."

Hope lifted Felicity.

Lady Blackstone pointed. "You, Mr. Wilmott and Mr. Dougherty and Mr. Bentley, carry him out to the shed where we keep the printing press. Then lock the door."

"Oh no, please! You can't take him out there like this. He might never regain consciousness. And these men might kill him as soon as your back is turned."

"What are you suggesting?" Lady Blackstone tilted her head to one side. "That we put him on a feather bed and give him access to the stable? He means the death of us all! Don't you understand?"

"Very well. Yes, I understand, but . . . his mouth is bleeding. He could choke on his own blood and die."

"And save us a lot of trouble," Mr. Cartwright said.

The other men laughed.

"There's no need to mistreat him. Hitting a man with his hands tied behind his back, when he cannot defend himself, is neither civilized nor sporting."

Lady Blackstone motioned with her hand. The man holding her back released her. She darted to the table and picked up a napkin, soaking one corner with water.

"You, Benson." Lady Blackstone motioned to one of the footmen. "Drag that old mattress from the storage room into the shed. Then the rest of you carry him to it—after Miss Mayson is satisfied he won't choke on his own blood."

Everyone left the room except three of the footmen, who stood by the doors watching her, and Lady Blackstone and Mr. Ratley, who whispered to each other a few feet away.

Felicity sank to her knees beside Mr. Merrick. She touched his temple with the wet cloth and whispered, "Are you all right?"

He didn't speak. Was he dead? Her heart skipped beats, and her stomach sank. She leaned down to place her cheek next to his nose and mouth to see if she could feel his breath.

"I'm all right."

His whisper startled an "Oh" from her lips. She sat up and wiped gently at the blood oozing from his lip, still leaning over him.

"Can you get the papers?" he whispered.

She looked around and spied the rumpled papers, with writing on both sides, lying on the table.

"I'll have to wait," she whispered back. Lady Blackstone and Mr. Ratley would surely see her if she tried to get them now.

"Is he still alive?" Lady Blackstone asked.

"I think so," Felicity said over her shoulder. When she turned back to Mr. Merrick, he was lying still with his eyes closed. His face was swelling and turning purple, his lip still oozing blood. Her heart twisted painfully inside her. She didn't know what else to do, so she wiped at the blood that had run down his chin.

Suddenly, it occurred to her that his chest was bare, as were his shoulders and upper arms. But it seemed silly to be embarrassed about such a thing at a time like this, so she ignored his state of undress and focused on his face.

She had to save him somehow. But he was more worried about the papers, the evidence against Lady Blackstone and the others. Wouldn't that evidence ensure the deaths of many people? She would have to think about that later.

"Get the papers," Mr. Merrick whispered, his voice so low she barely made out the words.

"I shall try," she whispered back.

He kept his eyes closed. Otherwise, she was not sure she would have been able to touch his face with the cloth. It was so personal, touching his chin and lower lip. But she had done many things in the past few weeks that she had never anticipated doing on this visit, or ever—deliberately lying and deceiving others; meeting a man who was virtually a stranger, alone, in a closet; becoming engaged to a man she barely knew; and allowing that man to kiss her multiple times so that he would not guess that she did not intend to marry him at all.

Her mother would surely take one look at her when she returned home and know that she had done many scandalous and unseemly things. How could she look her in the eye?

If things went badly now, Mr. Merrick would die. And in a few short weeks, all of England could be in chaos and deadly revolution.

Felicity glanced again at the papers, still on the table. How could she get them without being seen? Had Lady Blackstone forgotten about them? But in her mind, the spy was caught. They were safe again, so perhaps she *would* forget.

"I'll create a distraction," he whispered. He moaned and opened his eyes, and she backed away from him and stood up.

"Please don't kill him," Felicity pleaded again, turning to Lady Blackstone. Truly, her heart was in her throat, for she knew it was very possible that they did intend to kill him as soon as she was out of sight.

Lady Blackstone waved her hand at the footmen. "Take him to the shed."

The men strode over to Mr. Merrick and bent and put hands on him.

"Let me go! I can walk," Mr. Merrick said.

All eyes were on him now, so Felicity sidled toward the corner of the table where the papers lay.

The footmen helped him to his feet. He took a step, then sank as if in a swoon. While the men were scrambling to hold him up, Felicity bumped her hip against the table edge and took hold of the papers. Then she backed up to the sideboard that stood against the wall and slipped the papers behind a large urn.

CHAPTER TWENTY-FOUR

Felicity moved back toward where the three footmen were picking up Mr. Merrick's limp body and carrying him out of the room.

Lady Blackstone turned, as did Mr. Ratley, to face Felicity.

Felicity placed her hands on her cheeks. "I feel very faint. This is even more shocking than finding a dead body in the garden."

Mr. Ratley took out his handkerchief and tried to use it to fan Felicity's face, but it was not very effective.

"Let me fetch you some wine." Lady Blackstone stepped to the sideboard and lifted a decanter next to the urn where Felicity had just hidden the papers.

Would they be visible? Would she see them sticking out?

Mr. Ratley patted the inside of her wrists. "I saw a lady do this when a girl fainted at a party I was attending in Bristol. It's good for your circulation."

He was patting so zealously it was actually painful, but Felicity said nothing. Lady Blackstone brought her the glass of wine.

"Here you are, my dear. This should help settle your nerves. And please don't worry about anything. The capture of traitors need not concern you in the slightest. Forget you ever knew that man. Your Oliver and I shall take care of all the unpleasant details."

Felicity obediently sipped her wine. "But you won't kill him? You said you would hold him prisoner instead."

"Darling, we must consider what is best for everyone," Mr. Ratley said.

"We will not kill him tonight, at least," Lady Blackstone said, "so you may sleep well and not worry. And you will forgive me for searching your room, won't you, my dear?" Lady Blackstone peered into her face.

"Of course." Felicity looked down, hoping they would see hurt in her expression. "I understand that you must be very careful, for everyone's sake. I shall forget about the little thing of having my room searched, but if a man I have talked with, had dinner with, and danced with at a ball is killed while he lies helpless in an outdoor shed . . ." She lowered her voice to a whisper. "I'm afraid that would be much harder to forget."

Lady Blackstone huffed. Had Felicity gone too far?

"Go up to your room, Felicity. Get some sleep. We are all exhausted after a trying day."

"Yes, my lady." Felicity kept her gaze lowered as Mr. Ratley took her arm and led her toward the staircase.

"I am sorry you had to see that violence, my darling," Mr. Ratley said.

Felicity sniffed but didn't look up.

When they stopped in front of her room, he leaned down to kiss her, but she presented him with her cheek. He kissed it.

"When I close my eyes, I see that man's poor battered face. Good night, Oliver." She opened her door and went inside, shutting it behind her.

***

Philip lay on the mattress where they threw him. His rib was probably cracked, as every breath caused a sharp pain. Thankfully, all his teeth seemed intact. He moved his jaw up and down, but it didn't feel broken. His cheekbone was a different story. It was hugely swollen, and the pain was intense.

They had left his wrists tied. What would happen to him now? If he could not escape, they would surely kill him, despite what they had told Miss Mayson. That was just to placate her.

"Oh, Miss Mayson," he said softly, and moaned, since no one was there to hear him.

He had opened his eyes just a bit when she had been leaning over him, touching his face with the cloth. The compassion in her expression as she gazed at him . . . It had squeezed his stomach, but rather pleasantly, to witness her concern for him.

He shouldn't think of her that way—the terrified but fierce look in her eyes, the way her hair fell about her face, the tears threatening to fall. How much he wished he could touch *her* face.

But the first thing he had to do was get these ropes off.

It was quite dark in the shed, reminding him of the time he had been trapped there with Miss Mayson. They had been in several compromising situations that would have ruined her reputation if anyone had discovered them. Throughout, she had shown intelligence, strength of mind, modesty, and good character. She was exactly the girl he wished to marry. And if she were in here with him again, he would . . . but his prospects were far from certain. How could he ask her to take a chance that he might make his fortune someday?

What would happen to Miss Mayson if he died? She might be forced to marry Mr. Ratley. Or if she refused, Lady Blackstone was ruthless enough to kill her. He couldn't let that happen.

He made the effort to push himself into a sitting position. His head throbbed, but he did his best to ignore it. He looked around for something he might use to cut his bonds. If his hands were free, he might find a way to climb up to the window high in the wall and crawl out.

It was difficult to stand, with his sore ribs and bound hands, but a feeling of urgency spurred him to make the effort, and he managed to get to his feet. He stood still, waiting for his vision to stop spinning, then he started walking around the room, inspecting everything, looking for any kind of sharp object, a piece of broken glass, anything.

When he made it back around to the door again, he tried to open it with his hands, standing on his toes to reach the knob. It was definitely locked. Later he might try ramming his shoulder against it, but for now, he wasn't sure he could stay conscious if he tried that.

Suddenly, he noticed a nail protruding about an inch through the wall next to the door. He touched his finger to it. It was surprisingly sharp. He pressed his ropes against it, finding one particular spot, and rubbed with a sawing motion as hard as he was able to stand as the rope chafed his wrists.

Hope rose inside him as he stared at the window, planning and working at the nail.

***

Felicity lay in bed thinking of Mr. Merrick and how she might help to free him.

An hour after she had gone to bed, she put on a loose dress over her nightgown and went downstairs, planning to go out to the shed and see if she could figure out a way to get inside. But she heard voices near the door leading outside. It sounded like Lady Blackstone. That lady would surely deduce what Felicity was planning to do if she saw her. So she went back up to her room.

She tried to imagine how much pain Mr. Merrick was in. Would he incur permanent damage, having his hands tied behind his back for so long? Not to mention the injuries from the beating to his face. And when she thought of how he had saved her from the runaway horse, and how he might have escaped and been on his way to his own home at that very moment if he had not taken the time and trouble to save her . . . she couldn't hold back the tears, and soon her pillow was quite wet and cold.

She awakened from a nightmare just as dawn was breaking. Once more, she got dressed and walked quietly down the stairs.

The back door was locked, but the key was in the keyhole. Felicity turned it, and it opened. She slipped out and closed it as quietly as possible.

It was beginning to rain, more of a light mist, and Felicity ran along the ground to the shed. She tried the knob, but it was locked. "Mr. Merrick!" she called in a loud whisper. "Are you in there?"

She listened but heard nothing. She tried again, calling louder this time, "Mr. Merrick! It's Felicity Mayson."

Silence. Oh dear. Could he be unconscious? Or worse? She had heard of people expiring from head injuries. They simply went to sleep and never awakened. Surely that would not happen to Mr. Merrick. He was so strong.

She knocked on the door. "Mr. Merrick?"

She decided to walk around the building. On the west side, underneath the window, broken glass lay on the ground. She looked up. The window was completely out. She looked closer at the ground and saw a drop of red. Was that blood? She touched it, and the red liquid stuck to her finger. She held it close to her nose. The metallic smell was blood.

Had Mr. Merrick managed to crawl out the window, thereby cutting himself? If so, he was free, thank God. "Let him not be seriously injured," she whispered, clasping her hands.

After the quick prayer, Felicity ran back to the house. She'd nearly forgotten the papers behind the urn in the dining room. She went in and found them just where she'd placed them. She stuffed them up her sleeve and hurried to her room. Surely everyone else was still sleeping after the eventful day and evening.

But now, where could she hide the papers? Lady Blackstone had already searched her room once. Would she search it again? Besides that, Lady Blackstone would not forget the papers for long. She would go back to the dining room looking for them.

Felicity sat down at her little desk. She would copy the papers and then return them to the dining room. She took up her pen and quickly copied the names and places Mr. Merrick—she should probably start thinking of him as Mr. McDowell—had written in his masculine handwriting. She wrote as small as she could while still keeping the lists legible. She wrote until she was nearly out of ink, but she finished copying everything on two sheets of paper.

She looked about her room. Aunt Agnes was still asleep in her bed, so Felicity did her best not to wake her.

She spied her own *Book of Common Prayer* beside the bed and folded the papers until they were small enough and then stuck them between the pages of the book.

Somehow, she needed to get her new lists to Mr. McDowell and the Home Office. This information had been important enough to him that he was willing to give his life for it.

Some of the servants would be up by now. They might see her returning the papers to the dining room. But she would rather risk that than risk Lady Blackstone discovering them missing and then finding them in her room.

Once again Felicity ventured down the stairs and hurried to the dining room. No one seemed to be stirring. She darted to the large table, tossed the crumpled papers onto it, and bolted out again.

Whistling sounded from one of the rooms down the corridor. Felicity slowed her step, trying to appear calm. But once she reached the steps, she hurried up as fast she could, until she was safe once again in her room.

Her blood went cold at the thought of Lady Blackstone and Mr. Ratley and everyone else there being hanged for insurrection and treason. But wouldn't she feel much worse if the royal family was murdered, along with the Members of Parliament and many other innocent people? No, she had to get those lists into the hands of the authorities, no matter the cost.

At least Mr. Merrick—Mr. McDowell—had escaped. She felt so comforted at the thought of him being safely back in London again, or at least on his way, she changed into her nightgown and went back to bed.

***

Felicity awoke to shouts outside her window. She'd only been asleep an hour, so it was still early. They must have discovered Mr. McDowell had escaped.

She considered going downstairs to ask what the commotion was about. Or was it better to remain in bed, pretending she had not heard anything?

Aunt Agnes continued her heavy breathing, oblivious to the noises, but Felicity couldn't resist going to the window and peeking down at the yard below.

Men were running around the shed, the door of which stood wide open. More men were going in and out of the stable, at least one leading a horse out. Lady Blackstone was speaking in a loud voice, turning this way and that as she stood in one spot.

Felicity moved away from the window and got back into bed. She clasped her hands and prayed. "God, I beg you to help him make it back to London safely. Don't let him get caught. Give him favor."

Felicity waited for someone to send for her or come to her room. Finally, when she could stay still no longer, she got up and began dressing herself. She was nearly ready when a knock came at the door.

Lady Blackstone burst in without waiting for an invitation.

"Felicity, I see you are up and dressed."

"I only need someone to button the top of my dress."

Lady Blackstone strode forward and buttoned the top two buttons. "I heard noises, shouts. Is something amiss?"

"Yes. Do you know anything about Mr. Merrick escaping?"

"He has escaped?"

"Don't pretend you don't know. The scullery maid said she thought she saw you skulking about the shed at dawn."

"I admit I did go out there. I couldn't stop thinking of what a terrible state Mr. Merrick was in when they took him to the shed. I went to ask him if he was well. He made me no answer, so I went back inside and back to bed."

"Did you help him escape?" Lady Blackstone leaned toward her and shook her finger in Felicity's face.

"No, I avow to you, my lady, I did nothing to help him."

Mr. Ratley suddenly entered through her open door. Poor Aunt Agnes was starting to rouse herself, sitting up in bed and saying in a groggy voice, "What is the matter? Felicity?"

"All is well, Auntie," Felicity said as pleasantly as she could. "Do not upset yourself."

Mr. Ratley approached Lady Blackstone. "It appears he broke through his bonds, which were lying on the ground, climbed up to the window, broke it out, and escaped through it. He somehow saddled and took his horse without anyone seeing or hearing anything."

"Traitors. I will question the groom who was supposed to be watching the horses. Bring him to the small sitting room."

"Yes." Mr. Ratley turned, then stopped and looked at Felicity. He nodded to her and left.

"Felicity, you seem to have some kind of infatuation with Mr. Merrick."

"Not at all. I do not know what you mean." She tried to remain calm and dignified.

"Be that as it may, you shall suffer the same fate as the rest of us if Mr. Merrick has us arrested."

"Do you think he will have us arrested?"

"He has no evidence against us," Lady Blackstone said. "It is only his word against ours, and thankfully"—she held up the crumpled papers Felicity had returned to the dining room and smiled triumphantly—"he did not get the information he tried to steal from me."

"Oh, that is a relief." Felicity placed a hand over her heart and sighed.

Lady Blackstone reached out and patted Felicity's cheek, as she had been wont to do when Felicity had first arrived at Doverton Hall. "Forgive me once again, my dear, for my suspicions of you. I know you would never want to see myself or Mr. Ratley hanged."

Felicity tried to look meek. "I understand. It is a difficult time."

"Yes, and now we must prepare for the worst because of that traitorous Merrick, or whatever his name is." Lady Blackstone straightened her shoulders and slapped the papers against her palm. "We have to move the guns from the shell grotto where he knows we have hidden them. We will have to send the men out to warn everyone. And we will strike sooner, rather than later. Our plans will not be thwarted, no matter what Merrick does."

"You are so clever and brave, my lady."

Lady Blackstone's expression turned grim. "I have had to do many things that most people would shrink from, just to ensure my own survival. No one knows, but I killed my first husband." Her dark eyes fastened on Felicity, boring into her. "It was done in self-defense. He lunged at me, the drunken fool, with a knife in his hand. But I never drank in excess, and that gave me an edge—I've never forgotten that." She stared at the wall before turning back to Felicity. "I took the knife away from him and stabbed him. It was so easy, I was surprised. And it was equally easy to convince the constable that he'd fallen on his own knife."

Felicity stared back at Lady Blackstone, her fingers tingling uncomfortably and her toes going cold.

"And that is why I am so well suited to revolution. I know I am able to kill when necessary. So many people are unsure if they are capable of what is necessary. But I know that I am capable."

"Did you kill that man in the garden?" Felicity whispered, holding her breath as she waited for Lady Blackstone's answer.

Lady Blackstone said nothing for a moment, staring back at Felicity as if they were speaking of dress patterns or wallpaper. "I could have killed him—it was necessary—but I insisted Mr. Ratley do it. He had to show me he was capable, after all, before the revolution began, and we all were depending on him to be able to do whatever terrible deeds were necessary. For killing is terrible, Felicity. But sometimes it is necessary for the good of others."

Felicity swallowed and nodded. "Yes, of course."

Lady Blackstone smiled. "I must go. Mr. Ratley and I shall stay at Doverton Hall, but nearly everyone else will be leaving."

Felicity took a breath to ask her if she and Aunt Agnes could also leave and go home, but she stopped herself.

"We need to pray," Felicity said. "May Aunt Agnes and I go to church today?"

"Church?" Lady Blackstone looked confused for a moment. "It is Sunday, isn't it?" She said it more as a statement than a question, then stared at the window. "Very well, but you should take a manservant with you, and don't talk to anyone. We'll be moving the weapons today. Perhaps, for that reason, it is good that so many people will be at church." Her expression lightened as she said, "Yes, tell the rector, Mr. Birtwistle, that my guests have all gone back to London to enjoy the rest of the Season, and I am unwell. That is why I was not able to be at church today."

Felicity smiled and nodded, and Aunt Agnes said from her bed, "Very good, Lady Blackstone. You may depend upon us." But as she sounded as meek as ever, with her shaky voice, it was no wonder Lady Blackstone did not see her as a threat. Perhaps Felicity could use that to her advantage.

CHAPTER TWENTY-FIVE

Felicity and Aunt Agnes walked the short distance to the parish church with one of Lady Blackstone's footmen escorting them. Felicity clutched her *Book of Common Prayer* to her chest and had to take several deep breaths to calm her racing heart. Aunt Agnes, however, barely even plucked at her sleeves.

They sat through Mr. Birtwistle's sermon, and he impressed Felicity with his heartfelt sincerity. The man even referenced Miss Hannah More's latest book and quoted her, making Felicity like him even more. And Aunt Agnes never took her eyes off him.

When the service was over, Felicity glanced over at the footman. He was watching her and Aunt Agnes, and he turned to follow them out of the church.

Felicity was careful not to make eye contact with anyone in case they tried to talk to her. Although that was unlikely, since she didn't know anyone at this church. Finally, they were exiting, and she let Aunt Agnes move in front of her to speak to Mr. Birtwistle.

The rector's face lighted up as he caught sight of her. "Miss Appleby. How good to see you. I trust you and Miss Mayson are well."

"Very well, I thank you. Though Lady Blackstone is not so well and wishes me to give her regrets at not being able to attend this morning's service. And here, I have brought back your book, which you were so good as to lend me, and I have included something inside it for you."

Felicity's heart skipped several beats as she prayed the footman had not heard the latter part of Aunt Agnes's speech. But it was just as they'd rehearsed, so she could not find fault with her aunt, who continued to surprise Felicity with her calm competency.

Mr. Birtwistle took the book from her, and his eyes widened. Would he be scandalized that a woman unrelated to him would give him a gift?

"I shall be happy to inspect it when I am home. And did you enjoy the book?"

"Oh yes, it is one of my new favorites." Aunt Agnes smiled.

"Perhaps I shall call on you and Miss Mayson later this week."

"I would like that."

Felicity shook his hand as well, and they were soon moving down the lane toward Doverton Hall, the footman close behind.

Aunt Agnes smiled at Felicity and winked. Felicity grinned back as they walked arm in arm.

***

As Felicity sat in the drawing room with Aunt Agnes that Tuesday, her body seemed almost light enough to float up to the ceiling. Her mind wandered from the book she was reading, and she imagined how shocked Lady Blackstone and Mr. Ratley would be if they knew that she and her aunt had outsmarted them. Mr. Birtwistle had undoubtedly found the papers and read the note they had included in the book Aunt Agnes had returned to him. Perhaps he had already sent the all-important papers to Mr. McDowell in London.

Was Mr. McDowell well? Was he suffering any serious consequences from his injuries? Did he appreciate and admire her for risking her life to get that information to him? She liked to think he did, that he was thinking fondly of her at that very moment.

Of course, it was much too dangerous for him to try to help her or even to make sure she was safe.

But the more she thought of him, the more she realized . . . he might not think so highly of her at all. She was ashamed for anyone to know she had engaged herself to an insurrectionist who wanted to kill innocent people and wage war on his own government. And Mr. McDowell knew it all, had even seen her kissing Mr. Ratley.

She had behaved foolishly and unseemly. Was there something wrong with her, that she had fallen in love so easily? That she had trusted someone so quickly who was so greatly flawed? That she could agree to marry a man such as Mr. Ratley?

No, she wouldn't let these thoughts tear at her heart. Yes, she had foolishly engaged herself to the wrong man, but she had also done many brave things. Perhaps no one would ever know the things she had done for her country and her king. But she knew, and Mr. McDowell knew. She had risked her life. She had done what she could to save Mr. McDowell's life and mission, and to save her aunt and herself.

She admired Mr. McDowell so much. He'd been so strong and heroic and selfless. And just thinking of his handsome face made her heart flutter. The blue of his eyes, the masculinity of his square chin and rigid jawline, and even his red hair appealed to her in a powerful way. But most of all, there was a gentleness in the way he had touched her, including the last time they'd met in the closet in the library when he'd clasped her hand. Her heart had pounded as he gazed so intently at her, as if he was about to tell her something important. But then Mrs. Cartwright had opened the door and caught them.

Felicity sighed. It was not to be. Mr. McDowell would not want her any more than the other gentlemen, both with and without fortunes, had wanted her. She might as well start studying Chinese again.

Besides, she would probably experience something of a scandal for having been engaged to Mr. Ratley, once the truth came out about his involvement in a group to overthrow the government. And the newspapers would no doubt refer to the fact that she had been at Doverton Hall with Lady Blackstone, the leader of the group, for weeks. The damage to her reputation might be irreparable.

Lady Blackstone's voice carried down the corridor. She sounded strident and serious.

Everything had been chaotic since they had discovered that Mr. McDowell had run away. Many had fled Doverton Hall, fearing the worst, and the rest seemed poised to leave as well. Was Lady Blackstone giving them last-minute instructions?

Felicity tiptoed into the corridor. When she was only a few feet from the dining room, she stopped and listened.

"We must strike now," a man's voice said, "before the Home Office sends out troops to seize our weapons and arrest us."

"I think Mr. Rowell is correct." Lady Blackstone was speaking now. "We will keep our plan exactly as it was, only we will begin to put it into play on the twenty-sixth of April instead of the twentieth of May."

"That is only seven days away," someone said.

"Yes, so we must get word to everyone else. I don't trust the post, so I am sending you all as messengers to inform the others. We will have to make haste, but we are ready, are we not?"

Voices rang in agreement.

Lady Blackstone began telling each man where she wanted him to go to spread the news of the date. Their voices were quite animated as the plans they had been making were finally about to come to fruition.

Felicity turned and carefully hurried back to where Aunt Agnes sat engrossed in a book.

"Auntie," she said quietly, "is Mr. Birtwistle supposed to call on us again today?"

"Why, yes. And I have his book here that I promised to return today."

"I need to put a new note inside. May I have it?"

"Of course, but he will be here soon."

"I shall bring it back presently." Felicity carried the book up to her room.

She hastily grabbed a sheet of paper and used the edge of her desk to help her tear it in half and then again in fourths. On one she wrote, *Please get word to Mr. McDowell at the Home Office that the plan has been moved up to 26 April. It is urgent.*

Felicity folded the paper and stuck it inside Mr. Birtwistle's book and carried it back downstairs.

She handed the book to Aunt Agnes, who nodded.

Felicity could only hope Mr. Birtwistle understood by now what was at stake. No doubt he had been shocked to get their first note on Sunday. Had he sent the papers to Mr. McDowell by post? Had he gone to London himself? Or, as she thought most likely, had he given the papers to the magistrate, who then took them to Mr. McDowell and his superiors at the Home Office?

There was no way to know, but as the two days had passed, she'd had to ask God to take care of it for her, because the burden of worrying about it was too heavy. Besides, she had done everything she could.

They sat in silence for a while longer, and then the servant announced Mr. Birtwistle. Lady Blackstone must have intercepted him in the corridor, because she heard that lady say, "How good of you to visit us again. Did Miss Mayson and Miss Appleby inform you of my ill health on Sunday?"

"They did indeed, my lady," Mr. Birtwistle replied, his voice sounding rather shaky. Would he give them away?

"Well, I am much better now, as you can most likely see."

"Oh yes, quite."

They arrived in the doorway of the drawing room. Aunt Agnes had closed her book and was smiling up at Mr. Birtwistle. If that man only knew how infrequent it was for her to close her book for anyone, or for her to wait in anticipation of a visitor.

Lady Blackstone entered the room with him, and they both sat.

"Mr. Birtwistle, we are delighted to see you again." But Lady Blackstone's eyes had a certain hardness about them, and her lips were decidedly straight—not a hint of a smile. And she seemed to emphasize the word *again*.

"Why, thank you, Lady Blackstone. I was on my way to call on some other sick parishioners, and I thought I would call on you first, since you are nearest to the parsonage."

"I am quite well now, thank you."

She was giving the rector such a hard, direct look, he seemed to squirm a bit in his chair, but then he turned to Aunt Agnes.

"Have you been well, Miss Appleby?"

"Oh yes, quite well. My dear niece and I have been able to take walks in the garden every morning, and we enjoy reading. And I have just finished reading this book you loaned me."

Aunt Agnes held up the book.

"Oh yes. And did you enjoy it?"

"Very much. You have excellent taste in books, sir. I have never thought I would enjoy a book of essays, and though I cannot get through them as quickly as I can a novel, I did enjoy it."

"I am happy to hear that you have such an open mind." He smiled.

"Mr. Birtwistle, will you be staying for tea?" Lady Blackstone asked.

"Oh. No, I thank you. I should go. Thank you."

Mr. Birtwistle stood to leave just as Aunt Agnes held out the book to him. He reached for it, but somehow it slipped out of their hands and landed on the floor, with the spine of the book facing up. Mr. Birtwistle picked it up, but when he did, the note Felicity had written fell out of it and fluttered to the floor.

Felicity's heart stopped. She bent and reached for it, but Lady Blackstone got to it first.

Lady Blackstone snatched up the small piece of paper and examined it. Her eyes went wide, then immediately narrowed. She expelled an audible breath through parted lips. Her face began to take on a reddish hue, and her chest rose and fell rapidly.

O God, help us, help us. Please let her not kill us.

"What is this? Felicity?" Lady Blackstone fixed her eyes on her.

Felicity's head began to throb and her vision to blur. "I—I don't know. What do you mean?"

"Mr. Birtwistle, what have these two ladies been doing? Did they have you send a message to . . . someone?"

Mr. Birtwistle rose from his chair. "Send a message? Why should they do—do a thing—a thing such as that? I should be going now. Forgive me." He practically ran to the door. "I can see myself out. Good day, Miss Appleby, Miss Mayson, Lady Blackstone."

Lady Blackstone never took her eyes off Felicity except to glance at Aunt Agnes, who sat frozen, eyes wide, staring back at her.

How could Felicity possibly explain this? Her cheeks tingled, a burning sensation in the bridge of her nose. She didn't need to faint now. She had to think.

"You betrayed me." Lady Blackstone's voice was icy. "I trusted you."

Felicity's stomach sank to her toes. She took deep breaths to try to get rid of the black spots dancing in front of her eyes.

"Mr. Ratley!" Lady Blackstone grabbed Felicity's arm, her fingers sinking into her flesh.

Mr. Ratley hurried into the room.

"Your fiancée just tried to send a note through Mr. Birtwistle to a Mr. McDowell at the Home Office to tell him our plan was moved up to the twenty-sixth of April." She squeezed harder, bruising Felicity's arm as she turned her black eyes on her. "How many notes have you sent? What have you done? What does Mr. Birtwistle know?"

"N-n-nothing. I haven't sent anything." Felicity stood and tried to pull her arm free.

But Lady Blackstone held on. "Look at this note they put in Mr. Birtwistle's book." She held it out to Mr. Ratley.

Felicity cringed, her strength ebbing as Mr. Ratley read it aloud.

Mr. Ratley's face was deathly pale as he stared at Felicity. "You betrayed us? You want us all to hang?"

"No, of course not." They would surely kill her now. She had been caught, and she and Aunt Agnes would be murdered forthwith.

"How could you do it? I thought you loved me." He stared at her, disbelief in his big, round eyes and open mouth.

The color returned to his cheeks as they transformed from pallid to inflamed. "How could you do it?" he repeated. "I demand you tell me why you want me dead."

"Please forgive me, Oliver," she said. "I never wanted you dead. I was frightened. For you. For what might happen to you if you went through with this. Mr. Merrick didn't have any evidence to convict you of treason. He—he would only have made some arrests in London, and you and I could have gotten away. We can still get away, to America or France or—"

"What were you thinking? Did you think he could take better care of you than I could? He left you!"

"I know that. There was nothing between him and me. I am engaged to you."

"You would rather marry that Merrick fellow. And now we shall all hang." Mr. Ratley walked away from her, his shoulders sagging, and put his face in his hands.

Felicity was trembling all over now.

"Felicity still wants to marry you," Lady Blackstone said in a honeyed voice. "Don't you, Felicity?"

"Of course. As much as ever."

"Oh dear. What is happening?" Aunt Agnes was plucking at her sleeves. "I don't understand why Mr. Birtwistle departed so quickly."

"He departed because he caused your niece, Miss Mayson, to be caught betraying your host. Perhaps I should send someone to kill him so he doesn't talk."

"He doesn't know anything," Felicity said quickly as her breath deserted her.

"Doesn't he? Did you not pass information to him at church on Sunday?"

"How could we have done that?" she squeaked breathlessly. "The footman was watching us."

Lady Blackstone pressed a hand to her forehead as if she was thinking. "Mr. Ratley, what do you say? At least she and Mr. Merrick were unable to get the most damning information, which was the locations of our weapons and the names of our leaders. I still have the copy he made in his own handwriting."

But Lady Blackstone was wrong—or at least, Felicity dearly hoped she was.

"Well, Mr. Ratley? Do you still want to marry Miss Mayson, even after she tried to betray us?"

Mr. Ratley seemed to rouse himself and lifted his head. "How can I marry her now, knowing she would betray me at any moment?"

"Oh no, she will not."

"What makes you say that?"

"Once you are married, she cannot testify against her own husband. And murder is so messy. If you don't marry her, we shall have to kill her."

Aunt Agnes moaned, and then a hush fell over the room. Mr. Ratley looked first at Lady Blackstone, then at Felicity. There was a hard, dark, cold expression on his face. She waited for his answer. Was it to be murder? Or marriage?

"I have the special license. We can get married tomorrow."

"Or even today," Lady Blackstone said.

Felicity's heart hammered in her chest. Would she be forced to marry Mr. Ratley to save her life?

She turned to him. His face was unreadable.

"I shall have to think about it. I am still very hurt." He turned away from her, and she was reminded of a child, pouting because he had not gotten what he wanted.

But Lady Blackstone's expression was more akin to that of a falcon setting its sights on a field mouse.

"What else did you tell that rector?" Lady Blackstone hissed, striding forward and pointing her finger in Felicity's face. "Tell me."

Oh dear. She fought against the darkness closing in on her. She felt herself slipping, blacking out. She reached out for the arm of the chair, but her hand had no strength. She was falling.

CHAPTER TWENTY-SIX

Felicity awakened in her bed. Her head and eyelids were so heavy. Mr. Ratley was sitting beside her, his arms folded across his chest.

He fastened his gaze on her. "We were going to rule England together. How could you throw that away?"

She did not answer.

"Lady Blackstone says we should marry. But . . . I am unsure about you now."

How very astute of you. But sarcasm would do her no good. *God, help me.*

"Why am I so thirsty?" Felicity said, her voice sounding weak. "How long have I been asleep?"

"Lady Blackstone gave you something to help you rest. She said . . . well, she said if you didn't marry me, she could . . . she could make you go to sleep and never awake, and I would not have to worry about it anymore. But I still want to marry you, Felicity, if you still want to marry me."

Felicity laughed. It was a weak, quiet laugh, but she couldn't seem to stop it. Should she tell him she'd rather go to sleep and never awake? He would be so hurt. Poor man. He'd have to find someone else to marry. Why did she feel so strange? It must be whatever Lady Blackstone had given her.

The look on Mr. Ratley's face, similar to that of a thwarted child who'd broken his favorite toy, made her laugh again, even weaker than before.

"Why do you laugh? I see nothing amusing."

"It must be the laudanum," Felicity said. "I always laugh when the apothecary gives me laudanum." And she always hated it and refused to take it, even when the doctor insisted.

Mr. Ratley frowned. He reached out and squeezed her hand. "Do you care for me at all, Felicity?"

"I . . . I do not think so clearly . . . at the moment. Perhaps you could come back later?" She could pretend the medicine was affecting her more than it was. And truthfully, she was not sure how much it actually was affecting her. But her life, and that of Aunt Agnes, was dependent on what she and Mr. Ratley said and did.

***

Philip McDowell sat at his desk, busily writing arrest warrants for all the men on the list Felicity had somehow managed to copy and send to him. He felt himself smiling at what ingenuity she must have employed to get the list to him. But his smile quickly faded as he considered what it might have cost her. Was she safe? Her family could have no idea what danger she was in. No, he was the only one who knew. And it grated on him that he was leaving her there, unprotected. The Home Office was scrambling to round up enough men—constables and the militia—to carry out the arrests of all those on the list, but they were not yet ready to go to Doverton Hall and seize Lady Blackstone, Ratley, and the rest of the leaders. It was thought they still had about ten days or so before those leaders would leave Margate to carry out their plans.

God, keep her safe. She is much too kindhearted, too brave, too good in every way to be harmed. Please don't allow Ratley to force her into marrying. God willing, they still had a few days before the wedding.

He'd arrived back in London before sunset on Sunday, exhausted after riding hard half the night and all day. But he'd searched out the Home Secretary, the Viscount Sidmouth, at his town house to tell him what was happening at Doverton Hall.

Then late on Monday, the list he'd risked his life for had come by special courier, copied in Miss Mayson's handwriting. His heart had lurched with admiration and triumph.

But today, Tuesday, he couldn't dispel the feeling that her life was in danger.

He'd tried to ignore it, but it would not go away. He suddenly put down his pen, stood, and made his way to Lord Sidmouth's office.

"Sir, I feel I must travel back to Doverton Hall and insure Miss Mayson is well."

"I absolutely forbid it." Lord Sidmouth stood and addressed him. "Those people will shoot you as soon as they see you."

"I will not let them see me. The rector of the parish is the man who sent the list to me. He must be in the confidence of Miss Mayson. I can discover by or through him if Miss Mayson and her aunt are safe. And if I travel by coach, I can arrive there tomorrow evening."

Lord Sidmouth frowned and stared at the floor a moment, then said, "Very well. I shall assign someone else to write the arrest warrants."

"Thank you, sir." Philip was so relieved at having decided to go back to Doverton Hall that he shook the viscount's hand and had to stifle the whoop that had gathered in his throat.

He hurried out to make the necessary preparations.

***

"Felicity, wake up."

Felicity opened her eyes to see Aunt Agnes standing over her.

"What? What is it?" Her voice sounded quite sleepy. Then she remembered why. Lady Blackstone had come into her room and forced her to drink more tea laced with laudanum. Felicity could taste it. She'd tried to refuse it, but Lady Blackstone had threatened her. Lady Blackstone would hold her nose and force it down her throat. So she drank it.

"Felicity." Aunt Agnes was shaking her shoulder again.

"What? What?"

"I was afraid you would not wake up." Aunt Agnes was crying. She dabbed at her eyes with a handkerchief. "We have to get out of here."

"I think I can get out of bed. I am sure I can walk."

"You are too weak."

"No, no." Felicity raised herself to sitting, but her head began to spin.

"Darling, Lady Blackstone told me you were ill."

Felicity opened her eyes to see Mr. Ratley sitting by her bed. Had she fallen asleep again? The last thing she remembered was sitting up, talking with Aunt Agnes.

"Where is Aunt Agnes?"

"Darling, I'm sorry," Mr. Ratley said, "but we cannot risk calling the doctor. Our plans are coming to fruition very soon. But Lady Blackstone says she is taking good care of you, giving you the medicine the doctor gave her when she was ill with the same malady. I'm sure you will be better very soon." He picked up her hand and patted it in a most annoying way.

"I am very sleepy, and so thirsty. May I have some water?"

"Here is your tea Lady Blackstone sent up," Mr. Ratley said.

"No!" Aunt Agnes stepped into her line of vision. "Lady Blackstone is . . . um, that is, I don't think tea is the best thing for Felicity in her condition. Water is the thing for her."

Aunt Agnes seemed to be pouring a glass of water for her.

Someone was helping her sit up.

"Here, drink this water," Auntie said.

Felicity gulped the water, afraid it might be taken away at any moment.

She must have fallen asleep again, because when she opened her eyes, Lady Blackstone was standing over her, holding a cup in her face, while Mr. Ratley was holding her up in a sitting position.

"Drink it." Lady Blackstone pressed the cup to her lips.

Felicity was too tired to argue or fight with them. She drank it.

"Miss Appleby doesn't know what she's talking about. Everyone knows she's too weak-minded to know what is going on," Lady Blackstone said, apparently speaking to Mr. Ratley. "Keep drinking, dear Felicity," she crooned in her sweetest voice. Felicity drank it, even as her heart filled with dread. Lady Blackstone was poisoning her with laudanum, either so she would not protest or cause any problems, or with the intent of killing her.

"Please don't kill me," Felicity mumbled. "I want to see my mother again."

"My dear," Lady Blackstone said, amusement on her face and in her voice, "no one is killing you. This is for your good, some good medicine for you. You mustn't mind her, Oliver. She is confused, that is all. I know you wish to help her, but the best thing for her is to sleep. Come. We will be back soon to look in on her."

Before they exited the room, sleep was already dragging Felicity back under.

***

Philip went to the rector's house when he arrived in the little village outside Margate near Doverton Hall. He leapt from his hired carriage and hurried to knock at the front door.

The servant who answered showed him into a sitting room. He stood until Mr. Birtwistle came into the room.

"Mr. McDowell. I am Jonathan Birtwistle."

"Very good to meet you, Mr. Birtwistle. I am grateful for the information you sent to me. You cannot know how important and essential it was to the safety of this country and its people."

Mr. Birtwistle's brows rose dramatically. "I am dumbfounded. I never imagined anything so dangerous could be found in our little village."

"At Doverton Hall, specifically. And can you tell me if any other messages have reached you from that house?" Philip's heart pounded hard, as he was finally to discover if Felicity Mayson was safe.

"That is what I wrote to you of."

"You wrote to me?"

"Yes, I took the letter to the village myself to post. But I don't suppose it could have reached you yet. You see, I believe Miss Mayson and Miss Appleby may be in some danger."

"Why? What do you mean?" Philip wanted to grab the man's shoulder and force him to speak faster, but he caught hold of the back of the chair beside him instead.

"I'm not exactly sure myself. I called on Miss Appleby yesterday morning. We were having a pleasant visit, and nothing seemed amiss. Then Miss Appleby tried to pass a book to me, to return it. Somehow I dropped it. When I picked up the book, a piece of paper fell out of it. Lady Blackstone snatched the paper and read it. She seemed quite shocked and angry."

"Do you know what the paper said?" His stomach had sunk to his toes.

"I was not able to read it. I cannot fathom. The only thing I saw was '26 April.' Their first message was also passed to me in a book. Those were the papers that I sent to you, with the names and places, and there was a smaller piece of paper saying please send these papers as quickly as possible to Mr. Philip McDowell at the Home Office, Horse Guards, Whitehall, London. So I did. I sent it by special messenger so it would get to you as quickly as possible."

"I greatly appreciate that, sir. And what happened after Lady Blackstone read the new paper, the one which said the twenty-sixth of April?"

"She waved the paper in the air and said, 'What is this?' Poor Miss Mayson turned as white as a cloud on a sunny day. Then Lady Blackstone asked me if Miss Mayson and Miss Appleby had been sending messages to you through me. I did not answer her but simply said I had to go, and I showed myself out as quickly as possible. But ever since then, I have worried that my action was cowardly. Truly, I did not know that anything nefarious was happening at Doverton Hall, though it is always suspicious when a household so rarely attends church of a Sunday."

Heat spread through Philip's body. "Thank you, Mr. Birtwistle. I must go." He turned to leave.

"Where are you going, if I may ask?"

"To Doverton Hall. I need to rescue Miss Mayson." If it wasn't already too late. *Please, God, let it not be so.*

"Shall I come with you and offer my assistance?"

Philip considered the balding, slightly paunchy rector in front of him. His expression, at least, was very sincere.

"I would be pleased to have your help, Mr. Birtwistle."

***

Philip and Mr. Birtwistle stood behind some trees, watching the house. Philip was fairly certain he knew which window belonged to Miss Mayson and Miss Appleby's room. It was dark now, and the grooms seemed to have already retired for the night.

"It is time. All seems quiet." Philip looked at Mr. Birtwistle. "Are you sure you wish to come with me? The risk is great. They are desperate and have already committed murder. I am sure they would do so again."

"Yes, yes. I shall hold the ladder and assist the ladies."

"Very well. May God save us all."

"Hear, hear!" Mr. Birtwistle had the vibrant, wide-eyed look of a man going into battle for the first time.

Philip hoisted the ladder he had borrowed from the parsonage. He skirted around the stables, doing his best to stay in the shadows and away from the light shining from the house. Only a faint light shone in Miss Mayson's window, and he hoped that meant she was there.

He reached the spot underneath her window and placed the ladder against the side of the house, pressing it down into the soft earth and testing it to make sure it was level and steady. Then he started up, with Mr. Birtwistle holding on to the sides to keep it from toppling.

As he raised his head above the windowsill, he stared in through the glass panes. Inside, a candle was burning on a bedside table. Someone lay on the bed. Was it Miss Mayson? Then he saw Miss Appleby's small form standing beside it.

He grasped the window and pushed it open. He climbed up one more rung, and then sat on the windowsill before swinging himself inside, his boots making a light thud on the floor.

"Oh!" Miss Appleby seemed to shake all over, staring at him.

"Sh!" Philip put a finger to his lips, then whispered, "Gather as many of your and Miss Mayson's things as you can fit into two bags and throw them out the window."

"Oh!"

"Miss Appleby, I am taking you and Miss Mayson from this house immediately, but you must allow me to take you down the ladder."

"I am most agreeable to leave this place," Miss Appleby said, her eyes wide.

He strode to the bed. "Miss Mayson?" When she didn't look at him, he touched her shoulder. She opened her beautiful green eyes, and his heart started beating again. "Can you walk? Is something the matter?"

"Lady Blackstone has been giving her laudanum," Miss Appleby said. "I have been so very worried she's trying to poison poor Felicity with too much."

"Miss Mayson, are you able to walk?"

"I think so." She was rather pale, but still lovely, with her reddish-blond hair spread across her pillow.

"She cannot even sit up." Miss Appleby came hurrying over with two large carpetbags, one in each hand. "I have been packed these two days, hoping we would be rescued, just as in the novels I've read."

He imagined he saw a twinkle in her eye at that last declaration.

"And here is Miss Mayson's cloak." She took the dark-colored garment that had been draped over her arm and held it up.

Philip took it and laid it on the bed. "Miss Appleby, do you think you can make it down the ladder with my help?"

"Oh." Felicity's aunt stood at the window and looked down. "It's Mr. Birtwistle."

"Come." He took Miss Appleby by her waist and lifted her onto the windowsill. "I shall step out onto the ladder, and you step out after me." He quickly let himself out the window and climbed down to the second rung from the top. "Now step out onto this first rung, and I shall not allow you to fall."

To his surprise, the lady stepped out rather nimbly, placing first one foot and then the other onto the top rung. Philip held on to her side with one hand as they began making their way down the rungs of the ladder.

As soon as Miss Appleby's feet were on the ground, Philip climbed back up and through the window.

Miss Mayson's eyes were closed again, as if she had no idea he was there, or ever had been. Philip had a fleeting thought of the "Sleeping

Beauty" fairy tale, imagining kissing her lips and awakening her, dispelling the effects of the laudanum.

Instead, he touched her shoulder and said, "Miss Mayson, please forgive me."

Her eyes fluttered open. "Mr. Merrick?"

"Here is your cloak." He pulled the covers back and laid it over her. "I need you to put your arms around my neck. I'm carrying you out of here."

She blinked but then lifted her arms. He slid his arms underneath her and picked her up.

"You are always carrying me, Mr. Merrick." Her voice sounded groggy and weak.

"I hope you will not be too scandalized." He felt himself smiling. He had her in his arms again, and he would not rest until he had brought her safely home, God willing.

"Scandalized?"

"Yes, especially since you are still in your nightdress. Please forgive me for not allowing you to change first, but we must be quick."

He sat her on the windowsill, and, holding her arm so she wouldn't fall, he quickly wrapped the cloak around her shoulders and fastened it under her chin. Then he looked down. He'd have to carry her down the ladder.

With a hand against her back, he quickly climbed out the window and stood on the second rung. He carefully pulled her into his arms, then shifted her forward and over one shoulder. Holding on to her upper legs with one hand, he held on to the ladder with the other and made his way slowly but steadily, one rung at a time. Miss Mayson did not protest or even make a sound. He wondered if she was already asleep again.

How much laudanum had they given her? Had he come so close to saving her only to have her perish now?

CHAPTER TWENTY-SEVEN

All of Felicity's weight was resting on her stomach, making it difficult to breathe. Something was pressing against the back of her thighs. She was so sleepy—and so thirsty—but she was too uncomfortable not to open her eyes.

"Mr. Birtwistle."

The rector stood below her on the ground as she slowly moved toward him. Someone was carrying her over his shoulder.

"Mr. Merrick . . . no, Mr. McDowell . . . is that you?" Thank heavens. She was glad to feel the cool night air on her face. It had been so stuffy in that room where Lady Blackstone had been trying to poison her.

"Forgive me, Miss Mayson," Mr. McDowell said. They seemed to be floating above the ground but descending gradually. Finally, he set her feet on the ground, but only for a moment. He immediately lifted her, cradling her in his arms, and held her against his chest. She was much more comfortable now.

Felicity sighed. "I think this must be one of the dreams I keep having."

"What kind of dreams, Miss Mayson?"

He was walking with her now, and she was vaguely aware of Mr. Birtwistle and Aunt Agnes hurrying alongside them.

"I keep having these strange dreams. I guess it's the laudanum. It makes me so tired, I just sleep and dream. But I like this one." She laid her hand on his chest, beside his neckcloth. She could feel his body heat through the layers of clothing, even though it was a cool night.

"You must be very strong to carry me, Mr. McDowell. And do you not like how in dreams you can say anything that comes to your mind? You don't have to worry about rules or about being proper. Even my sweet and proper friend Julia Langdon would not object to speaking one's mind in a dream, since no one seems to remember it when they're awake."

He seemed to be walking quite fast and jostling her quite a bit, and his breath was coming faster.

"Perhaps you should stop and rest, Mr. McDowell." Perhaps she should rest as well. Her eyelids didn't seem to want to open anymore. Poor Mr. McDowell. She hoped he would not exhaust himself too much.

***

Philip heard the shouts behind them. Lady Blackstone must have discovered Miss Mayson and Miss Appleby missing from their room.

Philip glanced over his shoulder. The high hedges from the garden hid them from the house, and it was blessedly dark.

"Mr. McDowell, I hope you know of a good hiding place," Mr. Birtwistle said, breathing harder than Philip was. "I'm afraid we'll never make it to the parsonage before they catch up to us."

He was right. Philip couldn't keep up this pace for long while carrying another person, even if that person was as small and still as Miss Mayson.

"I have an idea. Follow me." Philip headed in the direction of the "shell grotto." The underground cave was easier to find since the conspirators had moved their cache of guns elsewhere. The entrance had been dug out, and their many footprints had made a very clear path to it.

The shouts behind them had grown louder and more numerous. It was dark, but Lady Blackstone and her henchmen might guess that they had gone to hide in the grotto. But he had no choice. He couldn't think of anywhere else for them to hide. He prayed the traitors would assume he had taken the ladies to the parsonage or that they had somehow gotten away on horseback. He could only hope they didn't find his hired coach and horses, which were waiting for them in Mr. Birtwistle's carriage house.

The muscles in his arms burned as he reached the entrance of the grotto, across which someone had placed a large, flat piece of wood.

Philip stood Miss Mayson on her feet. "Mr. Birtwistle, can you and Miss Appleby make sure Miss Mayson doesn't fall?"

They held her up, letting her lean on them, while Philip took hold of the board and shoved it away from the gaping hole that was the entrance to the cave. The small, round hole over the middle of the grotto that would let in the moonlight was covered by a branch, but he could not risk uncovering that.

Mr. Birtwistle seemed to be having trouble keeping Miss Mayson upright.

"Go on," Philip told him and Miss Appleby. "I shall take Miss Mayson." He picked her up again and followed them down the earthen steps, careful not to stumble with his burden. Once inside, he put her in Mr. Birtwistle and Miss Appleby's care and hurried back up the steps. He placed the board over the entrance and hurried down the steps into the pitch blackness of the underground grotto.

***

Felicity could feel herself being carried again, but when she opened her eyes, she couldn't see anything.

"Where am I?" she asked. "It's so dark."

The laudanum was still making her thoughts fuzzy, and though she knew, in a hovering sort of way, that she was in danger, she felt . . . buoyant and rather happy.

"We're in the shell grotto," Mr. McDowell's voice said, his chest rumbling against her ear. "We're moving to the inner chamber. I'm afraid there may not be any more light there than there is here."

She could hear his sleeve brushing against the walls as he moved. His breath was a bit labored. He must be exhausted from carrying her. She was exhausted, and she had not even been walking.

She heard herself let out a long sigh. "You are so strong." It was as if she was hearing herself while floating above her body—a very strange feeling but not entirely unpleasant.

"I have done quite a bit of fencing," he said. "And I boxed, but I was not very good at that."

"Mr. McDowell, I can believe that you would be good at everything you ever tried."

He laughed, a short, labored sound. "Flattery, Miss Mayson."

Was she speaking in an improper way? She rather believed she was, but she could not seem to stop herself. Besides, talking was keeping her from falling asleep again.

"You shouldn't have come back for me, Mr. McDowell," she heard herself say in a slow, drawling voice, still floating. "You are in great danger, and I do not want any harm to come to you. But I must say, I am grateful. For I believe my aunt and I would have been killed, or I would have been, at least." She laughed—it just bubbled up and out.

"Felicity," Aunt Agnes said from nearby. "You are talking nonsense. Poor Mr. McDowell."

"Am I vexing you, Mr. McDowell?"

"Not at all. For one thing, it is good for Miss Mayson to keep talking, because it is better to keep awake a person who has taken too much laudanum. And besides that, it is rare in our society to hear what anyone truly thinks."

"Mr. McDowell thinks women should speak their minds." Felicity heard herself laugh again. She seemed to have little control, so it was good Mr. McDowell didn't mind. "Perhaps we will scandalize Mr. Birtwistle. Are you here, Mr. Birtwistle?"

"I am indeed. I am very sorry, Miss Mayson, that you have been treated so ill by your own aunt, Lady Blackstone."

"She is not a blood relation, Mr. Birtwistle."

"Oh, I see."

Mr. McDowell seemed to be depositing her on the floor. She had been so warm in his arms, and now she felt a distinct chill.

"This floor is cold. Is it marble?"

"I believe it is chalk stone and possibly dirt. I'm terribly sorry."

"Oh, please do not be sorry, Mr. McDowell." Felicity was leaning against the wall of the grotto and could feel the tiny shells pressing against her back. "I was happy to be able to see this place. It is very beautiful, is it not, Mr. McDowell?"

"It is very beautiful," Mr. McDowell said.

"It's a shame it is too dark for Mr. Birtwistle and Miss Appleby to see it."

She heard a shuffling on the floor beside her. "Are you sitting by me, Mr. McDowell?"

"I am. And Miss Appleby and Mr. Birtwistle are resting beside me. But we had better lower our voices and speak in a whisper just now, as Lady Blackstone and her men could be nearby searching for us."

"Oh yes, very wise," Felicity whispered back. "Somehow it makes things seem very intimate, whispering in the dark, as we are doing." She smiled, wanting to laugh but fearing she would disobey their new rule to be quiet. "Gracious, but I am so thirsty."

"It's the laudanum," Mr. McDowell said. "I am sorry we have no water, but I shall get you some as soon as I can."

"You are so kind, Mr. McDowell."

It was dark . . . so dark in the grotto. No one spoke, and she felt herself drifting . . .

***

Philip could hear Miss Mayson's breathing change and knew she had fallen asleep again. She had obviously been talking with a great deal less self-restraint than she would normally use. Lady Blackstone must have been trying to slowly murder her with the laudanum, probably to fool Mr. Ratley, whom he could not imagine would sanction the murder of his fiancée—even though she *had* betrayed them.

Poor girl. His heart squeezed with sympathy at the thought of waking her. But he'd be much sadder if she never awakened.

"Miss Mayson?" He touched her shoulder, and she started to fall over.

He put an arm around her to straighten her, but then she slid toward him. He scooted closer and let her lay her head on his shoulder. After all, no one could see them anyway.

"Miss Mayson?" he whispered again. "Are you awake? Don't you have anything to say?"

"Is that you, Mr. McDowell?" She inhaled rather loudly and sighed. "Are you sure this is not a dream? Because it feels as if it were a dream."

"How does it feel as if it were a dream, Miss Mayson?"

"I suppose because it's so dark and I'm so sleepy. And it is so strange and dreamlike to be in the shell grotto, sitting on the dirt in my night-dress, with you, Mr. McDowell." She sighed again. "I thought I would likely never see you again, and though I was so happy you had escaped the dreadful end Lady Blackstone surely had planned for you, I was sad."

"Why were you sad, Miss Mayson?" He kept his voice low, hoping Miss Appleby and Mr. Birtwistle were not listening to this conversation, for he had an idea that Miss Mayson was about to say something very improper that she would regret—if she remembered it later.

"I was sad," she said softly, "because I was engaged to marry a man with questionable morals. I was sad because I was afraid you would not think well of me for having been engaged to such a man. I was sad because you are ever so much handsomer than Mr. Ratley. And I was sad because I would never kiss your wonderful lips."

He suddenly felt her hand on his chin, fingertips touching his skin through the day's growth of beard.

He should not enjoy her touch. He should remove her hand from his face. But . . . her touch was so gentle. He closed his eyes and pictured her face and imagined a tender expression on her perfect mouth. But then her fingers fell away. He squeezed his eyes shut and concentrated on remembering exactly how they had felt.

"I don't think you could feel about me the way I feel about you," she said.

"Why do you say that?" His heart was in his throat.

"You saw me kissing Mr. Ratley. I kissed him so you would not get caught and get killed, but I felt ashamed afterward." She expelled a forceful breath.

"Ashamed?"

"I didn't love Mr. Ratley. If I ever loved him, the feeling only lasted a day. But when I kissed him . . . I was only manipulating him. I felt . . . ugly and wrong."

"Please don't feel that way, Miss Mayson. I understand why you had to do it. It was very brave of you."

He leaned over until his nose touched her hair. She smelled of flowers and warmth. He pressed his lips lightly against her forehead. Her skin was as soft as he had imagined it.

"Mr. McDowell."

"Yes?"

"Did you kiss my forehead?"

"Perhaps."

"I hope you don't think I am a woman of loose virtue."

"Indeed, I do not. Forgive me if I have offended."

"I am not offended." She pressed closer and hugged his arm. "But I am very sleepy. And thirsty."

Voices drifted into the cave through the round opening overhead. Had they tracked them here, to the grotto? Or were they on the path to the parsonage?

"What will happen if they find us here?" she asked.

"I have a pistol in my coat pocket, and I will have to shoot them. That is, with your permission."

"Why do you need my permission?"

"Because they may shoot back. They could shoot us."

"Oh, then I give you my permission. But I don't think they could shoot us, because you will shoot them first."

Her argument was not rational, for several reasons, but he said, "Thank you, Miss Mayson. I appreciate that you trust me to shoot better than our enemies."

"I do trust you." She seemed to rub her cheek against his arm.

His heart expanded, filling his chest with warmth.

He had forgotten about the voices. He should be listening to see if they were coming closer. Straining to hear them, he listened until his ears roared with the silence. The voices had gone.

And Miss Mayson was asleep again.

***

Felicity was jostled awake as someone lifted her and began carrying her.

"Where are we?"

"We're leaving the shell grotto," Mr. McDowell said. "We will see if we can make it to the carriage I stowed away in Mr. Birtwistle's carriage shed."

"You shouldn't have to carry me everywhere. I should be able to walk." She had been walking for years, after all.

"Stand here. Miss Appleby, Mr. Birtwistle, make sure she doesn't fall."

Mr. McDowell held on to Felicity's arms until someone else came near and put an arm around her.

"I have her," Mr. Birtwistle said.

She heard rustling, and a bit of light filled her hungry eyes. She took a step toward that light, and Mr. McDowell came back and put an arm around her. He helped her up the earthen steps and out into the night air. He pulled her along, but gently, as he kept up a quick pace. Mr. Birtwistle and Aunt Agnes were close by—she could see them by the moonlight overhead. She held on to Mr. McDowell's coat to keep her balance.

If she had been at liberty to speak, she would have said, "I hope I remember this night forever."

They had been walking for a while when they heard horses coming, and Mr. McDowell directed them into the trees. They waited, and Lady Blackstone and Mr. Ratley appeared on horseback in front of them.

"They must have gone to London. Perhaps we can catch up to them," Mr. Ratley said.

"Check all the inns between here and London," Lady Blackstone said, an edge in her voice. "They can't have gone far on horseback, not with Miss Mayson, and there were no carriage tracks near the house."

Mr. Ratley nodded, and they both spurred their horses forward.

Felicity stared at Mr. McDowell's face, which was unmoving as he watched Lady Blackstone and Mr. Ratley leave. Such a handsome face. There was so much courage and loyalty and integrity in that face. She loved it. She loved him.

Just what she had been trying to avoid. And yet . . . it felt so good to love someone, someone who had proven he was of good character, even if he did not return her love.

The pain, no doubt, would come later.

CHAPTER TWENTY-EIGHT

Felicity sat in her parents' drawing room trying to study her book on the Chinese language. Her things had been sent to her from the Home Office the day before. Apparently, when the officials and militiamen went to arrest Lady Blackstone and Mr. Ratley the morning after Mr. McDowell's daring rescue, Lady Blackstone and the rest of their group had fled. But Lord Sidmouth's men had collected Felicity's and Aunt Agnes's things for them.

Three days had passed since she and Aunt Agnes had ridden back to London in Mr. McDowell's hired carriage. She remembered little of the trip besides waking up snuggled against Mr. McDowell's arm. She closed her eyes and groaned just thinking about it. What must he think of her?

Thankfully, she also remembered little of her rescue from Doverton Hall, but enough to know that she had said some very improper things. Felicity had asked Aunt Agnes, *Was I very improper? Did I say and do many terrible things?* Her aunt had blushed to the roots of her hair, coughed, and stammered, *It was only Mr. Birtwistle, Mr. McDowell, and myself who heard you. They are gentlemen and will never tell anyone.*

Felicity let out a pent-up breath. Well, it was not her fault, after all. She had been forced to take more laudanum than anyone should ingest. Hopefully, Mr. McDowell would not think the less of her.

She tried to concentrate on the images in her book. But instead of seeing Chinese, she kept seeing Mr. McDowell and all the events of the previous few weeks.

She sighed again and laid the book aside. It was no use trying to study. Her heart wasn't in it. She wasn't even sure she wanted to go to China to be a missionary, even if it was possible.

The front door opened and shut. Voices and then footsteps sounded on the stairs. Someone was here.

"Mr. Philip McDowell," the servant announced as Mr. McDowell entered the room.

"Mr. McDowell," Felicity acknowledged, her heart fluttering like a mad bird inside her chest. She had an irrational urge to throw her arms around him, seeing him again for the first time since he'd saved her, since he'd carried her in his arms, taking such gentle care of her. Only by his courage, strength, and cunning—and the favor and kindness of Providence—had she escaped being murdered. And when she remembered her laudanum-induced babbling, her face heated.

His eyes seemed even bluer than she remembered, with sunlight streaming in through the windows and highlighting the purple bruise on his cheekbone.

He bowed.

She did her best to remember her manners, but her heart had stopped fluttering and was now pounding so hard she wondered if he could hear it.

"Won't you please sit down?"

They both sat, he on the sofa and she on a nearby chair.

"I was hoping I could speak with you alone, just for a moment," Mr. McDowell said.

Her breath shallowed and her heart beat double time. How she had missed talking to him, as they had already had many private conversations.

He went on. "But first . . . I wanted to inquire after your health, Miss Mayson."

"Oh, I am completely recovered now, thanks to you, Mr. McDowell." Just as her cheeks had stopped burning, she felt herself blushing again.

"I am very glad to hear it. I was concerned about the effects of the laudanum Lady Blackstone gave you."

"No lasting ill effects, thank goodness. And you? Are you recovered from your injuries?"

"I am well. No lasting effects."

"Except for the bruise on your face. It looks painful." How she longed to let her fingers graze lightly over the skin . . . *Oh dear.* She must control her thoughts.

"The bruise will disappear in time." He smiled at her.

"Mr. McDowell, I want to apologize," Felicity said quickly. "I know I must have said some highly improper things the night you came to rescue my aunt and me from Doverton Hall."

"Please." He held up a hand. "Do not apologize for anything. I realize . . . you were not yourself. I could not begin to find fault with your behavior."

His look was so gentle and sincere.

"You are very kind, Mr. McDowell."

"And you were very brave, Miss Mayson. I am grateful you were there. No one else could have done better at thwarting the threat to our government and the royal family."

"Thank you for saying so." Had she been brave? Mostly, she had simply done what she had to in order to save herself. "You were the truly brave one."

He smiled. She hadn't noticed before how his eyes sparkled when he smiled.

"I was only doing my duty. But Miss Mayson, there is another reason why I came today."

"Oh?" Her pounding heart stole her breath.

"I also came here to say how sorry I am for the way I behaved toward you when we were at Doverton Hall."

"What do you mean?"

"I mean that . . ." He swallowed, his throat bobbing. His cheerful demeanor was quickly replaced by an intense look in his eyes, a tension around his mouth, and a crease in his forehead. "Under normal circumstances, I never would have put your safety at a lower priority. I am ashamed I did not take you with me when I escaped, that I left you there, in danger, to do the task I came to do, which was to get all the information about the insurrectionists back to the Home Office."

"You had no choice. Besides, you were the one who wrote down the information, risking your life to do so, and you were nearly killed trying to get it back to London."

"But I want you to know that I am horrified at the thought that I put you in danger and left you there, that you could have been killed. I thank God with all my heart that you were not seriously harmed." His hand was poised, clawlike, over his chest.

So many thoughts and feelings were tearing through her. He was sorry he had left her in harm's way, but did that indicate that he had feelings for her? Wouldn't he be sorry he had left any woman in danger, even if he felt no attachment to her?

"Forgive me if I have made you uncomfortable, but I need to know you forgive me for not keeping you perfectly safe. I could not bear to go another day without telling you, without asking your forgiveness. Nothing less than my duty to my country and concern for the lives of hundreds of people would have stopped me from taking you safely back to London at the first opportunity."

Her heart was thumping madly, but she managed to say, "You did keep me safe. You burned that first letter I wrote, which easily could have gotten me killed, and that is only one on a long list of things you did to keep me safe. And I do forgive you, though there is truly nothing to forgive. We both did what we thought best for our country."

"Thank you, Miss Mayson." Mr. McDowell expelled a breath, and the tension dissipated from his features, his mouth relaxing into a slight smile. "You are a great English lady, even if the history books never tell of your courageous deeds."

"Now you are flattering me." Felicity shook her head.

Her brother's loud voice boomed from the stairs. He was calling to Mother, then she answered him in a much softer tone. Soon they both entered the room.

"Oh, Mr. McDowell." Mother's face split into a pleased smile. "I did not know we had company."

"You have met, then?" Felicity asked, biting her lip at the way her brother was staring at Mr. McDowell with a goofy half grin.

"We met the morning he brought you and Aunt Agnes home from Doverton Hall, when he explained what had been happening there. How are you, Mr. McDowell?"

He bowed respectfully. "Very well, Mrs. Mayson."

"Won't you come and dine with us this evening?" she asked. "Mr. Mayson and I would dearly love to speak with you at more length and thank you for bringing our precious daughter and her aunt home. From what Felicity tells me, it was at great personal risk. Please do allow us to thank you."

"I would be delighted to accept your offer."

For the rest of his visit, he talked with Felicity's mother and brother, who asked question after question about his duties as an agent for the Home Office. He actually seemed different than he had at Doverton

Hall. Now a smile always seemed to be hovering on his lips, whereas before he had seemed much more sober and subdued.

When he left, he cast a wistful look at Felicity, then gave her a secretive smile before leaving and promising to come back for dinner.

***

When he returned for dinner, Felicity's large family kept Mr. McDowell occupied with questions.

"Have you ever killed anyone?" her youngest brother, Gilbert, asked.

"Gilbert!" Mother scolded, her tone and look severe.

Mr. McDowell's mouth twisted, then relaxed into a smile. "Fortunately, I have not."

"What did you do to get that bruise on your face?" Timothy, her fourth-oldest brother, asked.

"I can answer that," Felicity said. Everyone turned to her. "He was outnumbered twenty to one, and Lady Blackstone had a gun pointed at him."

Her brothers all seemed to exclaim at once, asking more questions, and suddenly Felicity's throat closed. Tears stung the back of her eyes as she remembered him lying on the floor with his shirt off and his hands behind his back, his face bleeding.

They were looking at her again, waiting for her to go on and answer their questions. She shook her head, blinking back the tears.

Mr. McDowell jumped in. "I was surrounded, the gun barrel pressed to my neck. They tied my hands behind my back, and then the largest man there—he must have been as tall as Goliath with giant hulking shoulders—pulled back his fist and . . . that's how I got this."

His cocky half grin enabled Felicity to let out a deep breath and the tears to dry up. He sent a concerned glance her way, such a gentle look, it tugged at her heart.

Just being in his presence, seeing his friendly smile and his easy manner with her brothers, all Felicity's sadness that had lingered since she'd returned home seemed to flee. How wonderful that he—that they both—were alive and well.

***

The next day Felicity was sitting at the small desk in the sitting room, writing about her experiences at Doverton Hall. She wasn't sure she'd ever let anyone read it, but it felt good to put her thoughts and feelings on paper. And perhaps when she was able to write out all that had happened, she would finally be able to start her treatise on society's egregious attitudes about marriage.

She had just finished covering an entire sheet of paper with her writing and was reaching for a second one when a servant came to the doorway and announced Felicity's friends Julia and Leorah.

Felicity stood to meet them, and she embraced them each in turn.

"Felicity, when did you arrive back in London?" Leorah cried.

"Four days ago, but I needed two days to rest." To wake up, more like.

"You should have sent word to us," Julia said, but not in a scolding way. It was difficult to imagine Julia scolding anyone, even her two children, once they were old enough to get into mischief.

"Now," Leorah said, putting a hand on her hip, "you must not waste time. Tell us, what are these rumors we're hearing?"

"What have you heard?"

"It's in this morning's papers that a gang of insurrectionists was meeting at Doverton Hall." Leorah's eyes were wide as she pinned Felicity with an intense stare.

With a little smile, Felicity said, "It is true, I'm afraid."

Julia and Leorah stared with their mouths open.

Felicity sighed and proceeded to tell them the entire story. Her friends interjected occasionally, but mostly they listened with rapt attention.

"Felicity, you have had quite the adventure," Julia said.

"I am impressed," Leorah said, "that you could be so courageous, thwarting an actual revolution and the murder of hundreds, maybe thousands—the Prince Regent and my husband included!"

"Oh, I am sure your husband and Julia's would have thwarted them if Mr. McDowell and I had not."

"Oh no, you cannot throw off the credit that easily. You are a hero, Felicity."

"Indeed, you are." Julia leaned forward and squeezed Felicity's hand. "And what of Mr. McDowell? Have you heard from him since he brought you and Miss Appleby home?"

Felicity nodded. "He called on me yesterday, and Mother invited him to dinner."

"Were you alone with him?"

"For several minutes."

"What did he say?" Leorah's voice was breathless.

"He said he was sorry for leaving me in danger."

"Oh," Julia said. "But it sounds as though he was very interested in getting further acquainted with your mother and father. Is that not so?"

"Perhaps."

Leorah said, "Then he will surely call on you again."

Julia placed a hand on her heart. "It is so romantic, carrying you out of a window and down a ladder, taking care of you while you were poisoned with laudanum." She sighed.

"Well, perhaps it would be, if . . ."

"If what?"

"If I thought he cared for me."

"How could he not?" Leorah and Julia both exclaimed.

"I have no fortune, and neither does he."

Both their faces fell. Yes, they had forgotten that fact.

"He did come back for you, though, did he not?" Leorah's brows lifted.

"Yes, but perhaps that was only because his superiors told him to. They probably needed me as a witness to prosecute Lady Blackstone and the others."

"Have they asked you to serve as a witness?"

"Not yet. But they surely will."

"I don't see how he could not be in love with you, Felicity." Julia pressed a hand to her heart again. "And you know, the Prince Regent is likely to reward you both for such heroic deeds. He will surely ask to marry you. You are so generous and kindhearted, so witty, and beautiful besides. He'd be a fool—"

"Mr. Philip McDowell," the servant announced.

All three of them jumped and turned toward the doorway.

Julia was blushing bright red, and Felicity's own face tingled as he made his way into the room.

"Lady Withinghall and Mrs. Langdon," Felicity said, swallowing the lump in her throat, "allow me to introduce Mr. Philip McDowell. Mr. McDowell, these are my dear friends, the Viscountess Leorah Withinghall and Mrs. Julia Langdon."

Mr. McDowell bowed. He made his way to a chair, and then Felicity's mother entered the room. He stood, and Mother greeted him, then they all sat and tried to think of things to say to one another. After a few minutes of inane comments about the weather and the roads that no one gave much thought to, Mr. McDowell cleared his throat and looked at Felicity.

Mother, Leorah, and Julia were watching them. But then they all three seemed to turn away and start talking quietly amongst themselves.

"I have a specific message for you, Miss Mayson."

"Oh?"

"The Home Secretary, Lord Sidmouth, wishes you to come to his office tomorrow and give a statement about everything that happened at Doverton Hall."

"Do they not have enough evidence against Lady Blackstone?"

"They do—we confiscated pamphlets that they had been distributing to the militia in an effort to convert them to their cause. It is more than enough to condemn Lady Blackstone and the other insurrectionists—as long as the incriminating literature can be tied to her and Ratley. However, most of their number have fled the country or are missing. They realized, of course, that they were about to be arrested and charged with treason."

"I see."

"But there is another reason for having you come and make a statement. I believe, for what you did to secure the list of leaders and their whereabouts, there will be a reward for you."

"A reward?" Until Julia had mentioned it a few minutes before, it had not entered Felicity's mind that such a thing might happen.

"You helped to save our royal family from the threat of execution, after all, though the public may never hear of your role in their salvation. The Prince Regent cares very much about his life and the lives of his family and Parliament, and he has the means and power to reward those he wishes to favor."

"I suppose he will wish to reward you as well. After all, you did most of the work."

"I can hope, at least."

"Mr. McDowell," Leorah said suddenly.

Leorah, Julia, and Mother were all looking quite bright-eyed and smiling.

"Lord Withinghall and I will be giving a ball five days hence. Will you be able to attend?"

This was the first Felicity was hearing of it. She very much suspected Leorah had only just decided to give a ball, and without consulting her husband.

"That is, the ball will be in either five or seven days. Would you be able to come either of those days?" Leorah grimaced a bit.

Felicity had to cover her mouth to stifle a laugh.

"Why yes, my lady. I can come either of those evenings." Mr. McDowell smiled. Such perfect teeth he had. Felicity had rarely seen them before yesterday. And how well formed his chin and jawline were. Even with the bruise on his face, he was the most handsome man she knew.

"And can you come tomorrow for dinner? At six o'clock?" Felicity's mother was looking at him with raised brows.

"Yes, ma'am. I would be delighted to accept."

This was becoming embarrassing. Did he see right through all the invitations?

Soon after, while the other three women were talking amongst themselves, Mr. McDowell asked Felicity, "Will you reserve the first two dances at the ball for me?"

"It would be my pleasure."

A few minutes later, when he took his leave of them, he gave Felicity a particularly long look that made her stomach flip.

***

After her friends left, Felicity received her summons from the Home Secretary and proceeded to his office the next day. Her mother went with her. She kept looking around for Mr. McDowell but did not see him.

Felicity gave a full account of all that had happened with Lady Blackstone and Mr. Ratley in the four weeks she'd spent at Doverton Hall, sometimes blushing at the parts pertaining to Mr. Ratley and their engagement. Finally, when they had written down her entire account and were dismissing her, she asked, "Do you know what has happened to them—to Lady Blackstone and Mr. Ratley and the others?"

"It will probably be in the papers soon, but we believe Lady Blackstone and Mr. Ratley fled to France, and some of the other members of their group took a ship to America before we were able to apprehend them. But it is just as well, I imagine," Lord Sidmouth said. "They are away from England—a very good thing—and we shall not have the awkwardness of a public trial and execution, which might excite sympathy for them and for their cause."

"Yes, of course. I am very glad to hear they are gone." And truthfully, she was relieved they would not be hanged, for many reasons, not least of which was so she would not feel responsible for their deaths.

***

In the few days leading up to Lord and Lady Withinghall's ball, Mr. McDowell dined with Felicity's family twice, and he came to call on her once. He was very attentive to her but also quite friendly to the rest of her family. She was never alone with him or able to have a private word, there were so many people in her house at all times.

Her brothers—the ones who were still living at home—all seemed to like Mr. McDowell. It was almost as if they had always known each other. They talked and laughed together. He even drew her father into their conversations. Everyone was cheerful when Mr. McDowell was around.

The day of the ball arrived, and even her brothers seemed interested in Felicity, looking in on her, commenting on her appearance, and asking her how she was feeling.

"Mr. McDowell told me his favorite color was blue," Gilbert said with a smile. "Don't you have a blue dress you could wear?"

"Be off with you and your fashion advice." Felicity laughed and shooed him out the door.

Her mother entered her room.

"What dress will you wear tonight, my dear? I wish we had ordered you a new one just for the occasion."

"There wasn't time for that, Mother. Leorah only decided to give a ball five days ago."

"Well, your blue gown is very becoming. But so is your green one. I do believe this darker blue gown is the prettiest, though. What do you think, my dear?"

Her mother calling her "my dear" brought to mind Lady Blackstone. Felicity shuddered. "Oh yes, that one is fine."

"What time should I send Millie up to dress your hair? I think about five o'clock. And you should be sure to eat something just before we go, since I don't want you to have a fainting spell. You know how you are."

"I'll be perfectly well, Mother." Felicity laughed.

Tonight, she would dance the first two dances with Mr. McDowell. Her heart fairly soared out of her chest. Tonight, she would not worry who might reject her or look down their noses at her. She would dance and laugh at every snub she might previously have cried over. She would remember all the times she and Mr. McDowell had assisted each other, had met secretly in the library closet and talked over how they would save the royal family and the government officials of Great Britain. She would revel in Mr. McDowell's smiles, the fact that he no longer looked serious all the time. She would hang on his every word, laugh at every amusing thing he said, and exult in every time she could make him laugh.

When Felicity and her family arrived at the Viscount Withinghall's fashionable home that night, she glanced around at the other guests. Just as Leorah came and embraced her, Felicity caught sight of Mr. McDowell speaking with Nicholas Langdon, Leorah's brother. They both had worked at the Home Office, she suddenly realized. No wonder they were acquainted.

"Mr. McDowell is looking very handsome this evening," Leorah said with a twinkle in her eye.

Felicity took a deep breath, suddenly wondering where all her joy and confidence had flown to. "He always looks handsome to me," she confided. "But let us talk of something besides him so that I don't feel so nervous. Tell me something about you."

"Oh well, I do have a bit of news, something I had been hoping."

"Hoping?"

"I am expecting a baby."

Felicity's heart gave a lurch, and she squeezed Leorah's arms. "I am so happy for you."

"Yes, it had been two years, nearly—I suppose that is not an overly long time—but I had begun to worry, but now . . . We are so pleased, as you can imagine."

Felicity glanced over and spotted Lord Withinghall, Leorah's husband, whom she had often thought frightening and intimidating. Today, he looked relaxed and was smiling at one of their guests.

"I cannot tell you how wonderful I think that is, Leorah. You and Lord Withinghall will be such wonderful parents." How happy they would be now, to share their love with a child. Felicity's eyes filled with tears.

"Now, don't you cry!" Leorah said, laughing. "You know I cannot abide tears, and I've actually cried myself, more than I wish to admit, the last two days since I found out. It is ridiculous."

They both laughed rather watery laughs.

"And wouldn't you know? Julia is pregnant again as well." Leorah rolled her eyes. "That girl will end up with ten babies before she's done."

"Or thirteen."

Leorah covered her mouth. "Forgive me, darling, I did not mean to disparage."

"Of course not, do not worry." Felicity laughed, but Leorah's "darling" stirred up memories of Mr. Ratley. She forced back a shudder.

They talked a few moments longer, with Felicity trying to stop herself from glancing at Mr. McDowell. Soon, she saw him glancing her way as well. When Leorah had to leave to greet some more of her guests, Felicity started toward Mr. McDowell, but he was suddenly surrounded by three young ladies.

Felicity could not expect that women would ignore him, but it did make her heart sink. Had she allowed herself to expect too much, that Mr. McDowell would pay attention only to her? Or was this to be like so many other balls at which the eligible gentlemen would show initial interest, only to ignore her when they discovered she had no fortune?

No, Mr. McDowell already knew she had no fortune.

She took a deep breath and proceeded down the hall to the room where refreshments were being provided, passing right by Mr. McDowell, whose attention had been captured by one of the ladies addressing him.

Felicity took a cup of lemonade and sipped it. What did she care if Mr. McDowell was talking with other women? She would not think of him at all.

He appeared in the open doorway, and his gaze caught hers.

"Miss Mayson."

CHAPTER TWENTY-NINE

Felicity's heart skipped a few beats as Mr. McDowell came to stand in front of her with the most attractive smile she had ever seen.

"Mr. McDowell, I hope you don't mind me saying that you seem so much more cheerful now than when you were at Doverton Hall."

"I think you are seeing me now as my usual self."

"Yes, of course. You had a job to do there, a very serious one."

"And which side of me do you prefer?" He raised his brows at her.

"I like your cheerful side very much, your smile, and how relaxed you seem. Although, your more serious side showed your courage and character." So seldom did she say these sorts of things. Was she being flirtatious? She wanted to converse with Mr. McDowell, to bask in his friendship, to remember how strong and capable he had been.

She also couldn't stop remembering how it felt when he held her in his arms. Was he remembering it too?

More people began to crowd in for refreshments before the dancing began. Felicity and Mr. McDowell were practically forced from the room and toward the ballroom.

When the music began for the first dance, Mr. McDowell escorted Felicity to the dance floor. How it made her heart expand to see him across from her, smiling, his gaze never wavering, intent on her. Every time his hand touched hers, her heart beat a little faster.

The second dance began just as enjoyably—even more so, since the pace was slower. He held her hand longer than necessary as they moved side by side and then faced each other to wait for their next turn. Was she imagining that he was looking at her in a way that was different than the way he looked at everyone else? Did she imagine that there was a questioning in his eyes, as if he was searching for something?

When the first two dances were over, a man came over to speak to Mr. McDowell. Felicity stood nearby, pretending to watch the dancers, but she was actually looking at Mr. McDowell, watching how he interacted with his friend, trying to imagine what he was saying and thinking as he spoke.

Truly, she was being ridiculous.

She moved away, and someone touched her arm from behind. She turned and found a woman smiling at her.

"Miss Felicity Mayson? You may not remember me, but I am Mrs. Ferguson. Your mother and I are well acquainted. I was just wondering about things I have been reading and hearing, some of it concerning you. You don't mind if I ask, do you?"

"I don't suppose—"

"Well, some say you are engaged to a Mr. Ratfield or Ratcliffe, whom you met at Lady Blackstone's home in Margate, and that you were all plotting to revolt against the government."

"Is that what some say, Mrs. Ferguson? What else do some say?"

"Oh, that Lady Blackstone and Mr. Ratcliffe or Rat-something fled the country together, that they are joining with the Jacobins in France."

"That sounds like gossip to me, Mrs. Ferguson. And if I *were* engaged to a Mr. Rat-something, I would be with him now. But I am not."

"What say you in reply to what these people are saying?"

"I say nothing."

"I hope I have not given offense."

"Not at all, but I am wanted elsewhere. Please excuse me." Felicity was already walking away, praying desperately she would see Julia or Leorah or—

"Miss Mayson? Are you well?"

She turned. Mr. McDowell was standing behind her.

"Yes, of course." She smiled, quite forgetting everything.

"Will you dance with me?"

She took his arm and he led her to the floor.

And so it went the rest of the night. In fact, other than Felicity, Mr. McDowell danced with no one else except Leorah once and his own mother once. He introduced Felicity to his mother, his father, and one brother, who were all in attendance. The rest of the night she was in conversation with his family members or him, but they were never alone.

Before she knew it, the night was over, and she was standing with her family, waiting for their carriage. Mr. McDowell joined them, bidding a good night to her parents and each of her brothers and sisters.

He came to Felicity last. "May I call on you tomorrow?" He leaned so close to her that no one could infer that he meant anyone else.

"I shall be home."

***

Philip walked the short distance to the Mayson home as soon as it was socially acceptable to make a call. When he was shown into the parlor, he could not have been more thrilled to find Miss Mayson alone.

"Let my mother know Mr. McDowell is here," she said to the servant.

But as soon as the servant was gone, Philip shut the door.

Her eyes were round as she stared at him.

"I have some things I must say to you, Miss Mayson."

He stepped right up to her and took her hands in his, staring into her sparkling green eyes. She did not pull away. Could she hear his heart pounding?

"Miss Mayson, the Prince Regent plans to reward me for my services to the country in searching out the members of Lady Blackstone's insurrectionist group."

"Oh, how very wonderful." She squeezed his hands.

"He has said he plans to give me a profitable estate in Cambridgeshire that is at his disposal, bestowing on me the title of First Baron McDowell."

Her eyes grew wider, and her pretty lips parted, tempting him. He ached to kiss her, his breath shallowing and making it more difficult to speak. But he wanted to do this right.

"The Prince Regent also plans to petition Parliament to reward me with twenty thousand pounds, and to reward you—"

"Me?"

"With the sum of thirty thousand pounds."

"Oh." Her chest rose and fell rapidly.

"You will not faint, will you?"

"No, of course not. But . . . oh my. You will be a wealthy man, a baron, and I . . ."

"You will be a wealthy woman."

She pulled her hands free and threw them around his back, hugging him. He slipped his arms around her and held her close, pressing his cheek against her hair.

She was in his arms again . . . at last.

***

Felicity could hardly believe what Mr. McDowell was telling her. Joy bubbled inside her, but . . . was it too good to be true?

"Just because he petitions them . . . that does not mean they will grant it, does it?"

She pulled away, realizing her behavior was quite unseemly and would be embarrassing if Mother or anyone else came into the room and saw them. She took a step back. But he grabbed her hands and leaned toward her.

"It is not a guarantee, but it is likely. And before any other men realize that you are to be a wealthy woman, I need to ask you something."

Her heart was pounding. Her gaze moved from his bright-blue eyes, which were strangely dark at the moment, to his perfect lips. Then he leaned his head down so his forehead was nearly touching hers.

"I need to tell you that I think you are the most clever, kind, unselfish, courageous woman I know. You are exactly the kind of woman I wish to marry . . . the only woman who could make me happy."

She could barely breathe. *Do not faint, Felicity. Do not.* "I hope it isn't only my new fortune that makes me appealing." She smiled to show she was in jest, but a lump rose into her throat, forcing her to try to swallow past it.

He seemed to go a shade paler, and his throat bobbed. "I can see why you would think that."

"It's only that . . . no one ever wanted to marry me when I had no fortune." Except Mr. Ratley.

The way he was staring at her made her bite her lip, wishing she had kept quiet. Her insecurity and fear had overtaken her. "I'm sorry. I—"

"No, I understand. I have felt the sting of rejection for my lack of wealth and status, and I do understand. But the truth is, I would marry you even if you did not have a shilling, though I may not be able to prove it."

"No, I was wrong. You are a good and honorable gentleman. I should not have insinuated . . ."

He leaned even closer. "The truth is, I wanted to marry you ever since you showed how brave you could be, stealing into Lady Blackstone's chamber and finding those papers. And when Ratley said those idiotic things about you, when he could have said how brave and intelligent and kind and good and noble and clever you are . . ."

He thought she was all those things? Her heart swelled inside her chest, pushing against her ribs, as she stared into his gentle blue eyes.

"Do you remember when we were hiding in the shell grotto?"

"I remember a little." Unfortunately, most of it had come back to her. Her cheeks began to burn.

"Do you remember when you said you were sad because you would never kiss . . ."

Your wonderful lips.

"My lips?"

She swallowed past the dryness in her throat. "Yes."

He pressed his cheek to her temple. She felt his warm breath against her ear.

"Will you let me kiss you now?" His head moved, ever so slightly, his chin brushing her cheek. "Will you let me call you Felicity? And will you call me Philip? From now until forever? Will you marry me?"

"Yes."

He didn't move.

"I will."

He turned his head and kissed her cheek, kissing his way down until his mouth slanted over hers.

Sweet heavens. His kiss turned her inside out and filled her with a strange feeling of . . . *Thank you, God, for this man's kisses.*

Her hands were around his neck as he ended the kiss and held her tight.

When he finally leaned back to look into her eyes, she very gently brushed her fingertip over his bruised cheekbone, barely touching the skin. "I could hardly bear to see them hurt you." Then she rose onto her toes and brushed her lips over the same spot. "I've been wanting to do that."

He kissed her forehead, then touched his thumb to the corner of her mouth. "Not as long as I've been wanting to kiss you."

He kissed her lips again, stealing her breath and sending her heartbeat into a rapid tempo. Mr. Ratley had never kissed her like that. It was not the same at all.

She wished she could kiss Philip again and again, but her mother or one of her brothers might come along and open the door. "Do you think my mother will be alarmed to see us like this?"

"I imagine she knows my intentions, why I'm here."

"My father said something to that effect last night."

"I shall go to him now, if you wish."

"Can you stay a little while longer?"

"As long as you wish . . . anything you wish." He kissed her cheek, then her lips.

Her heart seemed to float and take her with it, straight up to the ceiling and beyond. "I didn't want to admit I was in love with you, and I was afraid to hope you might love me." She caressed his shoulder as he touched his hand to her cheek. "I was so ashamed for engaging myself to Mr. Ratley. Are you not scandalized that people are gossiping about me being engaged to that insurrectionist?"

"That's all over now." He caressed her hair and pulled her even closer. "I don't care what people say. I shall make you my baroness, and then they will have to still their wagging tongues." He kissed her again, sending warmth all through her.

When the kiss ended, she said, "You were always so serious. I could not tell what you thought of me. And when you saved me from my runaway horse . . . It's my fault you were beaten and thrown into the outbuilding." She squeezed her eyes shut as a tear leaked from the corner of her eye. "You could have gotten away if not for me."

He wiped her tear with his thumb. "It's not your fault, and I would do it all again to save you."

This time she raised her face and kissed him. "I love you, Philip McDowell—Baron McDowell. I love you, and I always will."

EPILOGUE

The engagement of Felicity and Philip was announced, and a few days later, Felicity's aunt Agnes received a visit from Mr. Birtwistle. He was staying with the McDowells at their London town house, but after visiting Miss Appleby two days in a row, he proposed marriage.

The two couples were married four weeks later in a double ceremony.

Philip and Felicity learned a few weeks later that Napoleon had been defeated again and exiled to Saint Helena. Felicity gratefully received the news that her brother had come home whole and well from the war.

Four months after their wedding, the Baron and Baroness McDowell walked in the garden of their own estate in Cambridgeshire with their arms around each other, gazing over the hedges where the gardener was preparing a plot of ground under a mild October sun.

"Are you looking forward to your mother's visit in a few weeks?" Philip squeezed Felicity's shoulder and kissed her hair.

"Yes. But I've enjoyed being here in our new home, having you all to myself." She put both arms around him and squeezed.

"You haven't regretted giving up your freedom and your status as an independently wealthy woman to marry me?"

"No, I haven't. I like being a baroness."

"So you married me for my title, is that it?"

She smirked. "No, I married you for your sense of humor."

"Ah, then I should try harder to make you laugh." He leaned down and kissed her. But when he lifted his head, his expression sobered. "I received a letter today from Lord Sidmouth. He says that now that Napoleon is once again in exile, it will be more difficult to apprehend Lady Blackstone and Ratley, though it is possible they have fled France and have set sail to America. Either way, it's unlikely we shall ever see or hear from them again or that they will ever be tried for high treason."

"As long as they can no longer cause trouble. But what about all the men on the list, the leaders in charge of different counties and cities, and all their followers?"

"Most of them fled to America or elsewhere, as we had thought. But as for their followers . . . there's not enough evidence against them. The Crown has decided not to try them. The Home Office has agents who are keeping a close watch on them, and their stockpiles of arms were confiscated, so . . . that seems to be the end of it."

Felicity smiled and sighed. "It feels rather good to have saved Great Britain, its Members of Parliament, and its royal family." She gave him a sidelong glance.

"My wife has a sense of humor as well."

He tried to tickle her. Felicity squealed and ran. He gave chase and soon caught up to her. He lifted her off the ground and swung her around in a circle. Her squeals turned into laughter, dying abruptly when he started kissing her again.

How good God had been to Felicity, to save her from a dangerous engagement and give her so many blessings, not the least of which was . . . love.

AUTHOR'S NOTE

Regency England was a turbulent time of economic and social unrest. Many reformers advocated peaceful reform, and many others had given up on peaceful reform and favored violence. Government officials were afraid that these violent reformers would rise up and cause a revolution very much like the one that had recently taken place in France.

Though many of the records have been lost or destroyed, it was not without precedent for government agents to infiltrate these illegal reformers' groups to try to discover their plans and document who was involved. And if any of these groups had succeeded in revolting against the government, it's easy to imagine what might have happened to England's monarchy—the same thing that happened in France, Russia, and other European countries—mass executions and a chaotic time of transition. I hope you enjoyed my fictional story of how this fate might have threatened and then been averted in Regency England.

As for the Shell Grotto, it is a real place in Margate, Kent, England. This unique, man-made cave was not discovered until 1835, but I took the liberty to let my own characters discover it several years earlier. How it came to be, what it was used for, and even how long it has been in existence is still a mystery. I was so fascinated with it that I had to use it in my story. You can visit the Shell Grotto's website, www.shellgrotto. co.uk, where you may view photos, read facts, and even find out how to visit the grotto in person.

ACKNOWLEDGMENTS

I want to thank the whole team at Waterfall Press for all their hard work and support, including Faith Black Ross, Michelle Hope Anderson, and Sheryl Zajechowski, and Mike Heath at Magnus Creative for yet another beautiful cover. I also want to thank my wonderful agent, Natasha Kern, for all her awesomeness. Without her wisdom, effort, and business savvy, this series would not be written yet or published. Thank you so much!

I need to thank my friend Terry Bell for being willing to let me pick her brain and talk through my story. Thanks for brainstorming with me! I also have to thank my friends Katherine Bone and Mary Freeman, and family members Joe, Grace, and Faith, for brainstorming with me. I am so blessed, and I love you so much.

I'm also thankful for my friend Regina Carbulon for cheering me on and always encouraging and supporting me. Thanks for praying for me and being willing to listen to me talk about my stories, especially when I'm stuck. May God keep on blessing you. You are such a blessing to me and everyone who knows you.

And thanks also to all my readers who support me in so many ways, tangible and intangible—for sending me encouraging messages, writing and posting great reviews, telling others about my books, and praying for me. I love you all.

DISCUSSION QUESTIONS

1. Why was Felicity Mayson ready to give up on marriage at the start of this story? What did she want to do instead of attending balls and dinner parties?

2. What was it about Mr. Ratley that impressed Felicity so much? How was he different from the other men she had met?

3. What had Lady Blackstone assumed about Felicity that led her to trust her enough to invite her to the place where she and her henchmen would be planning their illegal takeover of the government?

4. What was it about Mr. Ratley that made Felicity almost immediately second-guess her decision to marry him?

5. How long should a person take to get to know someone before they decide to marry them? Why? Can you be sure you're not making a mistake? If so, how?

6. Did Philip McDowell arrive at Doverton Hall feeling as if he had something to prove to his brothers? Why? How did he feel about being the youngest son in his family?

7. How did Aunt Agnes Appleby's character change? What was her reasoning for changing her behavior? How does novel reading change you? Or does it?

8. Have you or someone you know ever fainted? How do you imagine that experience would make you feel?

9. Felicity was very distressed over deceiving and lying to Mr. Ratley and Lady Blackstone. Do you agree with her reasoning that perhaps it was justified since she was trying to save her country and the lives of many people?

10. At the end, what did Felicity put aside to start writing down what happened to her at Doverton Hall?

11. How important is/should marriage be in any person's life? Why?

ABOUT THE AUTHOR

Photo © 2012 Jodie Westfall

Historical romance author Melanie Dickerson earned her bachelor's degree from the University of Alabama and has taught special education in Georgia and Tennessee. She has also taught English in Germany and Ukraine. Dickerson won the 2012 Carol Award in young adult fiction and the 2010 National Readers' Choice Award for best first book. Her novels *The Healer's Apprentice* and *The Merchant's Daughter* were both Christy Award finalists.

She lives with her husband and two daughters near Huntsville, Alabama. For more information, visit www.MelanieDickerson.com.